FAWNW, the Fellowship of Australian Writers-North West, has been operating for over sixty years. Our members are spread widely along the North West Coast of Tasmania and occasionally further afield. Meetings are held monthly and visitors are always welcome.

For further information, email the FAWNW President, Allan Jamieson: jamtin79@gmail.com

We have published anthologies of short stories and poems in 2012, 2019 and 2021. This 2023 anthology is our most extensive publication to-date; there are 112 contributions from members either of FAWNW or of the Fellowship of Australian Writers group based in Hobart.

I0587078

The World According *to Us*

Compiled by

Allan Jamieson

Table of Contents

Vale Democracy
Donna-Marie Koopman

I heard you haven't been well for quite a while now
And what I've seen lately verifies the rumour.
Then today I heard the news that truly shocked me;
You were dead!

You, who always supported the freedom of every individual
No matter colour, creed or political viewpoint
Every opinion mattered, therefore in every decision
The majority ruled.

The worst of this is, you died in a place that gave birth to you
Supported you, held you dearest of all
That life from that place was adopted, respected and upheld
In every corner of the world.

We clung to you, an anchor in a sea of unrest,
bigotry and hate.
What of us now?
My tears fall, as my heart breaks at your passing.

Vale: Democracy

Cookie
Dawn Meredith

The last time she'd felt this way somebody had died. The crushing, squeezing emptiness, compressed her breath and her thoughts. Numbness and disconnection would soon follow. Last time it was her brother, Caden, who had died violently in an attack while he walked home from work through the dark city streets. This was death of a different kind. Death of the soul. The death of all hope.

Carla reached out with a shaking hand for the water bottle sitting just out of reach on the hospital table, gave up and slumped back against the crisp pillows. Her nostrils flared at the onslaught of smells – disinfectant, vomit and worse. She closed her eyes, trying to block out the banging of trolleys against steel framed beds, the chatter of nurses, the endless beeps and alarms.

Perhaps if she'd bargained better, she thought, held her ground, her life wouldn't have come to this. If she'd been stronger, more forceful. But she had no strength left now and her brain was so confused by all the drugs that she could no longer rely upon it to express her thoughts coherently. Bargaining? If only. She had nothing left to bargain with.

As was her usual routine that morning, five months ago, she had grabbed her swimming bag and headed for the beach. That day the sun was too bright, stabbing through her eyes. She'd pulled her hat down as far as she could and stumbled down the steps to the sand, vaguely aware that the tide had washed up large humps of seaweed, branches, rocks and broken shells. She'd tried to step carefully but a wave of dizziness had swept over her and suddenly her bag had slipped off her shoulder and she found herself sprawled awkwardly, her left knee trapped underneath her, sharp bits of something pressing into her cheek. For a microsecond she was embarrassed, wondering if anyone saw her tumble so stupidly. Then the pain in her leg had hit her like a train.

The GP said it was probably just a sprain that would heal itself. No broken bones, after all. He seemed so confident. Dismissive. But as the days dragged on, with her stuck on the sofa or hobbling painfully to the loo she realised it wasn't healing. Something was wrong. And she'd have to deal with it. At times like this she missed Tim even more. He had a quiet, efficient way of dealing with crises that always made her feel safe. But her wonderful, compassionate, intelligent Tim, with those dark eyes and scruffy sandy hair, that way of smiling that made her melt... He'd left without an explanation, just a scribbled note on the kitchen table. I'm sorry. Have to go. One day I hope you'll understand. Anger flared at the thought. What the hell did that mean? What had she done to deserve this aching loneliness and despair? She'd never pressured him to marry her, or have the children she longed for. She'd let Tim decide the tapestry of their life together.

But the worst was to come. Caden had been her rock during those horrible days following Tim's sudden, inexplicable departure. Her little brother, the adventurer, the silly joker had been absolutely amazing. Dropped everything and moved in for a week. And just as she was beginning to see that her life could continue without Tim, Caden had been killed. There was no other family to turn to. She was alone with her grief. How she'd managed to keep going to work when her compassionate leave was up she did not know. She had been on autopilot for months.

Moving interstate had helped leave some of the memories behind, but starting new in an unfamiliar town by yourself was hard. She'd joined various groups; book club, gardening club, Art group and gradually inched her way into friendships and a social life. She didn't understand what people saw in her, why they bothered. She felt like a ghost of a person. But she tried to fit in, be part of things. And it had slowly worked. She was forty eight now. Too old to start again, have kids, watch them grow up. That familiar void was always there. But she had carved for herself a sort-of life that was sort-of fulfilling. Getting fit, swimming daily, had become what she looked forward to every day. That and coming home to Tabby, her stray ginger cat. When she swam, the tingling of the cold water shocked her body into waking up, cleared her mind, brought a smile to her lips as she swam effortlessly among the gentle swell of her favourite beach. No matter the weather, she was there. Sometimes she'd see others swimming too and they'd stop for a chat. Then it was home for a cup of tea and breakfast. It wasn't an exciting life. It wasn't the life of her dreams, but it was a life worth living.

Until her body decided to let cancer run rampant through it.

A pretty nurse came into the room and smiled at Carla as if everything was wonderful. How did she do that, day after day?

Where did she find the strength to smile when all around her was misery and death?

"How's things today, Carla? Had brekky?"

Carla shook her head. "No appetite."

Rachel reached into her pocket and brought out a bag of sweets. She handed it to Carla.

"Salted liquorice. Your favourite," she said, grinning conspiratorially.

Carla dutifully opened the packet and popped a lolly into her mouth. It did taste good. She sucked at it thoughtfully. "Thanks Rach. You're the best." She tried to smile. Rachel deserved at least that.

"So, I hear you're leaving us later today."

"Guess so," replied Carla.

"I bet Tabby will be glad to have you home again. You miss him, don't you?"

"Yeah. Silly old codger." Carla felt the liquorice lift her spirits. Chewing the last of it she popped another into her mouth. "Maybe I'll buy him a new collar or something."

"I reckon he'd look handsome in red," Rachel said, adding information to Carla's chart. "Well, better keep moving. Take care," she said, patting Carla's arm. "An orderly will fetch you in half an hour, ok?" Turning to the next bed, she greeted the patient cheerfully.

Carla dressed slowly. She was so thin now and had so little energy. What was she going to do all day at home? Wait to die.

She heard whistling in the corridor long before the orderly arrived with a wheelchair into the room she shared with three other women. He was a solidly built Pacific Islander bloke of about fifty, with slight greying in his curly dark hair. His name tag said, "Cookie." Cookie?

"Young Carla!" He greeted her with a radiant smile of perfect white teeth in his broad, handsome face. "Off back into the wide world again, ay?" He hummed as he put the brakes on the wheelchair and helped her into it. His arms were warm and muscular against her body. She felt like a calico bag of old bones. He could easily have tossed her into the taxi through the window.

Thanks," she mumbled.

"Big plans for tonight?" Cookie asked as he wheeled her expertly round trolleys and people to the lifts and reached out to press the button.

"No," she replied. "Just TV and bed." The doors opened and she was wheeled smoothly inside the empty lift, then spun round slowly.

"That doesn't sound like much fun," Cookie said, from behind her. Carla was glad he couldn't see her scowl. What difference did it make? She'd had all the chemo. It was downhill from here. Wait to die.

As she was wheeled to the front desk and checked out, Cookie greeted several people, equally effusive. It was starting to annoy her that people could be so damned happy all the time. They reached the front doors and went straight through to a waiting taxi. Cookie put on the brakes and came round to assist her into the car. After watching her put on her seatbelt he stood, his hand on the door, unwilling to close it.

"Listen," he said softly. "I take a group of ex-patients to the beach every Thursday. Interested?"

She wanted to say no, but his kind face stopped her. The beach. Her happy place. Would it be the same when you knew you only had months to live? But she found herself smiling a little.

"Ok. Sure."

He grinned. "Awesome! Pick you up at ten thirty, ay?"

She smiled again at his Islander way of speaking. "Sounds good. Thanks." He closed the door and waved as the car drove away.

Tabby meowed forcefully as she opened the door to her unit. Shuffling into the bathroom she noticed her neighbour, Alice, had kept the litter tray clean. In the kitchen Tabby's water bowl was full and a few of his morning biscuits remained. She eyed him speculatively.

"You're fat. I see you conned Alice into feeding you six times a day." Tabby waddled over to the bowl and sat down expectantly, gazing at her with his 'I'm just a starving kitty' expression. "No way! There's still bikkies in there, Tubby!" She made herself a cup of tea and shuffled to the window where her comfy armchair and side table waited. Easing herself down she looked around the room. She'd furnished it nicely in neutral tones with the occasional splash of red. The Artwork on the walls was her own and she was proud of that. Tabby jumped up and settled on her lap. He was warm and his purring thrummed through her aching body. She stroked him absently and turned on the TV. It was only three in the afternoon, but what else was she going to do? Within minutes she was asleep.

Thursday morning she woke with a massive headache and the pain in her leg was so bad she changed her morphine patch and took Panadol as well, washed down with toast and some homemade jam Alice had left as a welcome home gift on the kitchen table. Ten o'clock was fast approaching. She wasn't even dressed! Slowly and painfully she showered and pulled on something boring and comfortable. She didn't care how she looked.

The doorbell rang.

"It's open!" she called out from her armchair. She didn't have the energy to get up.

Cookie's smiling face peered round the door. He was dressed in bright blue cotton shorts and a Hawaiian shirt of purple and yellow flowers.

"There she is! Morning, Carla! And this must be Tabby."

Her cat wound himself shamelessly around Cookie's legs. Cookie grinned.

"Cats like me."

Carla snorted. "He's asking for another breakfast."

Cookie laughed. "My cat is exactly the same, ay."

"Oh, you have a cat?" Carla asked.

Cookie ruffed up Tabby's fur, to the cat's utter delight. "Yeah. Her name is Princess."

Carla laughed out loud, surprising herself.

"I never imagined you with a cat called Princess!"

Cookie shrugged.

"That's what she is. A princess. To me, anyway. So, let's get you into the van, ay?"

There were five other ex-patients in the van, who greeted Carla warmly. The drive was about forty minutes and as she watched the scenery go by Carla felt warmed by the sun, the pain in her leg subsided, for now. Cookie chose a beach with a gentle slope down to the sand and a coffee van in the carpark. Thoughtful guy, she mused. The other passengers, three men and two women, were all gaunt and slow like herself, varying in age from late teens to seventies, but all seemed cheered by the ride. They sat at the outdoor seating and Cookie took their orders. Carla read the menu on the side of the van and decided not to bother with any food. A regular flat white would do. A couple of the passengers ordered sweet treats with their hot drinks and started chatting about the weather, the last trip to the beach. The teen girl sat sullenly, her hollowed eyes dull, staring at the marshmallows floating on her hot chocolate. Carla looked at the vast sparkling blue ocean and took a deep, satisfied breath. I've missed you, she thought. After they'd finished their morning tea, Cookie opened the baggage compartment at the side of the van and extricated folding chairs and blankets. The men insisted on helping him and as the ragtag group made their slow and painful way to the beach Carla felt overwhelmingly tired. She forced her feet to keep moving. Just a few more steps. She paused by the railing, gripping it tightly and watched as the others moved on.

"You ok, Carla?" Cookie asked, his arms full.

"I just need a minute," she said quietly.

"I'll dump these and come back for you," he said, before she had the chance to say don't bother-I'm-fine. He settled the others into their chairs in the sun and jogged back to Carla just as she was letting go of the railing to prove she didn't need help. He took her elbow anyway and guided her the last fifty metres, settled her in a chair and spread the blanket over her knees. She pulled down her hat so that he wouldn't see her scowl. She wasn't an invalid, for God's sake! Cookie and one of the men started to play handball. Cookie ended up doing all the fetching but the man didn't seem to mind. He laughed as Cookie staged a fake fall and rolled over onto his back, laughing. The gentle splash of small waves against the sand was absolutely glorious, lulling Carla into a half-wakefulness. The sun was warm on her back. Her spine relaxed. Next thing she knew Cookie was rousing her gently.

"Time to go, ay Carla? Here, I'll take the chair." As she made her way back to the van Carla felt exhaustion descend over her and worried she wouldn't make it to the carpark. Suddenly Cookie was beside her, bending down to look into her face under the hat.

"Want me to carry you?"

"I'm not an infant!" she snapped.

"Ok. Whatever you want," he replied genially. "Some women would find an offer like that irresistible, ay!" He laughed. Carla set her mouth grimly as she focussed on getting her bad leg to function.

The ride home seemed longer and she was relieved to be home again. Cookie took her to the door and made sure she got in all right. He was fussing. She hated it. She mumbled a goodbye and closed the door. Then she heard him whistling as he returned to the van. Did the guy ever have a bad day?

Despite resolving not to go the next Thursday, Carla found herself once again seated in the van on the way to another beach. This one had a restaurant across the road and magnificent views of headlands and a lighthouse. They decided to have a proper lunch at the restaurant. Even the teenage girl, Meg, seemed to appreciate the food and the view. Her cheeks were slightly pinker and her gaze lifted occasionally from her hands to survey their surroundings. She ate most of her food, too. Perhaps her chemo had finished and her appetite had returned. The men had all introduced themselves again as Robbie, Mark and Justin. The other female was a woman of about sixty called Penny. They all sat together, passing the herb bread and condiments. The talk was almost animated today and Cookie, seated at the head of the table, beamed. He loves doing this, Carla thought. He gets a real kick out of seeing us interact. As if we're normal people. She tried to talk to the others but her gaze kept drifting to Meg, sitting at the end of the table in her own little bubble, giving monosyllabic answers when someone tried to engage her in conversation. She felt for the girl. Fancy being a teenager and living with the big C. In her short life she hadn't yet had a chance to do anything much, have a career or long term relationship and chances were the chemo would sterilise her, so no kids in her future. Carla wasn't ready to talk to Meg yet. Perhaps next week.

The following week Cookie took them to the riverside instead of the beach. There were picnic tables and a gas grill. He'd asked them all to bring some meat 'for the barbie, ay?' which they had all dutifully done. Cookie had made a massive salad and whisked out fresh fruit for afters. The river was wide and deep, fringed by majestic willows and dotted with ducks. The weather was perfect. Carla ate more than she'd done in a year and when she returned home she felt content. Realising her leg hadn't hurt too much today she decided these trips weren't such a bad idea after all.

The following Thursday Cookie called to cancel. He was very sorry but something had come up. Carla was disappointed. The van trips were the only bright part of her life. She structured her whole week around them, her shopping, her Art class and book club. What could the something be that had caused Cookie to cancel? He'd sounded unusually quiet, too. Before she'd really thought about it, she'd sent him a text.

Hope everything is ok. Missed seeing the guys today. You're the best part of my week. Cheers, Carla. To her surprise, a text came straight back.

Sorry about cancelling. My sister is having her baby today. Have to fly home. Leaving tonight.

Hope it all goes well! Kind regards to your family.

Thanks so much, Carla. You're the best!

The week dragged by with nothing to relieve the monotony. Carla wondered, should she see if Meg was all right? She sent a text to Cookie asking if it was ok to call Meg and he sent her Meg's number, saying that would be awesome. After almost ringing out, Meg finally answered.

"Meg's phone, Diana speaking."

"Oh, I was hoping to speak to Meg. It's Carla. From the van trips. To the beach."

"Oh, Carla, yes, she's mentioned you. I'm sure she'd love to speak to you. How thoughtful of you to call. She's resting right now, but I'll be sure to get her to call you back when she wakes up, all right?"

"Great! Thanks. Bye."

The chat with Meg lasted two hours. On the phone the teenager was a different person. They chatted about everything, from boyfriends to favourite foods, to soccer, which Meg had loved to play before she got sick. They compared notes on chemo and foods that made you vomit and foods that were ok and which movie stars were absolute hunks, although they had different opinions on that. After ringing off Carla felt good. She'd helped a lonely girl. And she felt as if Meg had helped her too.

The next week the van trips were back on and everyone greeted each other with enthusiasm and lots of excited chatter. Meg sat next to Carla and they talked like they'd known each other for years, despite the age difference. Carla hoped Diana didn't think it odd that a middle aged woman had befriended her daughter.

Autumn winds kept them indoors at a beachside coffeehouse, with Cookie organising and fussing over them all like a mother hen. Carla just had to giggle. "You all right, ay?" He'd ask each person in turn. As she looked around at the other ex-patients it seemed to her that they all looked healthier and happier and she realised they'd become her friends. She tried not to think that some of them would crash and burn at some point. Cancer was a bastard like that. She pushed it from her mind that Meg could be one of those who didn't survive.

A few months later, on a Tuesday night, there was a knock at Carla's door. Getting up stiffly, she went to open it. Cookie stood on the doorstep, his clothes rumpled, tears rolling down his face.

"I'm sorry," he said. "I didn't know who else to talk to."

"Oh, gosh, Cookie, come in!" Carla pulled him inside. "Here, sit down. What's happened? Would you like a drink?"

Cookie shook his head. Carla sat nearby and waited, watching him anxiously. It was a shock to see this man so dejected. After a moment he stopped twisting his fingers together and looked at her, his face full of anguish.

"The baby died," he whispered.

"Oh, no!" Carla went on her knees in front of Cookie and took his hands in hers. She stroked his arm. "Oh, Cookie. That's awful! What happened?"

"Brain aneurism," he said softly. "No one knew. It was so quick. He was doing so well, ay. And now my sister Ophelia, she's completely shut down, locked herself in her room. Won't even talk to her husband."

Carla squeezed his hands. "Are you going to fly over?"
He shook his head. "Brad said not to right now. She won't see me anyway. He said give it a week." Cookie's shoulders shook as he held in his sobs. Carla stood and pulled him close. He rested his head against her, held onto her and took several big, shaky breaths. Pulling away he looked up at her, embarrassed.

"I'm so sorry to bother you with this, Carla. You have enough on your plate already, ay?"

She smiled ruefully. "It's ok. My stuff is boring. This is important. Is there anything I can do?"

He shook his head and wiped his dripping nose on his sleeve, like a small boy. Carla smiled, despite herself. Men could be so childlike at times.

"Coffee?"

"Sure," he replied. "That'd be nice. White with two thanks." He got up suddenly. "Want me to make it? You shouldn't have to…"

She waved a hand peremptorily. "Don't be silly."

They sat, cupping the steaming mugs, lost in their own thoughts for some moments.

"Will you go over for the funeral?" Carla asked.

"Yep. It's a big family. We're all behind her. All fifty three of us."

"Goodness, that's a huge family!"

Cookie grinned, looking like his old self. "Islanders. You know. Eat a lot and procreate a lot and sing a lot and fight a lot."

"Sounds like you do nothing by halves," Carla remarked, thinking of how small and dull her own life was.

"Hey, Carla," Cookie said softly, his eyebrows raised. "Would you come with me?"

"Me? To your nephew's funeral? But I…"

"It's ok. You don't have to. Never mind. I shouldn't have asked. It's just that you're the closest friend I have."

Carla frowned. Surely someone as outgoing and friendly and likeable as Cookie would have loads of friends? She looked at him more closely. Cookie was in his fifties, unmarried, as far as she knew, had a good job, cared about people. Why wasn't he tripping over friends?

"Are you upset with me?" he asked. "It's because I asked you, ay."

"No, not at all. I'm just struggling to understand why you're not swamped with friends, Cookie. You're so likeable and cheerful and helpful and…"

He grinned. "Thanks. But you know, I have lots of acquaintances, but not many people I'd actually call friends. And you're at the top of the list."

Carla thought back to the van trips. Had she paid Cookie special attention? Had private conversations? Shared confidences? Hadn't she spent most of her time lately talking to Meg?

"You know," he continued. "You're a great person, Carla. You never complain. Always ready to listen. Calm. I like that."

She shook her head, smiling, thinking of all the anger and resentment festering in her heart about cancer, losing Tim and Caden, her career. "Me? Calm? Are you sure you're not confusing me with someone else?" She laughed.

"Nup. You," he said, looking into her eyes. "You're a good influence on the group. We all value you. The way you care. I didn't just pick this bunch of people randomly, you know. You're all people I feel a connection with. Like a surrogate family, I guess." He went quiet.

"Well, they say you can choose your friends, not your family," Carla said, trying to lighten the mood. She still couldn't understand how the group thought of her like that. Wasn't she just a boring, self-obsessed cancer patient?

"You're in remission, aren't you?" Cookie asked suddenly.

"I…er…don't know," she replied.

"Well, it's just that I've noticed how much more mobile you are now, how your skin looks healthy and how shiny your hair is."

Carla blushed. My hair is shiny?

"Have you been back, you know, to see if the cancer is gone?"

She pulled a face. "No. I've missed my appointments. I thought it better not to know, not to get my hopes up." Tabby jumped up on her lap and after scrunching her clothes with his claws, settled down, purring. She stroked him.

"Could be good news, though," he said.

"And could be bad," she countered, feeling stupid for saying that.

Cookie got to his feet. "I'd better go. Sorry for disturbing you, Carla." He suddenly hugged her and pecked her cheek. She felt her face flush hot instantly. He was already opening the door.

"Text me before you leave?" She said.

He smiled. "Sure thing. Thanks again, ay."

"You're welcome."

"And if you change your mind…"

"Well I… They don't know me. How would your family feel about you bringing some strange woman to a family funeral?"

"Oh," he waved his hand. "They already know all about you." His eyes twinkled. "It's as if they've met you already. See ya later."

"See you."

Carla sat, stunned by the conversation. So much to think about. Decisions she had to make. Things she ought not to put off any longer. Stirrings of hope swelled in her brain. Maybe, just maybe…

Three days later, Cookie stood in line waiting to board the plane, dressed in board shorts and a loud shirt, sandals and a straw hat. He looked every bit the islander boy. Beside him stood Carla, in a bright summer dress, snazzy new sunglasses and sandals and wearing makeup for the first time in years. In her hand was her boarding pass. In her bag were the test results of her last scans.

Cancer free.

The Noble Art of Bluffing*
Brenda Slavoff

*Registered Trade Mark

When is a lie not a lie? No, I'm not kidding, I'm (only) bluffing!

Yes, those exaggerations, evasions and omissions that hold together the façade we present to the world. What would we do without them? And who has not been fooled by them?

Yes, I'm sure I can make a positive contribution to the company's profit margin.

(What am I waffling on about?)

My children would love to meet you; they are handling the divorce very well.

(How am I going to prevent murder?)

Dad, I won't be late. You don't have to worry about me.

(I leave this to your imagination.)

These are polite evasions, not lies. Life would not be comfortable without them.

Exaggerations are entirely permissible when telling a funny story from the past. In fact, reminiscences of the past are seldom true, even when totally serious. History, even personal history, is what we want to believe about the past. Never read over old diaries. It is totally disillusioning.

Omissions are extremely common. What is said is just the tip of the ice-berg of what is not said. No one wants to hear what is not said.

Reality is a scarce commodity, and that is how we like it. Who can say what is reality, anyway? We sincerely come to believe our bluffs. Who can prove them wrong?

Bluffing cannot be measured scientifically, and though counsellors spend much time and earn much money getting people to deal with their problems honestly, maybe they just help them come up with a more comfortable or practical bluff to believe in. The psychoanalysts try bravely to go where no man has gone before and discover the hidden secrets of the human psyche. It all makes interesting reading. I do not know whether they will ever reach the tortuous ends and discover the Minotaur they seek. I hope not.

Anyone who has ever seen a smaller animal standing up to a bigger one, puffing itself up and, like the frilled lizard, making use of every extraneous feature possible, must know that bluffing runs through the whole of nature, with its finest flowering surely occurring in human beings. Human nature is a deep mystery, unfathomable even unto itself, and bluffing is still a tried and true survival tactic. It has been with us since the days of the mammoth when the first axe was fashioned.

What are you doing with that piece of flint? (or grunts to that effect.)

Oh, nothing. Just passing the time.

(This'll settle that rotten so-and-so when next I see him.)

to

This will be a war to end all wars!

to

We cannot lose.

Without bluffing, we'd scare ourselves to death.

Civilised society would simply fall apart without bluffing. Forget about Freud and all his followers: bluffing is the basis of the arts, not sex urges. It is legal – actually the legal profession have made an art of it; it is entertaining, necessary to the perpetuation of the species, and only those of a religious bent consider it immoral. And who are they kidding? Whilst I consider sincerity the greatest virtue, maybe I'm only bluffing myself. And of course, in the realms of politics, bluffing becomes of national importance.

Honesty is not outlawed by bluffing. It is valued all the more by being rare. For every now and then we stumble upon the truth and blurt it out. That means more than all the bluffing that preceded it. In fact, the bluffing is the stage upon which is set the truth. And that is priceless.

Using "Alfred Nobel's Candles"
Pete Stratford

Interrupted by loud crunching on toast, our breakfast table conversation centred around a problem facing some farmers in Victoria's Western district: how to build a fence across those damned stony barriers. Back when volcanoes were spewing out their innards to flow across the land, the molten stuff simply followed along the path of least resistance, just as flood waters do today. Having once flowed as liquid magma it then solidified into very hard rock, leaving some areas with rounded ridges of basalt. While much of the land is now arable, either between those ridges, or perhaps even covering them to considerable depth, building a farm fence across any exposed areas of basalt is a challenge.

Although having only recently arrived into the district, I was included in the deliberations about how to overcome the problem of "digging post holes" into what is now very solid rock, and enquired if perhaps they had a powered auger that was capable of drilling a small hole into it. When an affirmative reply was given my next query was whether such things as gelignite, detonators and fuse may also be available.

While assured that those items were available, but no one was capable of using them, there was some hesitation in accepting an offer that I was willing to do so. The others took some convincing though eventually agreed that with no other options they would go with my idea. With hindsight I think perhaps the others there may have felt that this newcomer wouldn't be missed anyway! Hence over the course of several days many drill holes were hammered into the hard rock, explosives then inserted soon followed by numerous deafening "booms" as post holes were created, resulting in taught wires being passed through posts to form a stock proof fence crossing those difficult areas of land.

With the job completed there was a celebratory beer or three, which brought about some mild praise to all involved until the question was posed; "where did you learn to use that stuff?" Their facial expressions changed somewhat to hear I had only ever seen it being used by others, but had watched very carefully indeed! Over following years those products proved very effective for such difficult tasks as removing tree stumps, and even creating drains through swampy land that would not support machinery on it. The latter often resulted in rather worse for wear eels and frogs hanging up on any overhanging branches, but it was an economical way to achieve the desired result of converting a swamp into more solid land.

An aside that I still ponder on, was when applying at a South Australian Police station for a permit to purchase & use gelignite, being informed that I was required to purchase a "Fireworks Licence"!

Firelight
Dawn Meredith

Firelight,
Your music reaches out to me with hissing fingers,
Glaring against the black hush of night.
Glowing memories, ashen tears of regret,
Crumple, twist and vanish in a flash of blue.

Summon me into the golden abyss,
Where all is consumed – the ache of eager, pulsing heart,
The raging tyranny of fear and loss,
The crackle of unexpected joys -

The texture of life,
Spiralling into numb tranquillity
Of pure light.

The Inner Clearing
Jennie Herrera

I'm sure I started to write it. I know it's somewhere here among my papers. Such a mess. The piles. But I know I started the story a couple of months ago. There was the house down a long lane, dark trees bending across. An old country place. A small verandah, hardly that, more a large porch. Three steps up. The creak of dried-out timber. The front door with a window into the rooms either side. So vivid in my mind. And the family there. I'm certain I had them thought out. The why. The how. The lives they led. The darkness at the centre of the whole plot. The way the shadows crept in every afternoon. The nightjars in the black-trunked trees. The sense of the house in its clearing. Of the encroaching darkness. Of the world around them, not precisely hostile but not welcoming either.

I know they had a struggle with poverty. But money there somewhere. Or the value of the land. I know I had that worked out in my mind although I don't think I'd got that far with my story. It was on my mind as I woke up this morning. The thought—why didn't I go on with that idea? Why did I put it aside? But I put a lot of things aside recently. I tell myself I'm just slowing down a little. I probably won't get everything finished. But this story … I felt certain, as I blinked in the early greyness, that it was a good story, a good idea, and I couldn't think why I'd put it aside. Too tired perhaps. And I do forget …

I've forgotten where I put those first few pages. I know they're in here somewhere. I set it aside because … it must've been just before I had to have a few days away. Things overtook me. But I knew it would be waiting when I came home again. But where the heck did I put it? I'm sure I don't need half this stuff I've kept. All these early drafts, these notes I've made for stories that are long since done and gone … or the ones that were never written. I've got an ideas book here somewhere. But half the time I forget to use it … or I can't find it when I want it …

But I hate to waste a good story started and there was something about this one. The atmosphere. Something dark and fearful. It was more than my usual bland settings, my nice people, my little pleasant love affairs, my family sagas in which the families always hope for the best. I know this one was going to be different.

There was something about the way that rutted track wound inwards. It wasn't merely a track. It wasn't an appendage to the story. It wasn't like my normal beginnings when someone is merely arriving and the front door is there—and it opens and someone steps out— and the story begins. It is sometimes, I think, that I use my roads and tracks as the link between the title and the first important act. I like to have a door opening. No one knows until it opens who will step out, what lurks there behind it. No one knows until the key figure appears whether the heroine will step into happiness—or horror. Doors are more important than roads.

But in this story—if only I could put my hands on it!—I have the intuition the track is important. I lay there in bed, thinking 'is it time to get up or not' and deciding I could have another ten minutes, and this image of the road was so vivid. I don't know if I actually wrote it down with that sense of faintly lurking menace, nothing overt, not a gothic thing with the emotive adjectives piling up, just something in its turns and shadows and the house crouching in its grassy hollow. Was the house waiting? Was that what I wanted to capture? Or was it more that it was simply a house when the traveller expected something more dramatic? Just a house, a little shabby, neglected, run-down, a house that's been left behind by time, by its family, by those who lived in it … Those who lived in it …

I know I made a list of characters. I always do. Sometimes I change my mind once I start my writing. But I always start with an image of all the people who will matter in the plot. Sometimes I write them down 'long face with a chin running away to nothing', 'eyes sunk back into dim caverns, with eyebrows shading any reflected light', 'a little round button nose, too red for health and happiness'; and characters set out, sometimes even pedigrees so I won't get family members muddled up. I enjoy doing this. I keep my lists handy. But I must've put both lists and early draft away somewhere. I wish I knew where everything is these days. But it must be here. I know I didn't throw anything away.

Somewhere here. Put in piles. In boxes. Got mixed up with my old drafts. Slipped in the back of my ideas book. If I could only find it …

I know it was going to be a good story. I just felt it in my bones. And as I lay in bed gazing at the stained ceiling the feeling was so strong. I'm not very good on veiled menace. Something about me makes my stories come out sunny. A trifle bland. My villains are rarely villainous. I think I embrace the world around me with … I can't say kindness when I look around this room with all these yellowing books and papers. I know they have their significance still. A life lived through them. But tolerance perhaps. Yes I tolerate things.

But as I blinked my morning eyes I knew this story was going to be significant. I felt the way the road ran, twisting and turning, sometimes disappearing in the shadows of trees growing in too close, sometimes running ruttily with grass between the tracks, that it meant more than just the prop for a different kind of story. I felt a kind of shiver. Excitement. This story would be better than … than what? Apprehension. Could I do it justice? Then it all faded back into irritation. Where on earth have I put the pages already written …

I let my mind range over likely places. I know, occasionally, I put things in unlikely places. Now and then I can't find all the groceries and I've mixed them with things in the bathroom cabinet or my bedside bureau. But that's a minor aberration soon fixed. People dropping by. A kindly hand. But I can't ask them to hunt through piles of paper. And they wouldn't know it if they found it. More scribbled lines—

Did I write it up in longhand, I often do these days, or type it out? My hands seem to have lost their sureness but I like to type, it makes things clear. It makes things neat. But this wasn't a neat story. I felt it drawing me in. No simple cause and effect, no simple start and body and neat nice resolution. But I'm sure I did start to type it when the idea came to me. When was that? That might give me a clue where to look. Months ago. How many? Just after Christmas? No, that rings no bells. In the early autumn? I sometimes write less cheerful stories as the days draw in and there's a nip in the wind and the leaves fall. And then I was away … away for quite a while … that throws things out completely. My memory … but I felt so sure when I woke it was only about three months ago that I started it. It can't be far away. I really haven't done much since. I have ideas but I find it hard to organise them, to make my mind bend to the art of creation. My hands get tired. Maybe my mind gets tired and drifts away … and then I pull myself back, but the story's drifted on and I have to go back to my notes. It's just as well I always keep my notes. I do always keep notes, even months back, I'm sure of that. They'll be around even if ...

Am I confusing notes with story? Did I start writing it? Or was I just preparing to? When I had to go away for a little while. The notes'll be around. And even if I hadn't written much I know my mind will have fleshed out the bareness of my notes. When I find them it won't be hard to remember exactly what I intended to write ... The story will come flooding back. They always do. I know there are little gaps, little hiccups, sometimes. Where did I intend to go from here? What was the next scene I had planned? But having notes in front of me will make all the difference. And the characters—once they come back clearly, once they're jostling round in my head again, it won't be hard to sit down to writing it all out. It's always been like that. Once I have those clear pictures in my mind, and those notes to refer back to, the putting of words on paper runs smoothly. People always say: how smoothly my stories flow.

It's the building blocks, the notes .... But I know the story's in my head somewhere. Such vivid images. A vivid scene writes itself. And I know this was a vivid story. The way I woke with it. As vivid in my waking mind as in my dreams. A powerful story even. Those images as I followed that track in through the glooming bush, each bend, each new scene opening, the house waiting, the shadows, last light on the small window panes, smeary, a little tired in this old place ... no, I added that in just now, a door crashed open, glad cries, a welcome ... I don't think it was ... not that kind of house ... I felt something that wasn't welcoming. I'm sure that's why this story won't go away.

I woke early. Perhaps the dream woke me. My subconscious said 'there's a story you haven't finished, a good story, a powerful story, a story you must finish' ... Perhaps I was thinking on it when I went to sleep. I don't remember doing so. I don't remember that at all. I wasn't working on it ... some time ago, yes, quite some time ago ... and then, because I had to go away, and they didn't think I'd be coming home again ... but I could ... that confused me ... made the months get mixed up ... and the stories along with them ...

I might've pondered on it, my plot, my characters, in the uncatchable moment between waking and sleep, a memory resurfacing: there's something you haven't finished. You mustn't let it go. It's important. It's going to be worth writing. And then, while I slept, my subconscious added something. Told me it lacked something and I couldn't think what. And all this while, my conscious mind struggling with day to day things, my subconscious has been busy with that question: it needs something, what does it need? Place and people, plot and tone ... but something else ...

At first I thought it was a dream. What a strange dream I thought, that lane, those shadows, that small house waiting, no people in my picture, and then I knew it wasn't a dream. That I've visited this place before. I know I created it ... months ago ... was it months ... it might be more ... going away gets everything jumbled ... and home again ... and people popping in ... and thinking about tidying all this paper up ... what best to do ... it's enough to confuse a body. But something there, something definite, something significant. Not from my childhood, not a place where I grew up, not a place to visit, not grandparents, not neighbours ... I know I've never seen this house before ... except in my mind ... and written down ... I always write things down ... it's the only way to keep them when I can't trust ...

It's somewhere here. I never throw anything away. Not a scrap. I'll find my notes, my story, if it's the last thing ...

*

"Poor old soul," people said after the funeral was over. "The way she wouldn't give in to dementia ... The way she was determined to somehow keep going. You have to admire her." They all said things like that. The things forgotten. The things overlooked. The little problems the day carer noticed every time she went in. The muddles. The mix-ups. And, finally, saddest of all, the fire. All that paper, people said, old and dry. An accident waiting to happen. She hadn't written anything new in years. But those old manuscripts had a certain value. "In her heyday she was popular," someone said, and others mentioned the delight her sunny pleasant stories had given them. "Nice stories," someone else said. "No bleakness, no nastiness, no evil, no gutter language ... the world didn't seem to have a place any more for her kind of stories. I wonder if she felt everything had passed her by, the poor old soul."

One by one they turned and drifted away along the grassy path, shadowed now by the ancient pines, past the caretaker's hut, past the looming vaults and tombs and tangled weedy plots, through the wrought-iron gates, out into busyness again, still thinking back.

Due to Appear
Adam Stokell

Another hour yet.
Leave the car to stew in its juices.

It's a short walk to this bit of park
beside the Intercity Cycleway.
It's a thin wedge of daisy-starred lawn,
a few polite trees.
It's a few clean benches,
steel loops for bike chains / leashes.

Sit thought, sit. Stay.

Train slowed attention on these two dianellas,
bestsellers, fanged mauve flowers,
caged in a benchside half-moon plot.

It's harder than it looks.

More than the occasional cyclist cycling past,
it's the bees beyond the mesh fence that solicit.

Neither daisies nor dianellas make it onto their map.

The mesh fence separates the cycleway
from the old railway line that it rhymes
but would rather forget.

Beside the rails, despite the park,
a riot of weeds in high spirits.
Tight yellow minutes grow out of their minds,
bloom towards bees.

A Safety Demo
Jake O'Mara

On my inner left thigh, about forty-five degrees from straight ahead and not far south of my family jewels, I have two scars. They are each about two centimetres in diameter and five centimetres apart. How they got there is a bit of a story, so bear with me, you might learn something, as I did in acquiring them.

Now, droppers are the most numerous elements in the world of wire fences. Posts spaced every eight or ten meters may be the captains and the two strainer posts at the fence-ends like generals. Droppers though are the army proper, the poor bloody infantry, the cannon-fodder. They do the real work against marauding stock. They hold the fence wires a fixed distance apart, and without them even a six-wire fence would be next to useless.

In said six-wire fence there are at least seven holes through which the wires pass, the top one being to allow the barbed wire to be twitched on. Each of those seven holes pass through about 35 mm of hard timber, usually stringybark in the world of my youth. Now drilling those holes is quite a laborious task, and you can't buy 200 metres of dropper holes at the hardware shop, not nowadays. Old timers say you could, back before the war when a new crowbar cost two shillings, but the holes were always pricey and ordinary people could not afford them. Well, not more than a few centimetres at a time anyway, and such a tawdry amount was not much help when you needed kilometres of holes.

Because of the cost and the associated paucity of shop-bought holes my father had in his younger days drilled literally miles of holes in thousands of droppers with a brace and bit and wore several braces clean out in doing so. That, I suppose, is why he eventually bought a machine for the job. It consisted of a saw-bench about two metres long, and through it projected the 800 mm circular saw. In the end of the one metre saw shaft there was a hole to take what was known then as a blacksmith's drill bit of 15 mm diameter. The individual droppers were supported on a pair of wooden rails that held them at a height to meet the horizontal drill on their centreline and cause all the holes to be in a nice straight row, like proper soldiers.

So far so good. "Well, what about power to drive the drill?" you say, and I'm glad you asked. Grid electricity was then several years and a lot of miles from our farm, so power was supplied by a thirty-horsepower Ferguson tractor, via a power-take off pulley and a flat belt six inches wide. We had a few hundred droppers to bore, and I was assigned to the boring job, no pun intended. I was seventeen years old. Not a child, but not a proper adult either. Some say that's still the case.

I set to with a will on a warm day. The tractor roared and the flat belt slapped enthusiastically. There was a large pile of blank droppers to my right, and a place to put the punctuated ones on the left. I lined each one up on the parallel bars, held it at ninety degrees to the bit, and pushed. Too easy! The new bit fairly flew through the wood and each dropper with its seven holes was a done deal in less than a minute.

As the day wore on the tractor was keen as ever, but when our dogs realised that it was not going anywhere, they found shade and went to sleep. Our dogs were veritable da Vincis of sleep, but they also desired to be on hand should things suddenly become more interesting.

The drill got blunter as well. I had to push harder and harder to force the unwilling drill through the wood, and eventually took to using my upper legs to do part of the pushing. Those with the gift of advanced prophecy might be able to see where this could go.

I pushed harder as the drill got blunter, until I found a dropper with a fault in the timber. The drill broke through suddenly with my upper thigh right where the exit point was. The bit grabbed my jeans and with the sound of a minor explosion tore a square foot out of the denim, then went into my thigh perilously close to my virginal family jewels. The tractor never faltered, but the blood flowed freely, and I drove 40 km to the nearest doctor. He probed the wound for bits of wood or cloth, then pulled the ragged edges together with a couple of sutures. It healed remarkably well.

Now take yourself forward ten years to a motorcycle workshop in Darwin. The workshop was owned by the Honda importers for the Northern Territory, and they employed me as a mechanic in the aftermath of cyclone Tracy, when high-calibre technicians were very thin on the ground. I was the popgun of motorcycle mechanics, one of my duties was to assemble new motorcycles and do the pre-delivery work. One of our best sellers was the AG 175 farm bike, and for reasons I cannot remember, always needed a chain-guard to be fitted. This necessitated the drilling of a 10 mm hole in an existing bracket.

The workshop had a large and powerful electric drill, so I fitted a sharp 10 mm bit and prepared to do battle with the two newly un-crated bikes. The foreman stopped me and said,

"...You'd better get on with servicing that 400-Four. Get young Jim to do the chain guards."

Now "young Jim" was a particularly callow youth, thin and pale, with a brain that seemed to struggle to do two things at the same time, like breathing while standing up. He was, more than most of his kind, in that fateful hiatus between childhood and full adulthood. He was also seventeen years old.

Aware that I was handing him a tool capable of causing injury, I said, like Mulga Bill talking to his bicycle salesman,

"...Now see here young feller, you need to be careful with these electric drills. Have a look at this!" To illustrate the clear and present danger I used the tip of the drill to lift the hem of my shorts, intending to reveal the scar from the earlier encounter. The drill was plugged in and wouldn't you darn well know it, my finger was on the trigger. Perhaps minor prophecy skills will suffice here.

The drill started, caught the shorts and ran a couple of inches into my upper thigh, right alongside the scar from the earlier incident. The blood flowed and off I went to see a doctor. I often wonder if young Jim learned from the demonstration. I know I did.

A Marriage Reviewed
Ant Dry

James lay in bed, sweating, his wife Nora sleeping next to him.

He could not sleep.

He and Nora had had another robust discussion that evening, and he felt quite drained.

Was it always his fault, as Nora insisted, or was she to blame? What were they fighting about anyway? He tried to remember, but exhaustion made it impossible.

As he lay there, hands behind his head, staring at the ceiling, he considered. Was he happy? He'd been married to Nora for 40 years now and he could not remember a single day without conflict.

Was she happy? She liked spending the cash he brought home, but there was always a petulance about her. It seemed to James that Nora was disappointed with the amount he earned. She always made him feel that she had been short changed, that he was somewhat less than he could be. That she could have done so much better for herself.

There was even conflict over the kids. He couldn't work out what the problem was. He thought the kids were absolutely wonderful, but Nora was perpetually disappointed in them too.

James allowed his mind to wander.

A memory of his first girlfriend Yvonne came to mind. He smiled. Now that was a wonderful girl. They had met when he was a university student, and she was a student nurse. She was his first love. She did not know what misery was. Her job taught her that life was short, and could be painful, and she was determined to enjoy what she had to the full. Life with Yvonne was full of fun, laughter, and happiness. They had partied, made love and laughed a great deal.

He frowned. What had happened to Yvonne? That was over 40 years ago.

He felt a tear form, and he allowed it to run down his face, only wiping it away when it was about to drop onto the sheet. Ah, how his life would have been different if he had married Yvonne. She was loving and warm. She would never have made him feel worthless like Nora. She would have bolstered him up. Cheered him up, made him laugh. She would have loved their children as much as he did. Another tear formed.

He sobbed.

His wife sat bolt upright.

"What's the matter?" she cried in alarm.

In a blinding flash of clarity, James woke up, looked over at his wife of 40 years, and it wasn't Nora!

Yvonne sat there, looking dishevelled.

"What's the matter? Why are you crying?"

He pulled her into his arms; "I'm okay. I'm not crying at all. I'm sorry I woke you. I've just had the most terrible nightmare, and I'm so relieved you're here."

On the Beach
Meg McLaren

Oh Mother!
We are killing you.

My thoughts are dark.
Like a spine of black rocks
That sink down into salt pools
That splash and swirl.
Seaweed, bronzed copper,
Lies wavy over the shadowy pillars.
Small white waves near the shore
Languidly lap and lick at the sand.
The sea stretches out, unbelievably gorgeous,
Just the sea and the sky stretching out forever.

Here a child in a blue shirt plays,
And dreams bright dreams of the sea.
And the ships that pass by,
Like toys in a bath.
A small hand rests on the old, dark stones,
Fair and clean as his soul.
Like a blessing in the air.
I want to close my fingers tight around his dream
Lest it become a flutter of the past,
And will come back no more.

Stunning Coup for Cradle Coast Council
Ian Nettleton

In a dramatic and highly successful action, Cradle Coast Council (the new amalgamation of Burnie, Central Coast and Devonport Councils) occupied Wellington Parliament House, taking possession of New Zealand and declaring sovereignty over the former nation. This was prompted by habitual whinger, Mayor Cheryl Alison Conz, taking umbrage at a speech at the Australia Day Citizenship awards when a Kiwi-born new citizen boasted that migrants who arrive in Australia from New Zealand raise the IQ of both nations.

In a unanimous vote, councillors secretly declared war on New Zealand and assembled a flotilla consisting of the *Julie Burgess*, *Goliath* and the *Leven Explorer* trawler. An army of marines, consisting mainly of wild duck hunters and wallaby shooters, was recruited from local hotels and set sail for Wellington.

With serendipitous coincidence, that Saturday 11 March had been declared a public holiday in the Shaky Isles for rehearsals and practice drills in preparation for a possible earthquake, cyclone or plague of brush-tail possums. All military personnel, police and emergency services staff had been deployed to rural areas where most damage might be expected. Parliament House was unoccupied and guarded by a solitary Councillor. Distracted by a ewe that the invaders had brought with them, he was unaware that the building had been taken over by the occupying force. Phoning the local TV, radio and social media outlets, they announced to the populace that the North and South Islands had now been taken over by the West Island and the newly-created state would henceforth be known as New Van Diemens Land.

Assuming that a massive military invasion force must be responsible, Kiwis responded with a marked degree of apathy and inertia, philosophically concluding that they had become fellow-countrymen with most of their relatives who were already in Australia anyway. Cradle Coast Councillors are now determining how many Tasmanian gaol inmates can be deported across the Tasman Sea.

The Amusement Park Engineer
Edith Speers

Once upon a time there was a big city by the sea. The city was built all along the water's edge and the water curved in a big circle to make a harbour that was deep and safe from storms. Ships came over the sea and when they saw the two lights which stood on two cliffs at the entrance to the harbour then everyone felt glad. The ships passed between the two high cliffs and between the two lights that stood on the cliffs. Then they were safe in the harbour and all around them was the big city of many people.

There was a bridge across the harbour. At one end of the bridge on one side of the harbour there was the centre of the city. But at the other end of the bridge on the other side of the harbour there was the amusement park. The amusement park was called Luna Park. People went there to have adventures. When a ship came into the harbour of the city and when it saw Luna Park in the day time or in the night time it knew right away that Luna Park was a place where exciting things happened. That's what an adventure is. It's an exciting thing that happens.

In the day time or in the night time Luna Park looked exciting. In the day time when every other building and place in the city was white or black or grey or brown, Luna Park was red and yellow and green and blue and orange and pink and purple. These colours went up and down in curves like waves on the sea or they went in round shapes with points on the top like onions or they went in big round shapes that were made up of many tiny flat shapes like the face of a diamond.

At night time Luna Park looked exciting because of the coloured lights that were hung along every shape in the park. The lights outlined the shapes of the buildings and the rides. A ship coming into the harbour at night saw not the places at Luna Park and it saw not their colours. What it saw was the shapes of the places all in lines made up of round spots of coloured light. The ship knew right away that it was looking at an amusement park where there were exciting adventures.

At Luna Park you bought tickets to the different buildings and rides and each was a different adventure. But before you did this you had to buy a ticket to get into the park. This was called the admission ticket. On the ticket it said, "Admit One." The admission ticket was not expensive but there was a rule. You had to carry your own ticket by yourself as you went through a special gate. When you were at the gate you had to put your ticket into a slot on the gate. If you put the ticket into the slot the right way then the gate opened just long enough to let you through. Everyone had to do this for themselves.

Because of this rule no one ever went into Luna Park who was not big enough and smart enough to know that it was an amusement park and that all the places inside of the park were for adventures. The people who owned the park did not want anyone in the park who didn't understand this. There was a good reason for the rule.

People go to an amusement park for adventures. The best amusement park will make the most money. The best amusement park is the one with the best adventures and the best adventures are a very tricky business. They have to be real enough that people forget they are not real. But they must be unreal enough that people can remember somewhere inside themselves that they picked out and paid for this adventure themselves and that they will get out of it okay and still be themselves.

Adventures are exciting. But adventures are not always things that make you laugh. Adventures do strange things to people and sometimes they are very scary. In Luna Park the adventures were so exciting that while they happened, people almost forgot that they were not real. This was the best part of the adventure. This was why Luna Park was famous. These adventures were made up by a man called the amusement park engineer. He was the best in the business. He did not own Luna Park. He worked for the boss of Luna Park and the boss worked for the owners of Luna Park.

The best thing that ever happened to the boss of Luna Park was when the amusement park engineer came to work for him. It started very simply. This man came into his office one day and said, "You need me, I think." The boss was in the middle of adding up how little money the park was earning these days and he knew he needed something. He thought he needed money or maybe a strong drink. He didn't think he needed this man.

"Get lost," said the boss.

"I can fix your Hall of Mirrors," said the man.

The boss looked up and said, "What? How'd it get broken?"

"It's not broken," said the man. "It's boring. I can make it better."

It so happened that the boss had the accounts book open to the page where it showed that the Hall of Mirrors was making less money than any of the other places in Luna Park.

"If you can make it better," said the boss, "then you got yourself a job."

"I already work here," said the man. "I sell the admission tickets."

"You!" said the boss." Aren't you the one that invented that special gate for us?"

"Yes," said the man.

That's saved us a lot of trouble," said the boss.

What he didn't say was that the special gate saved them money, too. Every time somebody got too scared at the park and got too upset, it spoiled the fun for everyone. Or sometimes accidents happened. Scared people made a big noise about it. For a while afterwards other people didn't go to the place where the trouble happened. Also the park had to try to make the scared person happy and make that person shut up about the trouble by giving back their money or giving them free tickets to other things.

"I thought it was a good idea," said the man, "even though you said you'd sell fewer tickets and the park would lose money."

"Did I?" said the boss. "But I let you go ahead with it."

"Yes, but you said it was just for a week. That was a few months ago."

"Was it that long ago?"

"Yes. I remember because it was just after that crazy man tore apart the Haunted House. It was the same week that the baby fell in the water at the Tunnel of Love."

"Ah yes," said the boss. "Well, what about the Hall of Mirrors?"

"It's boring. Put someone else on the admission gate for a while and let me have a go at fixing it."

"There's no rise in pay," said the boss. Then quickly he said, "But if ticket sales go up there might be a bonus. And don't spend too much on new materials. You'll have to use what we got."

The man did as he was told. He did not need any special new things anyway. All he needed was electrical wire and mirror glass and coloured lights. There was nothing special about this stuff but the man did something special with these ordinary things. As soon as he was finished with the Hall of Mirrors the ticket sales went up and up and up. The boss couldn't believe it. He couldn't figure it out. He went to the Hall of Mirrors to have a look for himself.

He went inside the Hall of Mirrors and looked around. It looked the same as before. But it was busy. He could hear people shrieking and laughing all over the place. He couldn't see them because the Hall of Mirrors was built like a zigzag hallway with a different mirror at each zig and zag. Only a few people could walk side by side through the hall and only one at a time could stand on the foot-shapes marked on the floor in front of each mirror.

The boss went and stood in front of the first mirror. It made him look twice his usual size. It was a bit strange because it didn't make him look swollen or fat. In fact he looked a bit slimmer than usual around the stomach but a lot bigger around the shoulders and arms. And of course he was taller. Then he noticed a sign beside the mirror. It said, "Here is how you see yourself."

He frowned. "Very funny, I don't think," he said to himself. He didn't like that sign at all. It was okay to have a mirror that made people look bigger but it was not okay to put up a sign like that beside it. He'd say something about that sign to the admissions man. It had to go.

Then before the boss left the mirror, a little girl came up to the mirror and stood in the foot-shapes. She was sucking her thumb. She stood and stared at the mirror. The boss looked at her in the mirror, too. She looked about half her normal size. In the mirror she was as bald as a baby and she was wearing only a nappy. Outside the mirror she was about six years old with long brown hair. She was wearing a T-shirt and jeans and joggers. She took her thumb out of her mouth and she pointed her finger at the mirror and burst out laughing. "Hey mum!" she yelled to a woman who was just coming along. "Come and look at me!"

The woman put on a smile but she looked tired. She was a nice looking woman about thirty years old. She came and stood behind her daughter and giggled. The daughter said, "You have a go." The mother stood in the foot-shapes and stared into the mirror with round eyes. Her mouth fell open. In the mirror she looked about fifty years old and she was dressed in rags. Her hair stuck out and looked messy.

The boss waited to hear her howl at such a sight. But she only said, "Good heavens!" and touched her hand to her hair. Then she said to the little girl, "I see I need an appointment at the hairdresser and some new clothes."

The little girl said, "And I need some hair and some clothes, too!" They laughed together and walked along to the next mirror.

The boss of Luna Park followed them very slowly. He hung around inside the Hall of Mirrors. He looked at himself in the mirrors and he watched other people looking in the mirrors. All the mirrors had signs alongside them. Sometimes people didn't like what they saw in the mirrors, but then their friends or family laughed and made jokes so they had to smile and pretend it was all funny. Then at the next mirror things changed. The angry person laughed and the laughing person got angry or sad or thoughtful.

The mirrors also had signs that said things like, "How your spouse sees you" and "How your best friend sees you" and "How your boss sees you." Every kind of mirror was in the Hall of Mirrors and every mirror showed every person in a different way. The boss of Luna Park went and stood in front of the mirror that said, "How your girlfriend sees you" but he didn't have a girlfriend so there was nothing in the mirror. He stood in front of the mirror that said, "How your employees see you." He was not surprised that he looked ugly and bad-tempered. But he was surprised to see himself in a clown's outfit. He was puzzling over that when he came to the last mirror in the Hall of Mirrors.

Beside this mirror there was a sign that said, "The Truth."

"Good God!" thought the boss. "No one wants to know the truth!" He was so upset at the thought of such a mirror and such a sign that he stomped right past it.

But he couldn't go past it. A blaze of light made him stop and turn and step in front of the mirror. He stared. At first all he saw was a small bright light. It was white light and it was just at the height of his heart. It was a round shape made up of many small flat bits like the face of a diamond. When his eyes got used to the bright light from this diamond at his heart then the boss of Luna

Park saw that he could not see himself in the mirror, but he could see the shape of himself outlined in coloured lights. The lights were all different colours in round spots but the spots glowed and sent out small streams of light so the light seemed to burn like flames coming out of the shape of his body or like petals coming out of a flower.

The boss of Luna Park turned away from the mirror and went and stood by the exit door. He was thinking, "That was a trick. It was too beautiful to be me." At the same time he wanted to go out the exit door and pretend that what he saw in the mirror really was the truth. But he knew it couldn't be the truth. So he stood and watched the next few people come up to the mirror. When they left he watched the next few people. Every person was different in the mirror. Every person had a bright diamond light but at a different height according to the height of the person's heart. Every person had coloured lights outlining the shape of their body but the shapes were all different according to the shape of the person. Different people also had different colours of light.

As he walked back to the office the boss was thinking, "If I go back to the Hall of Mirrors after a few weeks or a few months maybe I will look different in the mirrors." Then he knew why the ticket sales were going up and up and up. A lot of new people were going to the Hall of Mirrors when they heard about it from friends. But also the same people were going back again and again to see how they were changed.

The boss of Luna Park hired the admissions man as the amusement park engineer. He gave him a big bonus and also a big rise in pay. He told the engineer to do whatever he wanted to do in the park and to buy whatever things he wanted. But the amusement park engineer didn't want anything special. He could make exciting adventures out of ordinary things and he liked doing it.

He made a Tunnel of Love where people really fell in love with each other but only as long as the ride lasted. People climbed into little boats that floated on a stream. The stream went in a circle and most of the circle was covered by a tunnel that was very dark inside. But along the way there were niches in the tunnel wall and in each niche were 3-D moving pictures that acted out all the different famous love stories from books and from history and even from ordinary life. The people in the boats sighed or smiled or laughed and compared themselves to the stories. If they liked each other already then the people in the boat had fun being in love. If they didn't like each other then they remembered this and yet they still fell in love. This was puzzling and it was also annoying, but most of all it was exciting. Going into the Tunnel of Love with someone you didn't like was even more exciting than going in with someone you liked. This was strange but people kept doing it. Ticket sales went up and up and up.

The amusement park engineer also made a Haunted House where real ghosts moved through real walls and where real poltergeists really threw things around and scared people. But the scare only lasted while you were in the Haunted House. People staggered out of the House with their hair standing on end and their knees wobbling. They said to each other, "That was great! Let's do it again..." Ticket sales went up and up.

The amusement park engineer changed every game and every ride in Luna Park. He made them all better. He made them all real. In the shooting gallery you could shoot at real animals but also they could fight back or escape. You could shoot at real soldiers but also they could shoot back. You could kill them but also they could kill you. But after the game was over then you were fine and they were fine. You could ride real horses in real horse races on the merry-go-round. You could ride real cars at the dodgem cars and you could really crash and you could really die. But only as long as the ride lasted. Then it was over and you climbed out into the real world and you said to each other; "That was great!"

Every adventure at Luna Park was a great adventure and all of the ticket sales kept going up. But for the boss of Luna Park the favourite thing of all was always the Hall of Mirrors and his favourite mirror was The Truth.

One day you will get on a ship and cross the ocean. When you see the two lights on the two cliffs at the entrance to the harbour you will feel glad. When you pass between the two lights and the two cliffs you will be inside the deep safe harbour and you will see the bridge over the harbour. At one end of the bridge you will see the centre of the city. But at the other end of the bridge you will see Luna Park. You will see right away that it is a place where exciting things happen.

The Umbrella
Angela Bischof-Joseph

The monsoon season in the tropics is known to catch people unawares with a deluge of rain at the most unsuspecting time. Shan and his wife Lita had decided to go to their local hawker centre for lunch. In Singapore, hawker food is so cheap that sometimes Singaporeans don't cook at home, opting to eat out at every meal. Why bother with the fuss and work?

"I shall take an umbrella," Lita said to Shan and reached to the umbrella holder inside their front door to select a foldable one. Taking the lift down their high-rise public housing block to the ground floor, they stopped at the traffic lights obeying the red stop light. Jaywalking in Singapore incurred hefty fines, and they did not need one. Large raindrops started falling on them, and Lita opened her umbrella. The traffic lights changed to green, and they ran along the crossing. When they reached the other side, their legs and feet were wet, and Shan had one shoulder soaking wet. The umbrella did not provide enough shelter for both of them. The hawker centre was just fifty metres away. Shaking the excess water from the umbrella, she folded it when they reached the centre.

They walked around the different stalls, looking for the type of cuisine they wanted. The enticing aromas of mixed-race foods wafted through the air as they passed one stall after another. Chinese Hokkien Mee, Malay Rojak, Indian Roti Jala and Curry. There were over thirty stalls to choose. The ever-popular Hainanese Chicken rice won the competition. They ordered their meal and settled at a table to wait for it to arrive. Rows of tables with plastic stools lined the front of the stalls. About two tables away was a policeman in full uniform eating his meal. Looking at his bowl, he was concentrating on transporting his noodles to his mouth with a pair of chopsticks. Lita's seat faced the policeman while Shan's back was to him.

Lita, while seated, decided to open the umbrella and place it on the ground to allow it to dry. She held it up and pressed the button. The umbrella's canopy did not open; instead, it became a projectile heading straight toward the unsuspecting policeman leaving the handle in Lita's hand.

Horrified, Lita watched her umbrella top, thankfully, land at the policeman's side and burst open.

The policeman threw down his chopsticks and shot upright, both hands by his sides, ready to pull out his gun and baton. The shocked look on his face was priceless when he realised that what was beside him was just an umbrella top.

Quickly looking around to see if anyone was watching him, he sat down and returned to eating his bowl of noodles with an expression of embarrassment. Lita had watched the event happen over Shan's shoulder. Shan had witnessed the umbrella top shoot past his shoulder and had turned to watch it land beside the policeman. Even though the policeman did not look up, Lita hid behind Shan's frame and burst into silent laughter, covering her face with her hands. Shan was laughing, too, although in a more restrained manner.

Signalling Shan to get the top, Lita pretended to look into her handbag to disguise her laughter as she could no longer hide behind his frame when he went toward the policeman to pick up the top. The policeman did not move or say anything. Shan said, "Sorry," picked up the top, and returned to his seat. The policeman finished his meal minutes later and left the Hawker centre, walking with his head held high.

Lita dumped the umbrella in the nearest bin as they left the Hawker centre. Thankfully it did not rain on the way home.

Sharp Love
Dawn Meredith

I'm risking everything to come here,
every blood-red, panicked moment.
Your world is a midnight place
where I pick my way over sharpnesses,
the taste of a wild, soulless wind on my tongue.

There's a certain rhythm here,
as you stride across this desolate landscape,
metallic fears swinging along beside you,
phantoms of what you've lost, hovering.
At other times you huddle behind obstructions,
waiting for the jagged, dirty-blue ceiling to fall in.

Yellow eyes are everywhere –
Sneaky, desperate, incredibly sad and vicious eyes.
No wonder you're suspicious of everyone
If this is where you live.

You keep everything up top brightly packaged,
With silk ribbons and cellophane.
Look, but don't open.
Admire, but don't ask questions.

No one else seems to realize you're adrift
on this bruised ocean of pain.
I tiptoe across to you, but it's unstable for me.
I could lose my footing at any time,
Any moment.

I don't know why I'm so desperate to reach you.
You hold no interest for me,
Stretched thinly across the face of your shallow values.
But I feel compelled to say
That you can't go on living like this,
cracked fingernails embedded in this landscape.

You've tucked yourself away in crevices so deep
that you can no longer see the surface.
But I see soft glimmers of the real you –
something quirky, something joyful,
something so tiny and forgotten.

I search in the bleakness, cup my hands
around those petals of purest you
that spring up briefly – a flash of colour in the gloom.
You keep shrinking away from my touch.
I am compelled to love you, rescue you,
But I can't wait forever.

You have to show me a sign that this is worth it.
Why should I inhabit this dark place with you?
I've been somewhere like this myself, once.
I fought to escape, believe.
No. You must come out into the light, to me.
Release your grip.
Fall into my embrace.

Morning Song
Brenda Slavoff

All the grace of the morning
Is returning from a long, dark sadness
As your voice is silvered with singing,
Every note sure as hope and gladness.
Small harbinger of sunrise, in a race
For the first burst of clear rejoicing,
Fluttering dull feathers as you chase
The early worm; my breath stills as you sing.

Loop-De-Loop
Hank Koopman

"Have you ever experienced a loop-de-loop before?" he asked me over the intercom.

"No Sir," I replied, a little apprehensively, as I'd been told this aircraft was not really built for aerobatics. What fifteen tonne bomber is?

My divisional officer asked if I'd like to fly with him today on a dummy bombing exercise in the Southern Highlands near Morton National Park. Thrilled at the prospect as flying has always been a passion of mine, there was no hesitation in my reply in the affirmative.

I was about to commence a career as an aircraft fire fighter, and part of the course was to gain knowledge about the aircraft we would become involved with at HMAS Albatross. These included Wessex and Iroquois helicopters, Vampire and Sea Venom jet fighters. Fitted with ejection seats, these needed specialist knowledge to disarm them prior to attempting any rescue of aircrew.

A Gannet unfolding its wings while preparing for take-off. (Image via Jeff Chartier. NAAA)

Fairey Gannets were not fitted with ejection seats, however we were still required to familiarise ourselves with the harness and quick release buckles with which aircrew were strapped into their seats. It also had an internal bomb bay capable of carrying a variety of explosive ordinances, including bombs, mines, torpedoes and depth charges. Electronic sonar buoys could also be dropped to seek out and find enemy submarines. Fairey Gannets were the RAN's primary anti-submarine warfare deterrent from its first introduction into the RAN in 1955, until it was phased out in 1967.

The Gannet was a revolutionary aircraft, being the first turbo-prop aircraft to come into service featuring the Double Mamba turbine engine, driving the contra-rotating propellers via a central shaft and gear box which made it look like it only had one engine when in fact there were two.

Excitement mounted when I was issued with a flying suit and helmet at the safety equipment store. Included in today's issue was a parachute pack that became a backrest for the cockpit seat into which I'd be strapped. A dinghy pack was used as the seat cushion in case it became necessary to ditch into the ocean.

Ambling out to where our "ugly duckling" (so named by many in the Fleet Air Arm) was parked on the tarmac; she posed a formidable figure, standing thirteen feet and six inches high.

With a length of forty-three feet and a wingspan of fifty-four feet and four inches, this aeroplane would not ordinarily be considered capable of performing loop-de-loops. Now, I was soon to be informed by my young erstwhile divisional officer, that he took pleasure in doing this manoeuvre whenever he could on most of his sorties.

When it is stowed away in the hangar, the wing configuration resembles a letter Z. Therefore, you immediately come to the conclusion that there has to be an inherent weakness in its structural integrity with a wing that has two folds along its span. This deduction was further amplified when, after clambering into my cockpit and getting strapped into the seat harness, then attached to the intercom jack and oxygen supply, the pilot conducted a walk-around check of the aircraft before climbing up and into his cockpit to begin running through his pre-start check list.

A starter cartridge was fired to start the first engine, bring it up to the correct revolutions to then enable it to engage the second engine. As soon as the second engine whined into life and increased its revolutions, the whole aircraft shook and seemed to dance on its three wheels in the one spot. With engines fighting against the chocks and brakes, vibrations began shaking the whole airframe violently. Looking outside my Perspex bubble, the wings were bouncing around in rhythm to the continued increase in power being generated by the engines.

Over the intercom I could hear my pilot relaying his intentions to the control tower for a one-hour flight to Morton National Park. With clearance given, he waved "away chocks" to the ground crew, pulled back on the throttles which quietened down the vibrations, then released the brakes. By re-applying a small amount of throttle we taxied to the duty runway.

"How are you doing back there Mr Koopman?" he asked. Officers all seemed to do that in the navy; call subordinates by their surname. Was it just so they could keep ratings in their place? We always had to reply to them as "Sir". After a while it was just a given, I suppose, so I dutifully replied,

"Fine thank you Sir."

"OK then. We'll get airborne shortly," he concluded, further concentrating on his pre-flight check list. At the end of the apron leading onto the duty runway, he once again brought the two engines to maximum power; I presumed to make sure they wouldn't flame out on take-off. Held only by the brakes this time, we bounced around on the one spot again. Our wings seemed to be shaking and flapping even more eagerly than before, in quite an alarming fashion. I heard the pilot make one last call to the control tower for permission to enter the duty runway and line up for take-off.

With clearance given, we rolled forward onto the runway, lining up the centre line. Suddenly I felt myself pushed back into my seat as the powerful turbo-prop engines were released. Barrelling down the runway we reached 120 mph and became airborne, commonly referred to as "rotating" in the aviation industry. Wheels were retracted almost immediately after we left the runway, a habit that carrier-borne pilots seemed to share as part of their training when being catapulted from the deck of their floating airfield. Anything that caused drag was seen as a disadvantage to get the aircraft powering away and clawing for altitude.

For such a heavy aircraft she effortlessly started climbing at 2000 feet per minute. At level flight she had a top speed of 299 mph (485 kph) which is remarkable for such a leviathan. On attaining 10,000 feet the intercom crackled into life again.

"So, what do you reckon, Mr Koopman?" He referenced his earlier question to me again; "Should we go for a loop-de-loop today?"

"I wasn't aware this aeroplane was capable of performing aerobatics Sir," thereby letting him know I was apprehensive about his suggestion.

"Yeah, I know they say that it can't be done, but I've done it just about every time I go up," he divulged his secret to me, sounding sure of his ability to achieve this dare-devil manoeuvre. After all he was my divisional officer, a lieutenant with wings on his tunic to signify that he was a pilot. That placed him well above my pay grade. I was about to turn twenty-one and I figured he might be about eight or nine years older than me, which isn't that much older when you think about it. He must've been a lot smarter though, or else he wouldn't be a pilot, would he, I convinced myself. Trouble is I thought his attitude was somewhat "gung-ho" and it didn't sit too well with me.

Then I thought about the training he must have completed to be placed in command of an aircraft in the RAN. These guys were exceptional pilots, landing on one of the smallest aircraft carriers in the world at that time. Landing on a flight deck measuring 690 feet long by 80 feet wide and travelling at 20 knots away from your aeroplane's projected point of landing, didn't leave much room for error. Landing on an aircraft carrier at night, being bounced around by waves, was even more dangerous, requiring extraordinary skill as an aviator. These guys were exceptional pilots.

We were now well away from the airfield and prying eyes. He surmised that if he did his practice bombing run first, he would disappear from HMAS Albatross's radar screen for an instant only. So, he contacted the tower to let them know of his intentions. Then switching to the intercom he told me what would happen next.

"I'll do the bombing run first," he said, stating his decision. "I'll be peeling off to port in three." (Left in lay man's terms in three seconds). I was pushed to the right of the cockpit as he side-slipped the plane on one side and dropped out of the sky careening down into a dive heading for what looked like a deep canyon.

The air speed indicator in my cockpit revealed a speed of 320 mph with the ground rushing up to meet us. With my face contorting into what felt like a rubber mask because of the G-forces, my arms pinned down beside me, I wondered how he could still function himself, to pull us out of the dive. I gasped a sigh of a relief when he pulled out at 5,000 feet. Considering the terrain was about 3,000 feet above sea level, we were about 2,000 feet above the actual ground.

"How was that?" he yelled in an excited voice, showing that even they still get a "buzz" out of performing these exciting pretend war games we used to play as kids in our back yards.

"There's a 'barf' bag jammed under your seat if you need one," he jokingly reminded me.

"No, I'll be right sir," I replied with an equally excited, but reserved quaver in my voice.

"You handled that OK then," he continued being quite chatty, "so now I think we'll finish the day's flight with a loop-de-loop." It seemed like I no longer had a say in the matter. He was determined to execute one.

Once again, we climbed to approximately 10,000 feet. In our last dive the wings had remained intact, though there was a lot of vibration felt throughout the airframe. I'd be lying if I didn't admit to being scared. Not terrified, just unhealthily frightened out of my wits. The intercom crackled. "Keep your head back hard against the headrest. As we reach the top of the loop, observe the earth by rolling your eyes back to finding an inverted horizon, then relax as we level out again. Ready? Going into the dive I'll jerk back on the column when we reach 320 knots. Here we go!!!!"

Unlike the bombing run, we didn't peel off. This time it was a full power dive straight down. Once again, the face becomes distorted as the G-forces build up with intensity. Performing a loop-de-loop is best described as being on a roller coaster ride, though I don't think they reach 320 knots. At the required speed the yoke is pulled back hard and for the passenger it feels like your stomach is being squashed into your anus and the contents of it are about to squelch out through your mouth.

"Yeeeehaaa!!!!" he bellowed out an exhilarating yell as we levelled out again. "Wasn't that the greatest feeling," he enquired of me? "Didn't use the 'barf bag'?" he asked inquisitively.

"It was great sir," I concurred excitedly; under my breath thinking something else entirely. What sets these dare devils off? They are entrusted with an expensive aeroplane to play with by our government, then treat it as a fun ride at a fair ground. However, in time of actual war, these pilots have to know what their aircraft are capable of doing. What better way to find out on a practice bombing run.

"Great. We'll do a couple more before we head for home."

I thought to myself, "You and your big mouth!" I was subjected to another two loop-de-loops in a bomber that wasn't designed for aerobatics at all.

(Of the 37 Gannets purchased by the Australian Government, 15 were involved in crashes. Sadly, six aircrew lost their lives.)

Home
Graeme Hetherington

Teetering timidly on the edge,
Afraid to take the plunge, immerse
Myself in blood and sweat, I seemed

Misplaced, born all wrong for the rough
And tumble of Tasmania's West,
The physicality of fights,

Preferring distant combat in
The form of throwing stones. And when
My younger brother took my part

I'd turn tail, leave him to it, then
Reward with jealous rage. But I've
Endured all this, self-hate, the shame,

Unbroken by reproaches from
Judgemental parents teachers, peers,
Consequent alcoholism,

Loss of wives, children, friends, my life-
Long unsuccessful searching for
Where best to live, during which I've

Learnt to look cowardice in the eye,
To never cut and run as I
Wrestle with words to create from

The mess that seems to be myself,
Poems, that sublimate, transcend
Childhood's defeat and are my home.

The Priory
Kathleen Bentley

Jill and Colin were married at All Saints Church in front of their families and friends, with a buffet lunch afterwards at the church hall just a few steps through the garden at the rear of the church. It was a glorious sunny day with a warm breeze and a cloudless blue sky. Everyone smiled and looked happy as, of course, were the Bride and Groom.

Jill and Colin had decided on a delayed honeymoon as they had just built their house so were keen to move into it and complete their furnishings – unpacking the last few boxes of crockery and hanging paintings. At last they were farewelled by all as they drove to their new home.

The house stood amid lovely countryside of green paddocks and tree copses on the gentle slopes of the Titmus Ranges, with a creek running along the rear boundary of their property. Legend has it that a Priory once stood on the site but was robbed and burnt to the ground by William III. Jill was interested in history and thought the story was quite charming, meaning to research the history of the Priory when the unpacking was done and the house in order.

These tasks duly completed, the couple celebrated with a champagne and crayfish picnic at the side of the stream. They lay back and enjoyed the ambiance of the day, discussing their future plans. They still had four weeks before they had to return to their respective places of work. While Jill was keen to learn more of the mystery of the Priory, Colin was eager to plant a rose garden for Jill.

Colin hired a backhoe to do the heavy work of removing the wild grasses, bushes and many large stones which he believed were part of the old Priory. He had fertilized the wide circle which was to become the rose garden and had called at the local gardening centre and had chosen 20 Peace rose bushes to plant.

Jill on the other hand, had discovered some interesting facts about the Priory and its occupants. They were of the Congregation of Marian Fathers of the Immaculate Conception of the Most Blessed Virgin Mary, an Order established on 11 December 1670, by Saint Stanislaus Papczyński. He was a Polish Priest, supported by the local Bishop, in his bid to establish a community of men dedicated to spreading the honour of the Immaculate Conception. The Order was to have a profound effect on the Catholic Church as this dedication spread throughout Europe and today there are almost 400 men in this Order. William III's attempts to destroy this religious order appears to be only a hiccup in its continuing strength in spreading the message of Divine Mercy however; William was ruthless and put many priests to death. The last protester, a young Initiate, was bound to the church alter and died amid the blaze that turned the church into a heap of rubble. Rumour has it that the Initiate still roams the long gone halls of the Priory and can be seen tending the trees which line the gravel road to its entrance – now the driveway to Jill and Colin's home – on Mid-summer Eve.

Jill delved further and found the story of the Saint and the rise of this Order intriguing and an idea of writing a book soon took root. Colin was as enthusiastic about the book as was Jill, and Jill thought the rose garden, although yet to flower, just wonderful. Colin turned his attention to other parts of the land he wanted to develop as gardens and Jill continued to research the religious order at the Priory.

It was Mid-summer Eve and the couple were enjoying an early dinner in the rose garden. Colin had laid concrete paving stones within the circle so the roses encircled these. To pay tribute to the Priory's previous existence a design based on the Congregation of Marian Fathers of the Immaculate Conception of the Most Blessed Virgin Mary emblem, with the Virgin Mary at its central point and the motto For Christ and the Church underneath this image, had pride of place at the centre of the paving's perimeter, in appropriate coloured tiles. It looked beautiful, and a fitting memorial to days gone by.

Sipping their coffee as the sun began its descent and the stars began to distinguish themselves Colin saw a movement on the driveway, close to the trees. He was surprised to see a thin, dark young man clothed in a monk's habit. The man was apparently checking each tree and removing new buds growing too low on the trunk of each one. He waved to Colin and Colin waved back. Colin thanked him and asked whether he would like some wine, but the young man just smiled and shook his head. Colin and Jill watched the man as he walked through the circle then stopped suddenly in front of the tiled figure; dropping to his knees he clasped his hands together in prayer. Jill and Colin looked at each other as the man stood with bowed head.

Suddenly the circle was full of monks! They sank to their knees in prayer then arose and bowed their heads. The hair on the back of Jill and Colin's heads prickled as, with one voice but in perfect harmony, the monks sang to the Virgin Mary: praising her grace, her services for the glory of mankind, her strength to those in need, and comfort for the sorrowful. They also attributed their prayers to their devotion to the Virgin Mary, to her mercy towards them, and her unfailing protection to those who sought her help.

Jill and Colin were overcome with the camaraderie of this shared moment with the monks, yet astounded when – one by one – the Peace roses began to bloom. The air was not only filled with the monks' chant but also of the beautiful perfume of the roses. But as suddenly the monks had appeared, they disappeared, and all was quiet within the rose garden. Jill and Colin looked at each other with tears in their eyes. The evening had descended and a cool breeze had sprung up. Without saying a word, both packed the dishes and took them into the house with the haunting melody of the monks chant echoing and the roses perfume following them. They were overwhelmed by their ghostly choir and the reverence of the choral offering. Both Jill and Colin knew they would never experience anything like that again – unless they were still living in their home during next Mid-summer's Eve.

Jill and Colin felt privileged to share in that incredible moment of pure joy which had filled the rose garden that enchanted mid-summer evening; a memory which would be etched in their memories for evermore.

Late Afternoon Walk 2007
(After a painting by David Keeling)
Graeme Hetherington

So taken was I by the light,
The lyricism of the scene's
Blue clarity of summer sky,

Its sunny green expanse of lawn
And golden smooth-limbed she-oak grove
That seemed aspiringly to stretch

And strain upwards away from earth,
I failed at first to spot within
The undergrowth the two bald heads,

Dark glasses wrapped around despite
Shadows almost engulfing them.
And once the visual rot began

A yellow bike came quickly in
To view, festering against a tree,
Its back tyre like a snake curled mouth

To tip of tail contagiously
Thought of as black as buggery.
And round the copse hiding the pair

The grass became as rusty as
Needles used too often for drugs
Instead of gloriously lit,

Such blindness caused by need to see
The pure before the human burst
Upon the naïve eye and fouled.

Man or Monster
Ant Dry

Very occasionally when it is known that I come from Zimbabwe, some wag will ask if I ever met Mugabe. The same goes for our African friends who, acknowledging that we now live in Australia, will ask if we have ever met Shane Warne.

I do not like to include Mugabe and Warne in the same sentence, as they are different in every sense of the word, but it does make sense here, as theirs are some of the first names that spring to mind when the respective countries are mentioned.

The fact is my wife did meet Shane Warne – at Sydney airport. She did not want to intrude, but he noticed her looking at him, introduced himself and casually chatted for a while, forever, cementing him in my wife's heart, and in her sporting hall of fame.

And ....The fact is, I did meet Mugabe – twice in fact.

The first time was in 1981, the year after independence. My father was Headmaster at Lord Malvern School in Harare, one of the first previously whites only schools to admit Black students. Dad invited him to watch the school play. It was a play written by a Ghanaian, and Mugabe's first wife, Sally was from Ghana. Much to everybody's surprise, he accepted the invitation.

During the interval, he was invited to the staff room for tea.

He was quiet, extremely well dressed, and attended by only one security officer. He was quickly surrounded by the other attendees, eager to overhear what he had to say. Conversation was very stilted. Most of the attendees were white, with very little in common with what they thought of as an ex-terrorist they had spent their lives fighting.

At that time I worked in an office that was opposite the Houses of Parliament, and the street had recently been blocked off to provide free parking for the parliamentarians. I had complained, tongue in cheek to my parents, that this was seriously inconvenient as I now had to park a block away.

Trying to thaw the ice, my mother cast around for a topic of conversation that our guest would find interesting. Inexplicably, she mentioned my parking problem. He looked completely bewildered, not understanding at all, but I noticed that he immediately turned his attention to someone else, leaving my mother gazing at his back.

During the awkward silence that followed, a teacher, actually an Australian on secondment, approached him, baby in arms, and asked if he would like to hold her baby.

It was an astonishing thing to see. His whole demeanour changed. He seemed to grow taller, more energised. Smiling widely, he held out his arms. His eyes, which had looked dull from exhaustion, lit up with joy, and he took the baby into his arms, well-practiced and at ease. He and the mother chatted for at least ten minutes before it was announced that part two of the play was about to commence, and he had to reluctantly surrender the child to its mother.

This from the man who Rhodesian propaganda had led us to believe ate white babies for breakfast, a terrorist who would kill without hesitation.

The second time I met him was 24 years later, in 2005. This was five years after he had encouraged the invasion of white-owned farms, and after he had started to suggest in speeches that white people should pack their bags and leave the country.

At that time he was universally hated in the Cities but had managed to retain the vote through intimidation and vote rigging. Everyone, including his Deputies, was frightened witless by him. For good reason: His opponents disappeared in equally regular and unexplained ways.

At the time I was the co-owner of a company that held the Mercedes Benz franchise. It was a lucky business to be involved in. Government wanted our product and supported us to obtain it. We were one of the few companies left to our own devices.

Mugabe had ordered a new armoured Mercedes, and it was my project to oversee. The process was exciting and lengthy. It involved the purchase of a standard vehicle, and the slow process of having it stretched, and armoured. It involved various trips to the factory, sometimes accompanied by the Secret Service.

Eventually the vehicle arrived and the Secret Service man, with whom I had become quite friendly, asked me if I wanted to hand the vehicle over to the President myself.

My secretary Esther and I had developed a running joke over the previous few years. Because he was hated so much, there were regular reports that the "old man" was ill and/or dying. On the morning I was invited to do the hand over, Esther had come in almost incoherent with excitement, over the latest rumour of the president's demise. It had really happened she insisted, quoting her sources, which she said were impeccable. She then, as was her habit, broke down into helpless giggles, and we laughed together, knowing that he would live forever.

The fact remained that the rumours gave us all hope, so when I was invited to hand over the car, I accepted, just to see if there was any basis to the rumours, and reason for hope.

He had married his much younger secretary and she had borne him two children, at that stage both younger than ten. The whole family came to see the new car, accompanied by about twelve security officers, all bearing weapons at the ready.

The security people were a little unnerving, but the family itself was absolutely charming. They were delighted to see the car, and they acted just as any family would when they get to see the new family car. They wanted to be shown all the fixtures and how they worked. All four of them clambered in and out of the car. The kids were particularly pleased with the DVD, as we had selected one that would appeal to them, and their mother had to drag them out, amid protests, just as any mother would.

Mugabe himself seemed, disappointingly for Esther and me, in excellent health. Despite being in his eighties, his hair was still jet black, and there was a definite spring in his step. I looked closely at his eyes however and noticed with some satisfaction that they were a little rheumy.

Towards the end, he jabbed me in the ribs and made a joke about how much money we must have made on the deal.

I smiled weakly. It was true.

Brief Moment
Brenda Slavoff

I held you
In my arms
Between two moments

Precious image
Of love
Unexpected –

You rubbed
Your eyes
And I was gone

But I left
My parting blessing
On your lips.

Every Olive Counts – Camping at New Harbour
Susan Austin

The wind flings my flatbread off my lap;
two olives land in the sand.
I'm instructed to pick them up, wash them off.

The departing tide arranges
thousands of translucent blue bodies
and long, opaque tails
on the sand.
A bluebottle invasion
shrivelling in the sun.

We skinny-dip in the creek's
thwarted mouth.
Breaststroke around in the metre-deep fresh water
backed up behind the beach.
The top two centimetres, warmed by the sun.
Below that, refreshing.
Paddle around, goose-bumped,
gazing at seagulls, eucalypts, clouds.
Drying off, we anticipate
a slightly less smelly night in the tent.

I am chastised
for snacking on lunch crackers
before bed.

This is the wild South-West.
Skies menace grey clouds;
cold wind whips into our bones
as we sit on the ground, puffed up
in down jackets, fleece beanies,
long pants and thick socks,
wondering where summer's gone.

Message to a Friend
Donna-Marie Koopman

You're inclined to be a dreamer
with your head in the stars.
Seeking something better for yourself
in life that you are.
Searching for that unknown thing
that even you can't find.
To calm stormy seas
that rage within your mind.
Looking far beyond the truth,
so very close at hand.
Not seeing within yourself,
there lies a special man.
So stop chasing others' rainbows
or envy them their lives.
Seek out the person you've imprisoned,
in the subconscious of your mind.

===///===

Count the things you have; not the things you don't.
Friends be they rich or poor; learned or just simple folk.
If they are good of heart, they enrich us.

Strange Events from the Journal of Louis Lamer
Brenda Slavoff

I had done some watercolours of the views from the house that summer, though I am no true artist. My friend Raoul had asked me to paint the scene for him to keep when the summer was over and we had all separated. He has an artist's soul, and yet he has never been away from his village or had much education. I, who have had an extensive education, travelled widely and mixed in society, am less of an artist at heart than young Raoul of this village on the Brittany coast.

The paintings were of the sea. On a sunny day I caught it in a laughing mood, the white-capped waves singing as they brought in the tide. The sky was crowded with seagulls. Gulls see more than we humans can, but cannot tell of it, to us – yet they tell each other, according to Raoul. Even Valerie, his old school friend, does not believe this! Valerie is too sensible. I am not sensible at all, so I like Raoul's ideas, but I think of them as poetic fancies.

I did a watercolour of the night too; a more difficult undertaking. I remember it was the evening our friend Edwin Knightley arrived. The sun had just set in red and violet; a full moon rode the horizon, splashing the waves with her borrowed light. An evening made for romance. What an anticlimax that we should be expecting only portly middle-aged Edwin Knightley, who is a prosaic English banker, to boot!

I like the sea – and so I should, for my surname is Lamer, French for "the sea". I am half-French, half-English, so I understand both Raoul and Edwin. They are my oldest friends – Valerie, too! Every summer I spend a month boarding at Raoul's house. I have done so ever since, as a boy, I came for the summer here with my father.

The night Edwin arrived everything was just exactly where we had left off the year before. I had just come inside with my finished picture, when we heard the carriage driving up to the door, the way it had last year.

"This is our Knightley ritual," I called out from the doorway where Raoul held up a lantern.

The carriage door was opened. "Louis Lamer, I see – the

same as ever!" came his answering voice.

We rushed forward, I treating him to my usual disrespect as to a forbearing uncle, and Raoul to the gentle familiarities of a friend who is above him in station. There were the usual laughing pleasantries, the questions about our lives since we last met. I have known Knightley since I was a boy of ten; he was my family's banker and my appointed trustee.

When I showed him my watercolours, he commented, "Humph! No change there, either. Your painting hasn't improved since you were sixteen."

I laughed, taking it all in good form. "And your taste is no more refined than it ever was. You collect pictures as investments, only."

"I'm a good judge of art," he said, with a twinkle in his eye.

"No," I contradicted, "merely a good judge of people!"

"Louis' picture is good because the subject is worthy," commented Raoul.

"Not like some of the modern works of art," I remarked. "I recently went to an exhibition where everything looked hazy, as if the painters were short-sighted. Some of the subjects were an error of taste, so perhaps it's just as well. Yet there were one or two that caught the play of light and shadow to a remarkable degree."

After dinner, Raoul brought Valerie over. They made a nice pair, these two, both dark and attractive; though there had never been any romance between them. Valerie lived with her widowed mother in the village, and worked as a casual domestic in some of the finer houses.

As soon as I caught sight of Valerie, I noticed at once how she had matured since last summer, and I expressed amazement at this charming, serious young woman.

"Now I've seen you," I said, "I must stop telling Mr. Knightley that we are all the same as ever, Miss Valerie."

She looked at me intently in turn. "You've changed, too," she said seriously.

I shivered suddenly, as if somebody was walking over my future grave.

"For better or for worse?" parodied Raoul.

Edwin cut through all this, coming over with a glass of wine for her. "I hope you still like to sing, Miss Valerie? Louis hasn't forgotten how to play the piano, and I should enjoy hearing all our old favourites again."

I struck up an accompaniment to encourage her. Valerie obliged, as did Raoul, while I played the piano and Edwin related amusing anecdotes, until Raoul's father and uncle returned from fishing. They too had tales to tell.

"If there is such risk and adventure in fishing, it is an honour to eat the fish!" I declared. "I'm afraid Mr. Knightley and I lead dull lives by comparison."

I sat down at the old piano and began to play the *Moonlight Sonata*. It too had a perfection of beauty, and a brooding as of death ..... How was I to shake off the strange dread?

Edwin was discussing Greek mythology with Raoul, and explaining its influence on poetry through the ages.

"Their gods were the personification of natural powers," said Edwin, "worshipped as divine."

"But you live in the city!" said Valerie to me. "*Paris*." She spoke the last word reverently.

I laughed. "I lead the dullest life of all. I have nothing to win or lose. Mr. Knightley can at least lie awake at night panicking that his stocks will come crashing down, or his pictures be stolen. I would be flattered if anyone bothered to steal my pictures."

I talked to Valerie about my life in Paris as we walked around the garden the next day. I had visited her home and her family, but she had never seen mine. I thought idly that I ought to paint a picture of her.

"I will paint her in this garden, under that old fig tree. I shall call it 'Portrait of a young woman in a Brittany garden' as painters do, making the personal general. As soon as I'm settled, I'll do it."

But one after another the days passed in lazy enjoyment and I was never settled. I did very little, mostly just wandered about on my own, sketching scenery and the imaginary figure of an elusive dark-haired woman. Every evening we gathered together in Raoul's parlour to discuss what we had done and what we would do tomorrow, and somehow I had less and less to say.

"How quiet you are these days, Louis," Raoul remarked one

evening.

"You certainly are not yourself," added Edwin in concern. "Are you sure you are not ill? You hardly ate any dinner today."

I laughed off the suggestion of illness; but I knew that Valerie was right – I was changed. There was a brooding in my heart as of something about to happen, for good or ill, I could not tell. I only sensed its shadow. Was something calling my soul, giving me a distaste for ordinary life? I saw the sun setting, and a mood of dread fastened on me; but even more strange, it was a mood I had been impatiently awaiting all day.

My friends' comments shook me up, and I was suddenly filled with a healthy urge to throw off this strange lassitude of spirit. In my desire to be my old self, I launched into the evening's conversation, describing the Paris art scene.

We compared modern art to traditional, and the talk turned to Renaissance statues of mythological subjects, and their perfection of beauty.

"But of course there are spirits of the earth, the sea, the air," cried Raoul. "There always have been! Life needs not just knowledge but understanding."

"Get wisdom, get understanding, Solomon told us," I murmured.

"It's like love," he continued. "You know when you love; you do not need to think about it."

"You speak like a man of experience," I said, smiling.

"That could be," he grinned back.

"You are making Valerie blush, you two," said Edwin hastily.

"Oh, not Valerie, she's not like other girls," said Raoul positively. "I have told her most of my secrets."

"That's true," she agreed dryly.

"I'd rather keep a diary that no one ever sees," I remarked.

"I keep a private journal of all my business transactions," said Edwin cheerfully, "so I can learn from my mistakes."

The time came for Valerie to leave us, and Raoul's father saw her home. We three friends were alone in the parlour. My uneasiness increased. I poured myself another glass of wine; and then made a resolution. I said abruptly:

"I must tell you about the odd dream I had last night!" I tried to sound light hearted. "It will make you laugh."

Edwin and Raoul looked at me in anticipation of an amusing story.

"Actually," I continued, "I've had three strange dreams; last night, and the two nights preceding it."

I paused. Having committed myself, I was aware of a desperate need to tell my friends the whole of it, but I was at a loss for words. I went on: "It seems I am being haunted!"

Raoul laughed shortly, but Edwin made no comment.

"I'm not sure whether I was asleep at the time or just dozing. But I started up in the night, feeling some presence in the room, and then a movement as of something jumping onto the bed. Quickly I lit my candle and saw it was a black cat. How had it come in? The door was closed and the shutters fastened. The cat curled up against my shoulder, and I felt its soft fur. Suddenly I knew the cat: it was Pixie, my childhood pet; she had returned to me! As I stroked her I remembered how I, an only child, before going to boarding school, used to make up imaginary friends and adventures. I might imagine myself to be a stowaway on a vessel captured by pirates, or a highwayman's apprentice, or companion to a prince at a Renaissance court. And then Pixie would wander in, and I would drop my dreams and cuddle her close to me with all the force of my cold loneliness.

"Feeling happy, I turned over and drifted back to sleep. But a short time later I started up in alarm. The cat was restless and growling, and in concern I stretched out my hand to her again and quickly let out a yell when she scratched me angrily. What had happened to Pixie? She attacked me again and again until I was forced to take her by the scruff of her neck to the window to put her out. At the first touch of the waning moonlight she seemed to shrivel in my hands; she was dead as I flung her out. That was three nights ago."

"Well, how odd," remarked Raoul. Edwin just listened carefully.

"The oddest thing about this dream is that it happened the following night again, in precisely the same way."

I had lain awake waiting for the cat that second night, knowing she would return, my every nerve tuned to the sound of padding feet across the floor. I felt the thump as she leapt upon the bed.

"The cat curled up beside the pillow as before, and as I heard her purring I thought, 'She will not change this time. Something must have upset her last night.' Reassured, I fell asleep – only to be woken sometime later by her warning growls. The cat was transformed again. She howled and scratched as if the devil itself had possessed her.

"As before, after a struggle I succeeded in throwing her out of the window. She was no longer my dear old playmate, but so filled with hatred of me that I was shaken. The cat did not die this time as I flung her out.

"In the morning I got up and looked out, just as I had done the day before. Once again, there was no cat outside the window."

"A dream," said Raoul. "Very odd."

"Yes, but the strangest thing about it is that my hands were covered with scratches that morning!"

I showed my hands to them. Raoul stared at the scratches incredulously.

"I do not know what to make of it," I said, shrugging. "Do you keep the Fiend himself as a pet, Raoul?"

"We have no cat like that, Louis! But it is possible that you were half asleep when some local scavenger came in. Close the shutters very firmly tonight, my friend."

"So I did before, but the cat still entered."

He was perplexed. "Do you sleepwalk, maybe?"

"No, I am sure I don't. Last night I even put a chair, and on that my trunk, against the shuttered window, though it did seem a pity to shut out the mysterious night like that."

"Night air is supposed to be unhealthy," remarked Edwin.

"What happened last night?" asked Raoul, apprehensively? "Did it come again?"

I sat at the piano and played a few chords as a mock-dramatic opening. I was more uneasy than I made out.

"Well *that*," I said, "is the most extraordinary thing so far. It happened again, but this time - ."

"I can guess what happened," said Edwin unexpectedly. He flicked his cigar ash carefully. "It happened again, but this time it was not a cat, but a woman."

I made a startled discord on the piano. "How did you know?" I exclaimed, astounded.

"I have some knowledge of such phenomena," he replied, smiling at my surprise. This calm acceptance made me continue. My fingers trembled so much that I abandoned the piano.

"She was a strange figure in the darkness," I recalled, dazed. "I couldn't see her clearly, but I had always known her; she was the reality of every dream. I wanted to lay my life, my soul, at her feet. It sounds stupid now, but it was so real then." I passed a hand over my forehead which was dewed with sweat.

"At first she was gentle and loving. She came to my side and it seems we talked for some time. She knew all about me, my hopes and dreams. I was so happy that I wished she would stay with me forever. I desired her love more than anything in the world.

"At last I held her in my arms, drunk with happiness.....but at that very moment it all turned to dust, for I saw that she had changed. The same transformation that had overtaken the cat had come over her. Even as I held her she began to abuse me, cruel insults, and it was in vain that I strove to pacify her. She struggled to get free, but I would not let her go until she told me what was wrong.

"I couldn't understand her – what had driven her to this?" My voice was as full of anguish as if it had happened with a real woman. "When I knew she could not be induced to stay, I let her go, but – " I hesitated at the memory.

"But?" Edwin prompted.

"But I would not let her go until I had kissed her once, no matter how much she now hated me. I knew she had loved me before! So despite her frenzied struggles and curses, I kissed her."

The memory made me shiver now.

"When I released her, she pushed past me like a fury and ran to the shutters. I don't know how she got out. When I woke properly, it was morning. It was a strange dream," I ended lamely.

"And do you believe she will come to you again?" asked Edwin.

I shook my head, shocked at the longing within me. "Oh no – surely such a dream could not be repeated!"

"Better stay up all night," suggested Raoul hastily.

Edwin crushed the stub of his cigar in the seashell that

served as an ashtray.

"I doubt," he said, "that even if you avoided your room it would do you the least good."

"I could leave on the first train tomorrow," I cried in a rush. "It is this place – this village. I've got superstitious suddenly."

"He who fights and runs away, lives to fight another day," agreed Raoul, who took it all seriously. "In this case, he'll dream better elsewhere."

Edwin shook his head. "No, no, that is not the way. Do you think the outside world would be a protection from such an influence?"

"What do you mean by 'influence'?" I demanded sharply.

"I mean that you are in danger of your life, and maybe more than your life. You know it, Louis. It was Providence that prompted you to tell us this tonight."

I sat up straight, my voice cold. "You think I am going mad?"

"That might be an easy explanation; but no, I am sure no doctor could help."

Raoul instinctively crossed himself. That gave me an idea:

"What about a priest?" I asked.

"A priest may be authorised to exorcise devils, but you are not possessed. Not yet."

"Then you deny me any help!" I exclaimed, almost angrily. "What is it, after all? Just a dream!"

"It is not just a dream."

"Then it's a nightmare – and I cannot awaken!"

"Steady," said Edwin, laying his hand on my shoulder. "You have, in fact, a friend who has some ancient knowledge. Secret things fascinate me. I have read many books on such strange subjects, though I seldom speak of them."

"You certainly have kept them hidden!" I said, surprised.

"But I remember reading a case just like yours....."

"What *has* happened to me, then?"

"Have you ever heard of the cat goddess Bast, Louis?"

"No, I haven't."

"She was worshipped in ancient Egypt and known in Greece."

"But this is France, the nineteenth century! What have I to

do with an ancient heathen cult?"

"She was capable," he continued, "of actually falling in love with certain mortal men and of taking human shape; and when she desired a man, she would take him, if she could. You have about two more nights to get through, I judge. During this time you are in the utmost danger. Her influence over you is extremely strong."

"Two nights?" queried Raoul. "Why two?"

"Two nights from now is the New Moon. Also, I doubt if she could appear in her form as a woman more than three times. You say she was a cat for two nights before that. Are you sure it wasn't three times, too? Could it have began four nights ago?"

"I don't know," I said gloomily. "It seems to have been going on some time. Perhaps it did."

"Yes, I could sense something was wrong," said Raoul in a low voice.

"Two more nights, then," repeated Edwin.

"And then Louis will be safe?"

"If he makes it, yes."

"If?" I echoed. "Edwin, what will happen if I don't – if she takes me – "

"If she takes you, you will die, Louis." Edwin spoke grimly. "Inevitably she will destroy you in the process. It will seem a natural death."

I repressed another shudder. "And if I die?"

"Then you will spend your eternity with her."

"No, no, this is not possible!" I cried, stunned. I tried to summon up common sense. "Things like this don't happen!"

"It is like the stories you hear of fairies taking children," said Raoul seriously. "They leave behind an image of the child that pines away and dies, so that people think it is a natural death."

"My nurse told me stories like that, too," I responded, trying to grin. No one spoke for a moment, and then I dropped all pretence. "What shall I do? Edwin, give me some advice. I know I can never withstand her on my own. I know it."

In two days I might be not only dead – but damned. At the realisation, all my feverish desire for the strange woman of my dream confronted me. There was a new fear, a distrust of my deepest self.

The clock chimed a quarter; I saw that it was quarter to

twelve

Edwin decided he would spend the night in my room, but we must not alarm anyone else in the house.

Raoul said, "Perhaps Louis should take another room, as well as have you with him?"

"No, no, there's no sense in playing hide and seek with the strange lady." Edwin spoke as if she were a real woman. "But we'll keep a lamp burning. We can read aloud all night. Pity I haven't my books on the subject – "

"Why not read the Bible?" said Raoul. "The scriptures will give you courage. Shall I stay with him too?"

Both of them, so brave in my defence!

"Yes, give us the Bible," I said, trying to sound normal. "I'll read over the psalms of David. I love them."

"No need for you to join us tonight, Raoul. You must keep up your strength as a reserve. We'll arrange this affair like an army campaign! Louis, when she comes – " I tried not to shrink from the thought "– call for help upon the names of Athene, Diana, or Isis. Isis might be the best. I'll talk to you about it when we're upstairs, and keep you on your guard."

These pagan names, at home in poetry and myth, roused my scepticism. "You believe these goddesses actually existed beyond the imagination of the ancients?"

"I do. They represent certain powers of the world and, as such, will always exist. But you must call upon the Virgin Mary, too. She has been loved and worshipped for nearly twenty Christian centuries."

To think of the Virgin Mary in association with the goddess Bast was so ridiculous that I struggled with laughter. And to think of calling upon goddesses for help!

"Perhaps," I joked, "I should have the dogs as extra protection! Watchdogs against the cat – "

Edwin's voice broke in seriously – "Take a grip on yourself, Louis! This is a time for presence of mind. Remember that you have two friends. Our friendship *must* be a protection for you."

He sounded as if he were trying to convince himself as well as me.

"I am sorry," I answered soberly. "I do realise that. Until now I have not known what a treasure I have in you two. No brothers could mean more. I want you to remember that."

"You need not ask us to remember. We will never forget any of this." Edwin's voice was quiet, and Raoul murmured agreement.

I was silent a while. Then I said, as I took out my watch to check the hour of midnight:

"I keep thinking of my mother. I remember how she used to come in to say good night; I can see how she looked, I can even smell the perfume she used. So long ago, now." My mother had died when I was ten; my father four years later.

Sometime after midnight I found myself in my room with the lamp burning on a small table between Edwin's pallet on the floor and my bed. I had offered him in exchange my proper bed as a concession to his older years, but he had quietly declined. As much as possible must be unchanged.

We talked for a while, then took turns reading aloud. I was reading 'The Lord is my Shepherd' when I noticed there was too much shadow on the page. "I think the lamp needs trimming or replenishing," I said to Edwin.

As I looked over, I saw that the shadow came from someone standing between the lamp and myself. The goddess Bast had returned. My heart began to pound with love, hope, and the full knowledge of what she was and why she had come.

The names of forgotten goddesses froze upon my lips. Edwin had not answered, and I called out to him urgently:

"Edwin! Edwin!"

There was no answer. For a moment I did not move, and I fought back the urge to beg the goddess to tell me why she had behaved that way last night, and did she return because she loved me? – instead I sprang up and went to my friend, who seemed to be asleep. No amount of shaking would wake him. 'That's because I'm asleep,' I thought; 'we cannot share the same dream.'

She was a powerful presence, with all the beauty and mystery of night, haunting as hopeless loss, enduring as cherished dreams. But I stepped back from her, shaking my head.

It tore my heart to see her eyes follow me with helpless hurt, to see her arms held out in warm offering, full of the love I had longed for last night. How could I resist the temptation to take now the love denied me last night?

"I came back because I need you." I could hear her voice in my head. "Say you love me."

"Why did you leave me last night?"

"I was mad, I can explain it. Say you love me."

"Do you love me?" I demanded.

"Yes! Do not doubt my love."

My heart cried out my love in silence, and for one supreme moment she was in my arms. I turned up her face to look lovingly at it – and saw that she had changed. Again!

I stared at her in horror as she twisted herself from my grasp. I released her quickly this time. I felt as if she could not help herself, that some terrible trouble had driven her to this, and it needed all my love and strength to save her.

Dear God, she knew all my darkest secrets, my deepest shames and most painful regrets. She revived all my failures in pitiless detail, playing on my every hidden fear and weakness.

The nightmare bickering left me utterly crushed. I returned to my cold bed, lying face down.

I woke that way to the sounds of morning. I struggled up and opened the shutters, first one side then the other. How grateful I was for the cheering sun! It could banish terrors, though it was the last morning I was ever likely to see.

I had come to the end of the road. How does one feel when confronting such a situation? I sat on the wooden chair at the window and pondered over my past.

The little things of life jostled for a place: college days in England, my interest in art, my friendships with the artists of Paris. Suddenly I remembered Winifred.....her pale intelligent face, her fascinating conversation. Then I banished her from my mind.

I found myself thinking that if only I had truly loved and been loved by one woman I would have been better off. Why? I did not know. I had always lived more by my instincts than my reason.

My mind went back to the only two love letters I had ever written, and the only two I had received. I still had those letters, amongst my papers in Paris.

I must write some letters now, I decided, and have Edwin

put my affairs into order. There was so much for me to do.....

Again the vision of the woman I had once been in love with came to mind: Winifred. She would not be banished. I could see again the sadness in her eyes. A gifted artist, she had been unhappily married to a wealthy man who never gave a thought to her talents. But how her more mature company had opened new doors for me!

Once she had written to me, asking for advice and the full understanding of her troubles had brought to life a new emotion in me. I had written back to her as a man in love. She had replied in the same manner of love. But I knew it had to end there, as she did.

The old pain returned, though I was no longer in love. There had been no other loves for me, just passing attractions of no significance.

The sun was stronger, marking the floor in patterns of light and shade. I let the breeze fan my face for a few more moments, then I woke Edwin to this grim new day.

"Edwin," I said, "the night is over."

He woke at once, and one look at my face was enough for him to know what had happened. Raoul came in. He looked at us for signs of hope, but we could give him none. The presence of my two friends was painful to me now, knowing that I would never see them after today.

I tried to give a rational account of my night, but it was hard to talk about it. All I could do was thank them both for their friendship, and then ask them how was I going to spend this last day?

Edwin jumped to his feet. "We will decide that after breakfast! I have no intention of giving up! And neither shall you, Louis!"

Raoul brightened at the command, like a captain at his post. They led me down to the kitchen and soon I found myself seated at the table awaiting breakfast.

The back door opened, but instead of one of Raoul's family, Valerie entered. Behind her ran a cat.

The sight of them both so startled my strained nerves that I jumped up with an exclamation. The tabby cat, beloved of Raoul's grandmother, ran straight towards me, and I instinctively shrank back. I noticed Valerie's surprised glance. I forced myself to remember my old fondness for cats and with an effort overcame my repulsion.

I tried to make amends to Valerie for not greeting her immediately, but the trite words "good morning" stuck in my throat. I could only study her with new eyes, taking in every detail so that I would never forget her. What would life bring to her? I wondered how my death would affect her.

Suddenly Raoul burst out: "We must tell Valerie about this. We must take her into our confidence."

I protested vehemently, but it was too late; I was over-ruled by the girl herself, who begged to know what had happened. With wide eyes she listened as Edwin calmly explained the situation in all its incredible details, the horror deepening in her face. Valerie wasted no time on disbelief; she joined forces with us at once. I did not like it, but my heart was fired with gratitude.

"Should we seek help from the church after all, Valerie?" asked Raoul.

"No," she shook her head. "Louis is not one of them. They would only consider us mad, or evil. And we have so little time!"

Edwin fumed over that. There was no time to send for more information or find someone willing to suspend disbelief to help us. He just had to try and remember what he had read so long ago, and began a campaign from that. He wrote out prayers and symbols, we gathered protective herbs and did ritual cleanses.

Valerie then announced that it wouldn't hurt to pray, and suggested I go to the church. That was a splendid idea, Edwin approved, it would get me away from this house and refresh me.

I took up my hat and accompanied Valerie out into the brilliant sunny day. It was just like an ordinary expedition on an ordinary summer holiday.

The walk to the village did not take long. As every footstep brought us nearer to our destination, so did every heartbeat bring those relentlessly advancing minutes to the end of my last day.

The church was cool and deserted. As we knelt, I found my mind wandering from my petition. My eyes went to the stained glass, to the image of the saviour on the cross, to the girl beside me, her eyes closed, her hands clasped. Would she be here again next Sunday, praying? I drew my hands together again and tried to follow her example.

When she was finished I took her arm gently, and we went out into the sunshine again. "The day has passed its height," I said. "Already I can feel the breeze from the sea that means the day is declining."

We passed children playing in the street, and there was a young man and woman sitting hand-in-hand beneath a tree.

When we returned we found Edwin and Raoul in consultation still.

"We will both guard you tonight," announced Raoul.

"And I've remembered the words of that special prayer of protection," added Edwin.

I spent the afternoon writing a last will – unhappily witnessed by my two friends – and in composing last letters. They were very hard to finish. Should I write to Winifred? No – it would be best for her to know nothing of me.

When I looked out of the window I saw that it was sunset, and I knew that until this moment I had not truly faced my situation, and that I must face it now. My last evening had come.

"Everyone is fighting for me, but it is I who must face the challenge," I thought, "and I do not trust myself."

The house was quiet, only the clock on the mantel ticked loudly. It was like the end of the world. And what comes, after the end? Where will I, Louis Lamer, be this time tomorrow?

Valerie had spent the afternoon in prayer and meditation. It was now time for her to leave.

"You must have my cross," she said, slipping it from round her neck. I could not refuse the gift.

"Adieu," I said.

She gave me a long look, then bid me au revoir, as if it were an ordinary afternoon. "Until tomorrow. I will keep praying all night."

As she crossed the lawn, I waved one last time.

We were to stay in the parlour all night, sitting up. I stayed where I was, then. My letters were done; my affairs were in order. I held Valerie's silver cross in my hand, then kissed it and put it carefully in my pocket.

"May life hold everything for Valerie," I said aloud to myself.

Edwin, Raoul and I played cards at the table to stay awake, and jokingly bet enormous stakes.

The night wore on; I had stopped noticing the quarter chimes of the clock. I glanced down at the score I was keeping and said, "Well, Edwin has won again; Raoul has now lost his boat, and I have only my library left" – when I heard soft footsteps behind me.

Someone had woken up, I thought, but as I turned I found myself gazing at Bast, now seen clearly in the lamplight. She was completely tangible now, and I felt that merely to view her immortal beauty as if it would kill me, so powerful was it. I heard her voice clearly:

"Come with me, and love me forever."

The cards scattered on the floor as I jumped to my feet and backed away. I said aloud the prayer of protection – nothing happened – I called out hopelessly, "Edwin! Raoul!" – but received no reply from this side of my nightmare. Had they fallen asleep? Their heads were resting on the table.

She followed me, holding out her arms. How could I turn away, wrench her hands from mine, when I saw the love shining in her eyes? I begged her to understand, I even found myself telling her she had been mistaken in her judgement of me previously.

"Prove yourself then; show me your true character and your love!"

"You will destroy me if I do."

"With me you will be immortal! What is life? A few meaningless years, living through the visions of other men, because you lack the power to make your dreams come true! I have to destroy that mortal part of you. But I shall breathe life into you that never dies."

How can I hold myself back until the morning? Impossible. Why not take the love she offers? It's true, there's nothing to hold me here..... But I knew that if I claimed her love, she would turn against me, just as before. My mind cried out for help.

The door of the room opened, and another light glimmered. A woman's figure appeared, holding a lamp.

I stared for a moment before I recognised who it was.

"Valerie!"

Resolutely she advanced towards me, towards the goddess Bast.

I cried out to her: "You shouldn't have come! Raoul should never have told you!"

"I had to come," she said. "Could I stay away when your very soul is threatened? I, who love you?"

"You, Valerie?"

"Yes, I know it's hopeless, but I love you."

We gazed at each other as if we were alone. But another voice broke in:

"Your love was always hopeless. He will never love you. He is mine."

The dark goddess turned her angry glance to Valerie, who shrank back but did not run away. I held out my arm, trying to shield her from Bast.

"No," said the brave girl clearly, "he is not yours. By virtue of my true love, you cannot destroy him. And after tonight you can never return, you know it. I have overcome –"

But before she could finish, the goddess, livid with fury, raised her arms and struck at Valerie, such a blow that the lamp not only crashed to the floor, but fell across the table first, upsetting the other lamp. We both collapsed onto the floor.

Fire leapt instantly to life. "We shall all be burned to death!" I cried out, aghast. My coat was lying on the chair; I snatched it as I got up, using it to beat out the flames that caught at the old carpet. The fire had started in two different places at once. I stamped it out, smothered it with the coat, grabbed a flower vase and emptied its water over the flames.

Never was a fire so difficult to subdue! I thought I had it out, then it sprang up again. The carpet was charred; thick black smoke choked me. Everything in the room was so dry.....

At last I managed to put it out. The whole room was plunged into darkness. I groped my way to the nearest chair and sank into it, coughing at the reek of smoke and oil. I leaned back and closed my eyes for a moment, trying to collect myself.

Suddenly I became aware of a luminous glow that penetrated my closed lids; it intensified into a definite yellow light, and with a gasp I opened my eyes, fearing that the fire had started up afresh. I jolted myself alert.

There certainly was light! It was morning; the risen sun was pressing in through the unshaded eastern window, casting warm beams over my face. I was sitting in one of the dining chairs, my body stiff and cold, and took some time to wake properly before I looked over the room.

Edwin and Raoul had their heads on their arms at the table; now I realised they were snoring. Birds were greeting the day outside, the clock was ticking, it was nearly six o'clock. I shifted in my chair and got up.

Suddenly I started, and looked fearfully around the room - where was Valerie? And the lamps!

Valerie was nowhere to be seen; the second lamp was nowhere. Nothing was changed from last night, no evidence of fire; my coat was on the floor, but not charred, nothing was upset. No - there was my lamp, on the floor. I must have knocked it over somehow during the night. It had fallen on its side, and the oil had drained out of it, drowning the wick and quenching the flame. Fortunate that it had, or it might have set the place alight.

In making for the door I slipped on some fallen cards, and the stumble I made woke both Raoul and Edwin.

Confused at first, they babbled out exclamations and questions, the first being wonderment at my being safe and sound. Understanding dawned on me of what I had escaped. Until now I had been too dazed to take in the wonderful knowledge that I was alive this morning, the day after yesterday.

"Yes, yes, I am quite all right!" Raoul was clutching my sleeve, Edwin thumping my shoulder. I began to laugh. "I am truly all right. Was it all a dream, these past days? Have we been the victims of our imaginations?"

"A very real dream!" exclaimed Raoul fervently. "But last night I remember nothing from the time we were sitting playing cards, till I woke up."

"I too remember nothing," said Edwin. "Was it all a blank for you too, Louis? Did she return, that dark creature –"

I sat again in my chair and explained everything that had happened last night, from the time of Bast's appearance to my waking.

"It was obviously all a kind of dream," I ended. "There is no sign of fire, no second lamp, no Valerie."

The thought of the girl, who had appeared so unexpectedly at that critical moment, was newly significant. A vision of happiness arose before me, and it was she who held it in her hands. What a revelation it was! What did it matter that our positions in life diverged so widely?

"Then we are all safe," Edwin was saying in amazement.

I happened to glance at Raoul's face and saw something there that struck terror to my soul. "Valerie – " he said slowly. "She was here – "

I froze. "Yes – but she is not here now! She's all right, you see – "

A growing terror was exchanged amongst us. "Oh no, not that," I heard myself saying.

Raoul jumped up and with an eye to the clock said, "We must get this over. Let's go. They'll be at breakfast by the time we get there "

I took up my coat.

"You go on ahead," said Edwin breathlessly. "Run all the way. I'll follow as soon as I can. Go!"

It is all a silly mistake, I said to myself as we dashed out. This whole affair has been mad! But I could not deny the reality of it. Yet, I reasoned, Valerie was away from it all; we are panicking for nothing. But how madly must I hasten, for my own reasons! Suppose she remembered nothing? No matter, I must tell her, without the loss of a minute, that I love her, that it is I who am unworthy of *her*.

I followed Raoul, whose feet seemed to have wings, over the short cuts he took.

At last we gained the house where Valerie lived. My heart was hammering with the exertion, and with the terror and delight of seeing Valerie again. As we jumped up the step, the door opened as if by itself. A child's face appeared in the doorway. We started back.

"Oh, it's Rene," gasped Raoul. Rene was Valerie's youngest brother.

"Let us see your sister Valerie," Raoul said directly.

The child stared at us in silence. I addressed him more demandingly -

"Where is your sister?"

"You can't see Valerie."

He continued to stare at us until I felt I must scream aloud to wake myself from this nightmare.

Raoul took the boy by the shoulders protectively. "Rene, what has happened?"

The child began to cry. "Mama sent me for the priest. Valerie's dead – I have to go – "

He pushed past us and ran down the street. Raoul and I were left with the blank despair in each other's eyes.

Edwin found us there some time later. Valerie was dead; she had been found in her bed that morning by her poor shocked mother. By this time neighbours had gathered, all protesting against such a healthy girl's death, and applying what comfort they could. No one knew why she was dead; they didn't know that the man responsible was standing before them. Raoul prevented me from blurting out the truth. I wondered if he would ever forgive me.

My love had been killed at its birth and could only find feeble expression in my saying to Valerie's mother: "I love your daughter, madame."

I wanted to pay for the funeral, but was only allowed to contribute to it with Edwin. I don't know what would have become of me if Edwin had not convinced me that the girl was nowhere near the menace of Bast. "She is safe, safe, Louis," he kept saying. Perhaps it was all just a strange coincidence?

I painted a portrait of Valerie from memory, with the background of Raoul's garden. It was not a good painting, as usual. I gave that first picture to Raoul. Though he is a tough, aging fisherman, whenever he catches sight of it, his eyes soften. Every year I return as I have always done, and I paint a new portrait of Valerie. She never grows older, and it is always summer behind her.

Ahead of the Bunch
Pete Stratford

Us small group of 'tradies" were all busily dismantling old metal shelving within a small storeroom at the back of a pharmacy. Dark, dusty, and very noisy conditions within the confined space didn't make it a pleasant task, but we weren't to be too bothered by that. In fact several very much lighter moments made it an enjoyable experience. Allow me to recount but two of them.

One of the younger chaps in our midst was a very studious teenager, and somewhat more naive than most his age. With us all making a din as we pulled apart the metal racks and shelves, plus rain hammering on the iron roof above, it certainly was very noisy environment, and he commented about it "hurting his ears." An older bloke tossed him a small object from amongst the numerous old items that had fallen down behind the backs of the storage shelves over many years and said, "stick those in your ears...but don't go out in the rain!" Having caught one of the objects thrown to him, he gazed blankly at the little white plug and its trailing white tail sitting in his palm, until slowly realising what it must be, then went scarlet with embarrassment.

A vertically challenged chap in our group, Lou, was also follically challenged, in fact by comparison, an egg was hairy. Due to his limited reaching ability he was working at the base of a stepladder while a young lad was working overhead. This chap above him was stirring Lou, just a little, saying how from his elevated position he could see trickles of perspiration on the top of the bald head below him, and was then running his finger along the lines of sweat. Only shortly afterwards Lou was nominated to go along the street to purchase our orders for smoko from the bakery nearby, which he was happy enough to do. On his return, as we sat around with our cuppa and were enjoying the goods we had ordered, Lou mentioned how almost everyone he passed on the street on his trip to the bakery and back had smiled at him, given cheerful greeting, etc, despite some being folk he'd never seen before. We assured him that it was just people being nice for a change, and left it at that. It wasn't until a while later, when Lou walked past a mirror in the pharmacy, that he realised the lad working above him had found an old stick of bright red lipstick and he could then see that his bald head had a large noughts & crosses game drawn on it.

The Wild Horses
Leigh Swinbourne

Rome, capital of Emperors and Popes, hub of European history and culture, so long Madeleine had dreamed of being here, ever since far-off schoolgirl Latin days. The Forum, the Vatican, Michelangelo, Raphael, Bernini... each successive crisp autumn day minted anew for her while Robert attended his conference. And yet, and yet she remained flat and unmotivated, unable to be astonished by all these astonishing things.

Armed with her apps, she dutifully roamed palaces, observed sculptures and paintings, and... well nothing much. Maybe her expectations had been so sky-high that some kind of advance unconscious reaction had set in, although this had never happened to her before. Giddy excitable Madeleine Bach, it was so unlike her not to be thrilled, not to be tripping over herself with enthusiasm. Just as well Robert never asked her about her day when he returned, for it would be such a wearying effort for her to dredge it all up again, try and fake what she did not feel.

Something was wrong, with her, but what? What to do? Just plug on until she finally snapped out of whatever, store away the multitude of impressions in the hope she would draw on them profitably times hence.

Post conference they hired a car, a flashy Maserati no less. Robert said he had done Rome as a backpacker student, couldn't be bothered with it all again— she was grateful for this— then he drove them both at breakneck speed, just like the locals, down the old Appian Way until Madeleine couldn't handle it anymore and made him pull up so she could take the wheel. No talk, Robert fiddled endlessly with his phone, just like he did these days at home. The plan was to tour down the coast to Naples and then Amalfi, but the souped-up vehicle over-heated and its engine seized outside Terracina, where the highway met the Tyrrhenian Sea. Madeleine vaguely remembered Terracina also from High School Latin days.

They rang an emergency number the hire-car company had provided, and miraculously within an hour a tow-truck appeared. The mechanic was a striking curly-headed youth, almost a boy, his beauty marred by a wall-eye. No English. Madeleine managed with her Google Italian, Robert left her to it, and they accepted a lift into town with the car. A water leak, the mechanic's father's garage could replace the tube by tomorrow they were assured.

Courtesy of the garage, they found themselves installed in a crumbling pensione, eating stale pizza and drinking rough chianti in its dark and dingy dining room surrounded by unwashed plates and cutlery, their unpacked bags beside them. Apparently, they were lucky to find this. There was a big soccer match on in town and everything was booked out. Crowds of youths with flags surged up and down the streets, shouting, singing, fighting. As she chewed on a crust, Madeleine read to Robert from a pamphlet with bleached photos lent to them by their hosts, dating from the sixties:

'For anyone coming from Rome, everything changes quite suddenly at Terracina; one has the impression of entering a country outside time, except that the huge wall overhanging the sea and the city, topped by the mighty temple of Jove, reminds us of the ancient history of Terracina, city of the Volsci. The Via Appia used to pass over the Acropolis up there, Terracina was the key to this highway. Anyone holding Terracina held the Gate of the Sun'.

'Let's check it out before we leave tomorrow,' she said. Her husband shrugged, eyes on his phone.

They couldn't sleep with the noise of the soccer celebrations, so they set off early. It was grey dawn and cold, a stiff wind blowing persistently from the sea. They walked towards the sea then climbed steeply up a wide rocky path to the temple, around which was the ancient slum area of the town. This was traditional, Madeleine reflected; poorer areas always used to be in the older precincts of European cities until the tourist trade pushed them elsewhere. But she and Robert were the only tourists here, ridiculously conspicuous, followed at a set distance by a raggedy group of urchins with gaping mouths.

A splendid courtyard fronted the temple of Jove, much of which remarkably still stood intact. Massive marble flagstones, elegant columns, what builders the Romans had been. The Gate of the Sun. A boy approached them from the urchins.

'He just wants money, Maddie.'

But it seemed he had a story to tell, his tourist English supplementing her Italian. A wall behind his grandfather's house had collapsed and amongst the rubble was a sculpture. Would they like to see it?

'Come on Rob. It will be an adventure. We've got hours to kill.'

Robert rolled his eyes. The boy had already moved to a back corner of the square, signalling them expectantly.

'Maddie!'

'I want to see what he wants to show us.'

'Jesus!'

She followed the boy, knowing Robert would have to follow her. They were led briskly along a bewildering sequence of paths cut directly into the rock, always rising, until finally they arrived at a sort of furnished cave, in front of which an ancient sat dozing on a cardboard suitcase. Was this his home? Bald pate, sunken cheeks.

'Nonno!'

The man quickly looked up at them, then at his grandson, and rose to his feet. Without a word, he climbed nimbly to a level above the cave where there was a makeshift storage shed with a huge rusty padlock. He unlocked this, pulled back the door and beckoned all inside towards a slab propped against the back, a classical frieze of some sort Madeleine saw. They all stood in silence before it.

The block, about one metre by two, was incomplete, both ends were jagged, and obviously from some much larger work. White marble, like the landscape all around. It had been cleaned carefully, by the boy or the man, gleaming in the shadow of the shed as though lit from within. It simply showed wild horses galloping left to right. Simply, but Madeleine wondered if she had ever seen anything so ravishing and moving. The details, forelocks and fetlocks, exquisitely rendered, the arched backs, strained withers, corded necks, dilated nostrils. Each beast, and the ensemble, a wonder. The work of a great artist. You might have stared at it for hours; you might have stared at it all your life, as perhaps the original patron had done. Which genius created this? What else did he do? Who would know? Freedom, exultation, grace, strength, energy. Freedom above all. She looked and looked, the casual sweep of muscle and sinew …

And she was eighteen months back.

'There!'

A herd of brumbies sporting on the horizon. In the dusk, with their moulded forms highlighted against the fading sky, they presented as a moving frieze, their fluid interactions as if they were underwater. To Madeleine they were mythical creatures, the brumbies of the high country, celebrated in verse and song, *The Man from Snowy River* and all that. An anachronistic Australia, a maudlin memory, she knew Robert would say. But what he said was...

'They're doomed you know,' snuggling his head into her neck. The rub of his bristles suddenly aroused her.

Of course she knew. A longstanding ecological debate that surfaced in the media periodically, one still in progress although the eventual end not in doubt. As she watched the shifting shapes from the snug warmth of the Kosciusko Hotel's bay window, their fate lent them a poignancy, added to the myth. They had revelled in their freedom for almost two centuries, but yes, shortly there would be a final round-up, or maybe worse. Still, for this time of her honeymoon, she could enjoy the occasional spectacle of these superb beasts ranging across the high wild landscape that they had made their home. Even then she had imagined herself sometime hence, in a stuffy Sydney suburb, reading of their demise, and saw herself remembering back to this, her and Robert, caught in their net of passionate love.

'What will you do with it?' she asked the old man carefully. She was sure her Italian was correct, but it wasn't clear he understood, perhaps he only spoke dialect. He shrugged, and answered incomprehensibly. The boy said: 'You like?'

'Si, molto bello.' Was that right?

Did the man want to sell it to them? He was an uneducated peasant but of course he could see what anyone could, this block, in itself, was a little masterpiece, a decontextualized fragment from some complete masterpiece, itself part of a mostly unimaginable world.

Madeleine could sense Robert's impatience. She paced back and forth slowly in front of the frieze, trying to take it in. What was she trying to take in? What did we have here? A chilly windswept morning in a nondescript Italian town. A young couple from halfway around the world. A poor man and his grandson.

And one random precious detail from a lost civilization; isolate, anonymous.

Now the old man was nodding his head like an idiot goat, except that his eyes were blazing with greed. The boy stood by non-committal, a little embarrassed, tracing the dirt with a stick.

'Come on Maddie, let's go. We can't buy it or anything; we're just wasting their time.'

Ever the voice of reason. She wondered how the story would eventually play out, whether somehow these two could ever manage to turn this incredible find to some recompense. Probably not, almost certainly not, they were too powerless. She and Robert should leave, they had to leave, but still, still, Madeleine just could not take her eyes off this *thing*, glimpse of some magnificent greater whole, which had gone, and could never be recovered.

Ice-Pick
Tatiana Petrovsky

The words strike
like an ice-pick to the heart.
It hurts, really hurts
as the reality of what is said
hacks at her precordium.

The pain pulsates
with each heartbeat.
Words can be weapons
ruthless warheads designed
to wound one to the core.

The ice-pick keeps stabbing
with word after word
as cruel as a cheek-slap
as killing as a knife-slash
until she can take no more.

Be still, the pain will pass.
Resilient, the heart heals
but small slivers of ice
remain imbedded, frozen
until the polar ice-caps melt.

A Bird Called Maggie
Hank Koopman

Wildlife has always intrigued us – particularly when human intervention becomes embroiled in its habitat, even considering humane circumstances.

Too often I have seen preventable, utter carnage on our Australian roads, where some vulnerable animal has been obliterated into tiny fragments of unrecognisable pieces of bone and meat. I question the mentality of people who have obviously gone to great trouble to kill an animal just for pleasure by even pursuing their quarry on to the verge of the road.

There should be more stories told about people like Ted and his wife Wendy who owned the Narooma Motel in New South Wales. We were accommodated there whenever we had bookings as a duo at the local RSL and Bowling Club. We'd developed a rapport with them over several years because their motel was one of the few that would allow us to keep our budgerigar in the room with us overnight. Taffy was part of our show for almost fifteen years. His cage would be open on stage and he'd either sit on it preening and chirping until he'd decide to fly to either Donna or me. Taffy sometimes flew out to the dancers on the dance floor and chose an unsuspecting couple to swoop on and spend time with dancing. After ten minutes or so, he always flew back to his waiting cage on the stage. He was unique for a budgie, however not as unique as Maggie!

On a return visit to Narooma, Ted casually came into the office to sign us into the motel for the night with a magpie on his shoulder. I was taken somewhat by surprise.

"Are you trying to outdo my act?" I whimsically asked him. This large black and white bird was so enamoured with Ted, it only gave me a cursory glance as if to say, "keep away from us." It seemed to be such a natural thing for her to be perched on Ted's shoulder.

"She fell out of the nest from the tree in front of the motel," Ted started to explain. "Completely helpless Wendy and me carried her into the house and started to look after her. Her own parents had deserted her when she fell out of that tree. As she grew bigger, we'd take her outside but she showed no interest in leaving."

"How does she get on with Puss?" was my next question. I knew Ted and Wendy had a beautiful Persian cat that ruled the house and motel. "Surely it would have shown some resentment about this intruder entering into his world?" I asked.

"No," said Ted, "they get on really well together."

Maggie and Taffy   Maggie and Me

He wasn't lying. This wild bird, known for swooping on unsuspecting pedestrians who might dare venture close to their habitat in mating season, displayed no such instinctive behaviour to anyone who visited or stayed at the motel. For almost two years Maggie would not leave the surrounds of the motel, even when pressured to by Ted. He knew it was a wild bird, and tried on many occasions to shoo her to another crowd of passing magpies. She stayed.

Puss.

Encounters with Maggie would be something to look forward to over the next two years as we were booked regularly every four months or so at a club in town. One day we arrived and there was no Maggie. Ted informed us that she was now a part-time visitor, finally finding a mate after being tied to Ted and Wendy's apron strings for almost two years.

"You should have seen it," he explained to us excitedly, "she came into the sitting room one day, followed by two young magpies, obviously her babies. They just marched in, as if they owned the place. She was chortling and calling out to her young offspring, who didn't hesitate to follow her into the house. It's obvious they communicate with each other, though the male bird she had mated with was wary and remained outside."

"That must have been remarkable to witness, Ted?" I put it as a question and a statement. "I don't mind telling you guys, it brought tears of happiness to our eyes," he said, once again holding back an obvious wetness around his eyes, rubbing them with the back of his hand. Ted explained to me how he could almost converse with Maggie. Certain calls were almost human. Not as clear as a cockatoo, but distinguishable enough to Ted and Wendy to almost understand what she wanted to convey.

Six months passed before we drove up the driveway again for another night's accommodation.

We'd been overseas as well as interstate touring, and were totally unaware that Ted had passed away, having had a massive, unforeseen heart attack. He seemed so fit last time we saw him, always out on his ride-on mower cutting the grass on the small golf course he'd developed as part of the motel. Golf was another passion he and Wendy shared besides their love of wildlife.

Entering the office, there was not the usual exuberant welcome we used to get from Ted or Wendy. This time there were new faces, strangers we needed to get used to and explain our situation with Taffy all over again. In our line of work, this happened all too often; having to get permission to take him into the room overnight. We carried a ground sheet and used a hand-held car vacuum cleaner to always clean up any spilled seed or feathers he might shed overnight. Most times we'd leave a room in a cleaner condition than what we found it in. These new owners were sticklers for the rules, which were primarily introduced regarding cats and dogs.

"No, I'm sorry, health regulations don't allow animals into the rooms," the new owners were insistent. Even trying to explain to them that we'd been coming there for four years with never a problem, they remained adamant that no animals were to stay in the motel.

"Does Maggie still stay here?" I asked.

"Who's Maggie?"

This answered my question without any further probing necessary. Some people are just not tuned into animal behaviour. Maggie knew when Ted had died, deciding she could now fly free, as that bond with her male human companion had broken. Her ties with the motel vanished and she had gone to return to the wild with her kind. We no longer stayed there either.

Wendy had been unable to continue running the property on her own, and moved away the last we heard. What a wonderful experience we shared with Ted and Wendy and also with a bird called Maggie.

Abby's Home
Ant Dry

We met Abby in the pub in Harare one warm balmy Zimbabwean night.

She was singing, and we were her audience.

She was our age and her choice of songs reflected it. We sang along with her, we danced, my wife Yvonne and I the only dancers, and we bought her a drink. In between sets she came and sat with us.

Abby was an American, a fact that did not register deeply, we were all foreigners in Zimbabwe, even if my wife and I were born there. She said her name was Abby and that was sufficient for us. We didn't probe – it was bound to be a brief relationship – next week there would most likely be a different singer.

We were not regular pub goers, but the next time we went she was there again, and we had a repeat performance. We laughed, we joked, and we swapped tall stories. She was from New York. We assumed she was with the American embassy or with a mission or some international NGO.

As far as it was possible in the circumstances, over the next few months, we became friends with Abby. We were her most appreciative enthusiastic and loyal audience members, and she regularly sat with us, but the relationship remained superficial, we never spoke of anything meaningful. There were no philosophical thoughts exchanged, and no private matters divulged, we just enjoyed the relationship on the level on which it was based. At times we tried to probe and to engage her in more meaningful discussion, but she was very coy, very reticent.

At one time I asked her where she lived, and she replied.

"Here, I live here, this pub is my home."

We laughed, and I didn't pry again.

****

Yvonne worked as a Nursing Sister for a gynaecologist. Some months after we met Abbey, there was a scene in the consulting rooms.

A Mrs Mudamburi had called in for an appointment. The receptionist, seeing the name, expected a black patient, but Mrs Mudamburi had turned out to be very white. This receptionist, an elderly white lady, after fumbling her way through the initial interview, which had not gone well, came bustling indignantly into the back office, bursting with outrage and excitement to share this shocking detail with the other girls.

Yvonne who had been busy with a patient came out of the consulting rooms to find the place abuzz.

The girls all peeped around the corner, and there, sitting waiting to be seen, and looking incredibly stressed, was our Abby, flicking furiously through a magazine.

She was Mrs Mudamburi. Abby was married to a black man.

Interracial marriage at that time in Zimbabwe was still taboo. Despite independence, the racial tensions were still too raw for it to be easily understood and accepted. Back then, forty years ago as I write this, we lived in unashamedly backward times.

Yvonne, however, had spent some time in Cape Town in the apartheid era, working in a multiracial private hospital, so she took in the scene, in her stride. She stepped out of the Nurses Station and welcomed Abby to the doctor's rooms.

Because they were obviously friends, the tension in the rooms immediately fell away.

****

The next time we saw Abby in the pub it was as if the flood gates had been opened. She joined us after her gig and spoke freely of her life.

She had met her husband Herbert in New York when they had both been students at university. He had been studying for a PhD in Chemistry and she was an undergraduate.

Her father, a New York Jew and owner of a string of jewellery shops, had not been impressed with his daughter's boyfriend and had made his views known on a regular basis.

Abby bitterly told us that her father had said that Herbert was only interested in her because she came from a wealthy background. He had said she was no more than a novelty to him, and that he would both move on, and never fit in to New York Society.

She had been outraged.

It didn't take much reading between the lines, for us to presume that she had married Herbert to spite her parents.

Their leaving New York to move to Zimbabwe had apparently caused a huge family uproar.

Herbert had secured a good job in Harare. Abby had asked her father to send them money to buy a house and he had obliged.

****

Abby had been appalled by the Shona/Zimbabwean way of life.

"People would just arrive" she said.

"It was as if they had a right to be there. They just stayed and stayed, and we had to provide everything. We had one aunt of Herbert's stay for six months, never lifting a finger."

"It was as if it was their home, not mine."

She and Herbert had also visited his relatives in the rural areas.

"I couldn't believe it," she moaned, "I had to sleep on a mud floor on just a blanket, AND in a hut with three other people."

"And his grandmother ordered me around like I was some kind of slave. I pretended I didn't understand a word she said, and I just ignored her."

"And that wasn't all. When I needed the bathroom, I had to go to an outside long drop. That wouldn't have been so bad if only the door would work properly, but it kept being opened by Herbert's Granny's goat. The door handle was made of string and the goat seemed to think it might make a tasty snack."

****

Eventually Abby and Herbert moved out of Harare. Herbert wanted to go farming, so Abby once again prevailed upon her father to send them sufficient funds to buy a farm.

To help with the farming costs, Herbert continued to work, and they would visit the farm over weekends.

We were invited to the farm on one occasion.

"Come and see my home" she said.

We went to the farm, and we had a great time. We made pizza, New York style (whatever that was – it seemed just like any other pizza we had ever had) and were royally entertained. We sang songs together, played board games, talked endlessly, made cocktails, and swapped stories of our backgrounds.

It would seem that Abby came from a very conventional and loving background, and that her parents doted on her. The house was furnished with pieces that they had sent over from New York. They were very fancy and seemed a little out of place in rural Africa.

Her parents had yet to visit them in their Zimbabwean home.

We only saw flashes of Herbert the whole weekend; he was too busy on the farm. I was not invited to join him in the fields.

It would seem that Abby's Dad had continued to supply funds to support his daughter. The barns had been built with his cash, and a brand-new tractor and implements sat gleaming in the sheds.

Apart from the furniture, there were very few decorations in her house – just a single family portrait of her with her parents and brother, which took pride of place on the mantelpiece over the fireplace.

****

After our farm visit, we lost track of Abby for a few months; and then one day she arrived at our home, with a collection of suitcases and look of grim determination on her face.

It would appear that Herbert was going to be a father.

But not with her.

Her visits to the gynaecologist had been due to her infertility. The visits and treatment had not helped her.

It would appear that Herbert had decided that since she couldn't have children, it would be acceptable to father one with someone else. From a Shona point of view this was perfectly acceptable and understandable, but from the point of view of a New York Jewess, less so.

He had announced his impending fatherhood to her as if it were something for her to be proud of. He had been staggered when she had been less than pleased.

"He said he didn't see a problem at all."

"He said I would always be his senior wife," she went on, "but what does that even mean?"

There was a brief silence. We had nothing to say that would help.

"So what are you going to do now?" asked Yvonne.

She shrugged and motioned towards her pile of luggage.

"I'm going back to New York." She said, "I'm going home".

The Ultimate Economy
Leigh Swinbourne

Raising his eyes from the desk's finely-tooled leather veneer, Stephen sees that his familiar office furnishings have assumed a kind of unreality. He considers something new: the world as absurd. Which nudges him slightly from his grief, although it is fully there, along with a physical pain in his throat and chest. The heart, that perennially sensitive organ.

He stands, right leg numb, needles and pins, waits for restored sensation, then limps out the office door, carefully locking it as ever, and over to the lift lobby. Up to the top floor and the short steep flight of metal steps leading to the roof. The safety rod seems unnaturally cold. He pushes open the outsized security-door (Authorised Personnel Only), and steps down onto wet concrete.

It was raining when he first read the email. Now it has cleared. Behind scattered cumulus a few stars shine, a mild spring night, slightly fragrant after the rain, even here in the coil of the city. Remote traffic noises meld into a general hum of life. Around him is the baroque paraphernalia of the antiquated air-conditioning system, also humming. Stephen meant to itemise its upgrading at the last Board meeting. Another little matter he has failed to address.

He weaves through this to the edge. He was right, it is simple. A flimsy railing. The street is empty and appears a long way down. Fifty storeys. When he first started working here, many years back, this was one of the tallest buildings in the city, a prestigious address. Looking down he is both exhilarated and fearful and a sensation lodges in his genitals that he has always felt at heights. Probably something to do with balance. Also the common fantasy of launching off. Now he will do this. He must ensure that he jumps well clear of the building. He buttons up his suit coat.

'Scuse me Mister!'

Always someone! Stephen turns and there perched on an air-conditioning tube is a woman, maybe in her mid-thirties, obviously a derelict of some kind, crazy or substance-abuser or both. She is an apparition as odd as unexpected, swathed in a filthy array of brightly hued overlapping cloths, some personal couture of odds and ends, like an oversize tropical bird. Although she is in shadow, all her physical details seem sharp as though he is seeing her through a suddenly focussed lens.

'Lovely evening,' he responds ludicrously, his voice sounding to him as if spoken by someone else. He can jump when she moves on, or just walk around to the other side of the building. No need to distress her.

'What you say?'

'Lovely evening.'

'What?'

'The evening.'

'You got the time?'

He slips out his phone. No messages.

'Ten-thirty.'

'Why you workin' so late?'

Why was he working so late?

'Do I know you Mister?'

'No!' But he does seem to recognise her voice. Maybe he's regularly walked past her without noticing. On the footpath with a sign or something. So many people in a life, even a truncated one. He peers closer: 'What are you doing up here, Madam?'

'I'm going to kill meself.'

'Well don't let me stop you!' What is he saying? He is not in control. But wait, did he hear right?

'Tell me again,' he says.

'Just makin' a few last calculations. Numbers never lie.' (Is that true?) 'Ten-thirty you say.'

Stephen moves in to examine this strange doppelganger. She is intently bent over a book, jabbing at it sharply with a pen or pencil. Older than he first thought, but how old is difficult to say. For while her body looks relatively young, the skin on her face is like very worn, soft leather. A lifetime of outdoors. Her ash-blonde hair is loosely gathered up in a crimson scarf. He can smell her now, sweat and urine. He clears his throat.

'Well, I'm going to kill myself too.'

At this she stops her jabbing and stares at him in unblinking silence, mouth open, jaws working back and forth. There is a glaze of saliva on her chin. Time passes.

'I've just learned my wife and closest friend are lovers.'

Was she waiting for an explanation? Why has he offered one?

'I sorta thought that type of thing went on all the time.'
'Not to me.'
Meeting her stare he recalls how from incomprehension, through incredulity, bewilderment, shock, jealousy and anger, he had arrived at the final station: grief. The end of the line. A slow succession of tears had flowed silently down his cheeks like a miraculous statue, blotching the leather veneer. He had not cried since boyhood, when he had cried regularly and copiously. On the day-by-day desk calendar, beneath his note to buy cat food, was a dictum of Aristotle's: 'The unexamined life is not worth living'. Up until the email Stephen would have thought this ridiculous, unmanly even. But with Aristotle's cue he had found himself forcing himself, a compulsion both voluntary and involuntary, through a complete re-appraisal of his entire adult life, the only part of his life that had seemed of any worth.

Their faces had materialised in the office gloom, almost hallucinatory. Joyce's, thin and fine, with large close-set chestnut eyes, like a deer's he'd always fancied, gentle but not tame, and with a wild animal's secretiveness. Whereas Craig's was the opposite, open and frank, a little flushed from his drinking, hail-fellow-well-met, a natural charmer's façade, behind which naturally also lay secrets. Then Stephen's brain had kicked into an unstoppable sequence of memories of Joyce, Joyce and himself, Joyce and Craig and himself. Could he identify any specific incident where betrayal was obvious? No. So then every act, even the innocent, must now appear guilty. The whole picture irreparably foxed.

'You goin' to punish them.'
'...Maybe.'
'Ya reckon they're worth it?'
'Probably not.'
'Probably they don't give a rat's.'
'It doesn't matter. There's nothing left.'
She snorts at this, which riles him somewhat.
'So why are you killing yourself?'
She brandishes the book at him.
'Save money.'

'What?'

'It's costin' me too much to live.'

Maybe she isn't crazy. She seems serious, not at all hysterical. People do kill themselves for rational reasons. Stephen feels a burst of sympathy.

'Listen, I'm well off, I've nothing further to live for, believe me. I really am going to kill myself. I have my wallet here. There's some cash, cards. At least you won't be poor for a while.'

Craig always his closest friend, especially throughout their wretched boyhood with the Brothers. Were those men still alive? Impossible. Warriors of Christ. Christ almighty! Here were the bloody demons alright; you had to conjure the angels yourself. Survival meant holding in, first lesson, at which he was not good. But when Craig arrived they bonded instinctively, perhaps only as children can, a bond that grew as they grew and suffered. The Monday morning they met, chatting casually in the library under Father Dominic's baleful watch. A morning of bright winter sun. Craig, a man so easy in his own skin, unlike himself. So much he had learnt from him, admired in him. Their success together a realisation wildly beyond boyhood dreams, although of course, largely through his own initiative and effort.

But then so typical of Craig's carelessness (casualness?) to send a personal file with a batch of business rubbish. The writing itself, intense and passionate, he found difficult to imagine from Joyce, although unmistakably it was hers. Certainly he had never received anything in any form from her vaguely resembling this, in fact had never sought it, and almost incidentally was surprised to discover her capable of such range and depth of emotion. The cursor blinking at him impersonally. Do you want to shut down? Yes.

'Aint poor now.'

'What?'

'Your hearin' crook, mate?'

'You said you were killing yourself because it costs too much to live.'

'Right.'

'Well?'

'What?'

'I'm offering you money.'

'Don't want it. Make my problem worse.'

'What's your problem?'

'Savin'

'Saving for what?'

'You see mister, I 'ate spendin', 'ate to think that what's mine has got to go to some other bastard.'

The cars, the clothes, the holidays, anything she wanted, even before they were married. He needed her to ask him. Yes, clearly he'd been papering over a gap. Her sequence of notes suggested some of this largesse had been diverted to Craig. A not uncommon business bind as it happens, money thrown at a problem, funding, not solving, that problem.

'But then if, as you claim, you've plenty of money, what does it matter?'

'It matters. 'Ad nothin' when I was a kid. I was a orphan. Just you try and think of that, you being rich and all. Learned what it was to be 'ungry, learned how to scrimp and save. 'Ad to bludge food. Steal it sometimes. No easy ride for me Mister. But you know, as time went on, I found I 'ad a real natural talent for savin' and bludgin', a gift, if I don't say so meself. I got along. No easy ride, but I got along. Bit of a natural.'

She breaks into a violent cackle, then hawks loudly.

'Bernadette's me name.'

'Stephen.'

Are they worth it? Are they worth his life, that's what she was asking. But the question he was asking was, does he still love them. The answer was, is, yes, of course. Life seems inconceivable without them as he is and always has been bound to them. So an evasion, is that what he is about? No doubt. An evasion of life. And what have been life's highest finest moments? Making love to Joyce, no, the deep calm after making love to her, even if, he must admit it now, and its implications, he more than occasionally sensed his feeling not reciprocated.

All he thought was his is now theirs, is no longer, perhaps never was. He has attempted to construct a complete life out of nothing, and it seems that the effort, enormous for him, enormous for anyone really, has not been finally successful. The walls of his beloved home have atomised from the heat of some immense alien passion. It is monstrous, inexplicable, yet it must be accounted for.

He must account for it, for in some tangential way he is partly responsible for it.

'...and I was a bit of a looker in my time too, so I made sure I hooked a good earner. Not that I ever let 'im spend any of it. Watched 'im with skinned eyes. Never wasted a penny. Only bought things on special. Search through the papers for hours for bargains, wait in line for hours to pick 'em up. Vinnies clothes, shoes from the tip, I 'ad it all down pat, economies of scale, economies of use, every way I could possibly avoid spendin'. Jim was always sayin': "Let your hair down a bit", but no fuckin' way. I says to 'im: "You never been poor. You don't know what's what". But 'e used to spend money anyway, fucked if I know 'ow, you know, without me knowin', though I'd always find 'im out in the end, after I'd done me sums. Aint the bastard born can pull one over me.'

She pauses for another extravagant hawk, followed by a protracted bout of spitting and coughing. So she is crazy, but is she serious? Maybe this is some kind of regular act, and he needs to work out from her what part he must play. To break the spell.

'Anyway, I quickly comes to realise you can't really save, not proper like, with another body around eatin' from the same plate as you. But there I was. Nothin' I could do about it, 'cause he made the money you see, just keep watchin' 'im. Then one day, 'e dies, just like that, stroke, and I thinks, well, I don't want his money, I can save better on me own, in peace, with no worries about some other bastard wastin' it. Whatever it is, it's mine, no-one else can spend it. Well, I 'ad quite a pile when Jimmy croaked. Always fightin' with the bank over the interest, and the fuckin' tax man! I 'ad me pension and me interest, but they were me rightful due, I'd be buggered if I was goin' to spend them. So, I started hoardin' stuff, you know, shop liftin' and like. I never bought any new clothes at all, new anythin'. I sold me 'ouse and moved into a little room. I never went out. If you go out it costs money. Began eatin' pet food.'

'What's it like?'

'What?'

'Pet food. I've always wondered.'

"Orrible, but it saves. Anyway, I did everything I could, every fuckin' thing, but I was still spendin'. It was gettin' away from me. I don't know 'ow. I'd dream about it you know. I just couldn't see where it was goin'. Drove me crazy! Then one night I 'ad a vision. God 'elp me! All at once it come to me what 'ad been costin' me money all these bloody years . I 'ad the answer right 'ere in the palm of me ' and. 'Know what it was?'

'Tell me.'

'Livin' Mister. Livin' costs. You can scrimp and save for all your fuckin' worth but while you're livin' you're spendin'. There aint nothin' you can do about it, except stop livin'!'

'But if you kill yourself now, what good will all your saving be to you, all that effort?'

'I don't care about that! I just can't stand to spend any more!'

'You're telling me you're going to kill yourself simply to save money? That's ridiculous!'

'Mister, you look after your death, and I'll look after mine.'

'Let me get this totally straight: you're going to kill yourself purely as an economy measure, right?'

'Right.'

'Well, what about this: if you kill yourself now, you'll never again know the joy of saving.'

'There aint no more savin' I can do mate, except this.'

'But it's such a waste!'

'It's the wastin' I'm tryin' to stop! I can see I'm getting' nowhere with you. 'Ere, 'old this.'

She rises from her perch, approaches Stephen along with her stench, and hands him a soiled spiral-bound exercise book. He flicks through it. The pages are covered in flamboyant numerical ciphers, all contained within neat red-ink double-margin lines. He examines them; none of them seem to add up.

'I was just sittin' here quietly, workin' out 'ow much I was goin' to save a week by doin' this. But it don't come to very much.' She shakes her head. 'Ardly worth it.'

She snatches back the book and strides to the edge.

'No!'

But she's gone! And he is shocked to his core! Horrified! How stupid! He leans over the railing but cannot locate her. Still, she couldn't have possibly survived. He takes it in.

Alright, she was crazy, but surely he could have talked her out of it. Surely he could have done something! The money, he shouldn't have offered it. He can't imagine how anything else would have made any difference, but it wasn't the answer. He hadn't learnt his part in time, whatever it was.

Suddenly he feels exhausted. He turns and slumps back against the railing. The pain in his chest and throat has eased. He listens to the night, the hum, then slips out his phone, rings triple-O and reports the suicide. The voice is shaky but it is his. It is a lovely evening. He pulls the printed email from his coat pocket, reads it again, steels himself—the phone is still in his hand— sucks in a deep draught of spring air, and calls his solicitor.

Greed
Donna-Marie Koopman

The man bent down and reached for the ground.
His heart raced as he guessed what he'd found.
He picked up the pebble, turned it around to the sun.
Greed came to the good man, that's how it begun.
"Gold" cried the good man, the cry went around.
All through the county to every small town.
So they packed their belongings, and headed on out,
to where precious gold was easily found.
And men who had worked hard all of their lives
for land and a home they left it behind,
Their dreams of riches were all coming true.
But for oh so many their greed they would rue.
For the greed in a good man he'll work off on a pick.
But the greed in a bad man he'll work off on the meek.
For just one golden speck, many would die.
And what they panned would span the rest of their lives.
And the devil's laugh resounds and rebounds
To see foolish men dig his spawn from the ground.
And the devil plants well when he plants his seed
and it grows and it grows, into greed.

Just Testing
Allan Jamieson

He was well pleased with himself. Work seemed never ending and it was definitely at least three weeks since he had last felt the direct rays of the sun on his skin. Today though, not only was the sun surrounded by blue sky – itself rare in this god forsaken country – but he had decided yesterday to come to the seaside today; serendipity?

He sat on a chair and looked out to sea. It was a calming sight, the waves approaching slowly before dissolving into the stones, for there was no sand here – just shingle. Sand would have been nice to feel between the toes, but where in this country could one find a sandy beach? He didn't know. Shingle was nice too in a way; although the stones were the reason why he was seated on a chair, because the stones gave off a constant tinkling noise when pushed by the waves; soothing.

He looked around. People! He had gradually become accustomed to never being on his own; always there were people following him, watching his every move. More, they were imploring him to give them advice. Every time he walked into a room, the chorus would always begin with flattery:

"You are the greatest man that ever lived," one would say. "There is nothing you cannot do," someone else would chime in with. Another would sing out "Nothing in this world dares to disobey you."

Two years ago he was quite unnerved by the constant attention; now he tolerated it, though he doubted that he would ever accept being their Leader, their Boss. He was a mere mortal; were his thoughts and decisions any better than those of anyone else? No, he said to himself. Why was it that nobody else could think for themselves? His pronouncements were not always successful, but anything is a winner when there is no competition!

Today's journey to the seaside would help resolve the situation, he reasoned. He knew that his presence at the sea's edge would generate consternation, "what's he going to do?" They'd say.

The tide had been out and was now slowly on its way back to shore. In twenty minutes the water would begin lapping his feet and he guessed the crowd would become agitated; they'd expect me to turn back the tide, he surmised. If he was wrong in this, it didn't matter because he could still steer the crowd in the direction he intended. Getting his feet wet today would be worth it!

The water was up to his calves and the crowd noise was rising in phase with the water level. One man was picking his way over the stones towards him. Eventually the man stood in front of him, wet to the knees. After hesitating, the man spoke:

"King Canute – Are you going to turn back the tide?"

Still sitting on the chair, he knew he'd succeeded; the people were not only starting to think for themselves; they were also starting to doubt if they should meekly follow his every word and deed. He smiled at the nervous man and said with a smile:

"Just testing."

Viv
Ant Dry

Viv has been Jack's friend for years. Actually to be more correct she had been Jack's wife Yvonne's friend for years, but Jack liked to claim her as a friend too.

The two girls had met when they started their nursing training together. Viv was one of the first of Yvonne's friends there that Jack had met, and she had become one of his favourites. She was vivacious (Jack always enjoyed how well she was named) noisy and great fun. She always had a boyfriend in tow. She slept with them all and was very open about it. Jack could remember how she had recounted once that she had vowed as a teenager that she would only sleep with a boy with whom she was in love. When Jack quizzed that with her and pointed out that she had slept with at least seven boys that he knew about, she was quick to respond with; "well, I fall in love very easily."

Once Yvonne qualified, Jack and Yvonne lost track of Viv for many years. One day Yvonne came home from a visit to the supermarket very excited, as she had, by chance, met Viv in the aisle. She was coming over for dinner that evening. The two ladies had obviously spent a good deal of time talking in the aisle, as Jack was told that Viv was newly divorced, had had two children, and was working in some dead-end job. She seemed very unhappy. Yvonne was very keen to cheer her up.

The path to cheering anyone up at that point in their lives, was paved with beer bottles, so Jack duly shot out and bought a case. They had a job to do.

Viv arrived and she did seem a little downcast. Jack and Yvonne set about cheering her up.

Knowing her as well as he thought he did, Jack was stunned to discover that Viv came from a very conservative background. Her father was a minister in the Dutch Reformed Church, very dour and very set in his ways. His view on women was that they were there to do men's bidding and little else. They were to be, at all times, bare-foot and pregnant and behind the kitchen counter. Her father had not approved of Viv's following the nursing profession and only allowed her to do so when she pointed out that caring for people was surely part of God's design for women.

That night was, Jack believed, very therapeutic for Viv. She visibly started to relax. She told the couple about her marriage breakdown. Mike, her husband, and she had had fundamental differences of opinion about a number of issues. These were not outlined and neither Jack nor Yvonne wanted to pry.

The conversation, beer fuelled, ranged wide that evening.

At one stage the topic of homosexuality came up, Viv suggesting that it was an abomination in the eyes of the lord.

Jack was amused. He momentarily forgot the earlier revelation that her father was a minister, and scoffed loudly.

"What a load of cods," he laughed, "Yea, Leviticus 18:22, everyone knows that one! That one's used a lot. What the Christians forget is that according to Proverbs 6, "haughty eyes" are an abomination, as are "a lying tongue" and "a heart that devises wicked plans." Tell me who hasn't had at least one of those in their lives? Deuteronomy tells us that women who wear Jeans are an abomination. Leviticus also says eating seafood is an abomination. I bet even your dad eats seafood!"

They had all laughed at that.

Later they returned to the subject. Jack pointed out that he was left-handed and that the Latin word for left-handed is "sinister" and that left-handed people had, for centuries been treated as if they were indeed sinister. He suggested that less than four hundred years ago left-handed people were burned at the stake just for being left-handed. He suggested that homosexuality was bound for the same end and that in the future it would be treated as no more odd than being left handed.

Jack tended to wax lyrical when he had a few beers under his belt.

They drank more; they laughed; they told stories; they reminisced. They had great fun. Viv spent the night in the spare bedroom, on a mattress on the floor as the couple couldn't afford to buy a bed. In the morning, she had a cup of coffee, and left to change and go to work.

Over the next few months, they saw a fair bit of Viv. She came around often, they all drank more beer and with every visit Jack and Yvonne could see that Viv was improving, relaxing coming out of her divorce induced shell and becoming more like the Viv of old.

Then, one day she simply stopped coming around. They didn't notice at first, they were both working, living busy lives, enjoying themselves. One day Yvonne remarked that they hadn't seen Viv for a while, and they worked out that it had been six months since they had seen her. They assumed she had found a distraction, possibly a new man in her life, and had no immediate need for their company.

Some years later, Jack was at a work-related cocktail party. Towards the end of the evening he looked up and saw, standing in front of him, a woman obviously waiting to gain his attention. She seemed familiar. In a flash he recognised her as another of their old friends from Yvonne's nursing days. It was Linda Baker. She's been a periphery acquaintance. Jack had known her only to the extent that they would greet each other and smile. He was surprised that she seemed to want to talk to him.

Once they were alone, she gave Jack a big hug and a kiss, and told him it was wonderful to see him again.

Before Jack could respond, she said, "I saw Viv the other day. I told her I was coming to this function, and that you were likely to be here. It's a bit weird I thought, but she specifically asked me to look for you. She wanted me to tell you that she says "thanks". She says you changed her life."

Jack looked blank.

"Thanks for what? Changed her life how?"

"Oh, she didn't say, she said you would understand."

"Understand? Really? Understand what?"

"She also said to tell you that she had come out. You knew she was gay, didn't you?"

Forty Two
Dawn Meredith

I gripped the pencil tightly in my hand and stared down in utter frustration at the mistake I'd just made. I'd been working on this drawing of a friend's dog for a couple of weeks and I hadn't enjoyed a single second of it. Why should I even bother continuing?

After many years of denying myself the pleasures of drawing for fun I had returned to Art after the breakup of my marriage, seeking the joys of my early life in an effort to comfort myself. As a high school student I had discovered I was good at it. Like a subterranean river it had flowed in my veins my whole life, unseen, unacknowledged. When I began putting pencil to paper in earnest for a school assignment, to sketch my own hand, I saw with surprise that I could produce something amazing. My teacher's jaw dropped and her eyes narrowed as she looked me over, no doubt wondering whose work it really was. In my final year of high school I was nervous, as I usually am during exam periods, but I aced my final exam and joined the elite group of the top Art students in the state. I could hardly believe it!

After I left school life took me through university, romances, marriage, ongoing training and a career which I thought had been fulfilling. But life at home was never easy. Finally, after years of loyalty to a violent marriage, I reached a point where I could no longer continue. My instinct to be faithful and loyal finally gave way to my instinct for self-preservation.

When a marriage fails it's like a death. It's the death of your dreams, the death of your belief in love. You have FAILED. And nothing can ever erase that failure. The divorce certificate is permanent proof that you are inadequate, flawed, wrong. And even in my situation where the violence I experienced at home brought me the sympathy of police officers and medical staff, it did not cancel out my sense of failure.

Now, I gazed out the window of my studio at the garden which I had planted many years ago and which had brought me so much joy and peace. The sun glinted on leaves wet with dew as furry bees buzzed around the flowers I had carefully selected. It was a haven out there, but in my mind I wrestled with demons. I glanced down at my hand, clutching the pencil so tightly the blood had fled from my fingers. I dropped it, took a deep sigh and pushed away from my drawing table. How does one deal with failure? How do you pick yourself up and keep going? In which direction? On whose advice? How can you be sure you won't make the exact same stupid mistake again?

I startled as something banged against the French door, followed by scratching at the glass panels. I looked up to see my little dog waiting, the tip of her tail wagging furiously, her adorable face looking at me with such enthusiasm. Smiling, I slipped on my shoes and pushed open the door. A breeze greeted me, carrying the scent of flowers heavy with nectar. A walk, that's what I needed.

"Come on, Daisy," I said, forcing brightness into my voice. "Let's go, bub!" She leapt joyfully at my side as I walked down the slope towards the lake. Somehow in the divorce I had managed to keep the small stone home that we had built together – our home, which had been created over five years whilst living in a caravan on site. How could such a journey of dedication be for nothing? I pushed the thoughts aside. The breeze lifted my hair, forcing a deep, satisfying breath into my lungs. Daisy ran down to the lake's edge and barked at some ducks, who flew off, quacking with annoyance. She nosed around bushes and dug underneath rocks, searching for excitement. I called her and headed for the wooden bench my father had built for me.

"Oh, Dad, I wish you were here right now," I whispered as tears trickled down my face. Daisy hopped up onto the bench beside me and I stroked her absently. Her coarse Jack Russell fur was a comfort. She licked my hand. It was almost like she was saying to me, but you have your freedom. Why are you still unhappy? You have so many commissions to do that there really isn't time for despair. It's what you always wanted, isn't it? I stared into her little button eyes.

"You're right, as usual, Daisy. Why don't I listen to you more often?"

I pulled the phone out of my pocket and called my dad. Disappointingly, it went to message bank and I didn't have the words to describe how I was feeling so I just hit 'end'. Who else could I call? Mum had died years before. My brother lived in Germany and the rest of my extended family was still back in the

UK. I didn't feel close enough to discuss my cycle of despair with any of them. I patted Daisy's head once more. "You're the only friend I have, you know that?"

Oh stop feeling sorry for yourself! I thought irritably. So what, that your marriage failed? So what, that you had no children together? You have a gift – a talent. And you've always found joy in your work. Just get on with it, woman!

I got up and walked among the trees that fringed the lake. I was only forty two. Wasn't that the meaning of life, according to *Hitchhiker's Guide to the Galaxy*? It wasn't too late for a beginning. Walking back up the slope to my stone house, which sat nestled in a vibrant garden full of life, I determined that I would no longer be a burden to myself and others. Sitting down at the kitchen table with my laptop I looked up local groups and decided to join an Art class. I had no intention of getting into another romantic relationship, but I did need company, people with a shared passion.

The following Saturday I turned up at the Art class, my backpack full of good quality paper and my best watercolour pencils and a smile plastered on my face that was completely fake. I greeted the person on duty at the door and scanned the room for an empty seat in a corner where I could sit by myself and not impose on anyone. The table in the far right corner was occupied by several chatty women and a couple of men. There was one space left in the whole room and it was at this particular table.

Come on, I told myself. You can do this. It's not school. You're a grown up for heaven's sake! I walked over to the table.

"Hi," I said tentatively. "I'm Janice." I was greeted politely and sat down trying not to take up too much space on the table. A woman in hippie style clothing sat next to me. She had a well weathered face and kind, green eyes. She was scribbling away with a black ink pen at a fuzzy drawing of a Tasmanian devil. There was flair and artistry in her work that I admired. My drawings were always so precise. Could I ever be as relaxed as this woman?

"Hi, Janice, I'm Sunny" she said, turning to me. "What do you like to draw?"

I placed my folder on the table and drew out the current drawing of a beagle. I had been struggling to get the tone right, the exact gingery colour of the beagle's face. I looked down at it.

"I like watercolour pencils and seem to be drawing animal portraits quite a lot lately," I confided. "But I'm not really happy with this one." Sunny looked down at my work and grinned.

"Oh my God, if that's what you're unhappy with, what does your best work look like?"

I grinned at her. I shook my head.

"I know. I'm my own worst critic," I replied ruefully.

Sunny looked around the table and, as if by some hidden signal, everyone looked up at her and exchanged knowing smiles and looks. She patted my shoulder gently.

"Well, we've all got to start somewhere."

I looked at her, confused. She leaned forward slightly and stared into my eyes as if she could peer through into my very soul.

"Do it because you love it, because you need to do it, because your hands rejoice in what your eye beholds! Do it because it makes you happy and distracts you from your pain."

I felt the tears welling up in my eyes and felt ashamed. What the hell? Crying in front of a bunch of strangers? What was wrong with me? Sunny squeezed my arm and smiled gently.

"We're all different, but we're all, somehow, the same. Everyone at this table is here for a reason. Don't be embarrassed. Your gift has brought you here, to a safe place, where you can explore so many things. The world, in fact!" She chuckled. "And who knows what you're capable of?"

I smiled back at her, feeling a sense of calm descend. My breathing deepened. How could she possibly know so much about me in ten seconds? I looked around at the others in the group, their heads down, beavering away, showing each other and asking for comments or searching for images on the net, sharing a joke.

Perhaps I'd found my tribe.

"And you've arrived just at the right time," Sunny said scratching away at her drawing. "At 12 o'clock we all go for lunch."

I smiled to myself, chose several shades of orange and brown and looked at my drawing with new eyes. It wasn't actually that bad. The beagle emerging from the page had a cheeky look about him and I'd caught the light just right. The owner was going to be very pleased with this.

"Did you hear Michael and Reese are going to Norfolk island next week?" Sunny said to no one in particular.

"I know!" replied one of the other women. "Isn't it amazing how this group has brought people together? Two years ago, Michael and Reese didn't even know each other and now they're travelling around together." She smiled at me. "Friends are just people you haven't met yet."

Extraordinary
Kathleen Bentley

I am not an extraordinary person
I am just as ordinary as the next person.
But then, they do not have you.
For you make every ordinary thing – extraordinary.
        Even me!

Each day is a new day of excitement
Something to discover, a wonder to behold.
It is almost like being a child again
Exploring our community, our environment, our universe
        Enchanting!

You take me to the 'wow' factor of every day.
Because you have opened my eyes,
My senses – and my heart.
Everything is new. It has an inner depth I had never seen
        Before you!

Thank you for putting the rainbow in my sky,
For bringing your sunshine into my world,
For uplifting my heart to embrace the universe.
And thank you for your belief in me. I am extraordinary
        After all!

'Safe as Lights'
Jennie Herrera

The keeper put the letter aside and got on with the job of storing everything which had come in on the monthly boat. Other fathers might look forward to a daughter coming home, but all he could think of was the disruption and noise she would cause. 'Women,' he thought sourly, 'got their tongues hung in the middle and clacking both ends.' But anyone who chose to disrupt his daily solitude would be resented.

He had been keeper of the light on this remote and tiny speck of rock for more than twenty years. Something about his silence, his taciturn face, seamed and brown, suggested a being which had ceased being fully human and begun to merge with the rock beneath the lighthouse. His movements were slow and careful. The dangers of the cliffs and boiling waves demanded that. But they also suggested something slowly slipping and weathering.

He poked the unwanted message into his coal-fired generator. The lighter had been and gone. Unloaded into the pulley boxes at the bottom, ratcheted up, cog by cog, tipped into his cellar at the top – that was the kind of conversation he preferred with the outside world. Several hours of creaks and bangs and shouts over the sound of a crashing sea. Then alone again with gulls and gannets and the ever-present waves. He wanted to sit down and dash off a scrawled plea: 'Stay with your aunt. There's nothing for you here. Stay where you can live your life.' But he didn't. He hated the thought of her coming. But he couldn't bring himself to refuse her. She would soon get lonely and want to leave again. Blessed peace would return.

But when his daughter seated herself and her luggage in one of the makeshift boxes and was winched upwards a month later it was worse than he expected. She was smart. She wore the new shorter skirts. She had a picture hat tied on firmly with ribbons against the constant tug of the wind. Her lips were red. She wore bangles.

He didn't know what to say to her. He wasn't used to conversations, except those occasional short bursts directed at the weather or the birds or the machinery that worked the revolving light, and his voice sounded odd in his ears. She didn't appear to notice, rattling on about how things were back on the mainland with her aunt, the voyage out, how good it was to see him again

He wasn't a subtle man and it didn't occur to him that she felt daunted in his unspeaking presence broken only by occasional brusque questions. Instead he heard her cheerful chatter and how it seemed to fill every nook and cranny in his small quarters.

"Gotta go down and feed the … "

He was in the habit of calling it 'the old black bastard', that great maw that took his feedings of coal, and now he couldn't remember its proper name. She busied herself with washing up and making herself a bed in the small storeroom.

The first night she was tired and slept easily. But in the weeks that followed she often lay awake, pondering on her decision to come home. 'It will take him time to get used to me again … I know that … and I don't mind that he sits there and scowls sometimes … but it's something more than that … I don't understand it and I must be imagining things surely … but I have the feeling sometimes that he actually hates me … '

*

He couldn't bring himself to admit it to himself. A secret hope that she would leave soon. An unnatural father? Probably. He gave out hints. 'A young thing like you.' 'Life there with your aunt … ' Sometimes his tongue simply dried up and he sat there mouthing sentiments which wouldn't fully form. Because deep down he felt something worse than simply wanting her to pack and leave. Coming down the steep stairs and seeing her below him he had found in himself a sudden terrible desire to push her so she would fall. Out on the rocks he wanted her to slip, to tumble, to be gone. As they ate their plain fare from the cans that had sat on shelves for months he longed for her to press her stomach and groan and need a doctor. When she offered to help him with the boilers he wondered if it was possible to blow them both sky-high and end all his miserable thoughts for ever.

Did she see it in his eyes? The way he sometimes glanced sideways when she was preoccupied? The way he put out his hands as though they had taken on this strange despair of their own and would happily push her out of their way? After her first cheerful days when she tried to get him to talk she gradually fell into long reveries herself.

All her happy imaginings before she came home, all the stories they would tell one another, all the memories they would share, all the things he could tell her about his work and the birds and seals and insects which shared his lonely post ... Now she knew all this had been wishful thinking. It wasn't simply the endless silence. It was a deep intangible fear that he actually hated her and wished her ill. Or, at the very least, wished she would soon depart again. Put like that it seemed absurd. Her own father! Of course not. It was just that it took time to get used to constant human contact. Ten years was a long time. And he didn't follow the changing news and fashions and ideas of the outside world. There was nowhere their minds could meet.

Little by little she grew more cautious. Not walking along the cliff edges. Not going downstairs in front of him. Not letting him cook. Standing away from the winches and pulleys. It must be her imagination. Of course it must! But that didn't mean she should become careless ...

And when they sat down to each meal the words dried on her tongue. He didn't care a penny for the world she had inhabited all through her growing up. They were two strangers suddenly thrown together on this tiny rock. Instead they both ate slowly and silently, only the bullying rushes of the wind round the stone tower and the endless crash of waves on the rocks and the lonely cries of circling birds to keep them company.

"Such lonely sounds," she said one evening, unable to keep back the sudden cry contained in her throat.

"To you maybe." His voice was a rusted growl.

"Yes, to me. I looked forward so much to coming back to you. But I am lonelier in the same room with you than I ever was when I merely went to bed over there, in the first days, and cried for homesickness."

"No one gets lighthouse-sick."

"Don't they? I did."

He didn't try to answer that and they finished the meal in silence. But as she rose to clear their plates and shake out the tablecloth she said suddenly, "You were just as quiet back then. You didn't talk from morning to night ... but you listened."

He grunted and got up from the table.

*

The evening sky was fierce in its purples and crimsons and dreadful wintry greys and he stood for several minutes at the lower door gazing out on the immense scene before him.

The question came unbidden. 'Did I listen?' But the child who went away was not the woman who came back. That child, with its artless prattle, its happy sense that this was home, every inch of it, had needed him. That child had no one else to turn to. That child had no comparisons. That child was a creature of this lonely place. That small girl never doubted that this rock was the centre of the universe.

'I doubt it.' The words had flowed by, as much a sound of this pinnacle as the sea and the storms, as much a backdrop to his world as the occasional foghorn.

'She expects more of me now.' Was it that rather than the invasion of his solitude? And he knew he had nothing to give.

No emotions. A rock, a light, an ocean, they don't expect protestations of love or hope. Something dried out and soulless, all it's being absorbed into the fury of this necessary place. 'I'm needed here. Someone's got to do it. I couldn't live with people rushing by and these new cars and trolley buses and phonographs and all the things she speaks of as though they are natural. I belong here.' A human being as necessary as the light, as silent, as real.

'Did I listen?'

*

"I never listened to you. I listened to the wind and waves, to the storms coming and the storms blown out." It was a long speech for him.

"I know you did. But you made me part of that world you lived in. But I know now we can never go back to that. So there's nothing for it but for me to go back on the next boat."

She said it without emotion. It was their failure. But tears could not turn them back to what they'd been to one another.

"Seems best."

He worked away at his usual duties. Perhaps it was imagination, and he didn't see himself as an imaginative man, but several times he thought he heard her singing on the gale. Mermaids were said to sing like that. Voices that could never be separated out from the world around him.

And there was the rustle of her movements about their rooms, the food on the table, the small clatter of spoons and knives, the deft way her still smooth young hands folded round things and did the small household tasks. There was the glimpse of her outside, her long tawny hair blowing in the wind when she grew tired of plaiting it neatly round her head, and the way her shawl billowed out.

She was the stranger here, the alien, but sometimes, too fleeting to be caught, he knew she belonged.

"It's for you," he said another evening. "Husbands and all that. Nothing for you here."

"No. Nothing. Just my father." He thought she was going to add something. He even found himself wanting her to add something. And he remembered her as a child holding his weatherbeaten hand as they went to and fro on the rocks below on a rare calm day collecting shells and marvelling at the great long strands of greeny-brown kelp.

*

Two days till the boat with stores and coal. One day. Six hours, five, four. She had her cases packed. Her hat set out ready. Several times she had looked out at the weather. Would the boat come on time? The weather was reasonable. She tried to summon up the joy of returning to her aunt's house. Its routines. Her aunt's expression. Her moments of kindness. Her acceptance. The boarder she might have given the spare room to. The kinds of positions she might seek. A shop. Companion to an elderly person. A library. None of them would have the fresh clean tang of the sea. None of them would hold her at the centre of each magnificent storm.

But she would live as other young women did.

There was no sign of her father. He had gone out somewhere. She assumed he had things to send on the boat. The wind tugged at the grass and shrubs that struggled for a foothold on this stack and crept down the sheltered clefts in its sides. In the smooth swell below a seal popped a whiskery snout above the water. She was distracted by watching.

Her father came up beside her. She turned and, without thinking, said, "Look at him! I wonder if it's Rocky?" As a child she'd had her own names for all the seals who hauled out on the wave-washed platforms.

He had forgotten. He was suddenly ashamed for forgetting. He thought of saying 'Don't go!' and quashed the thought. Of course she must go. For her sake. For his. And then it came to him. How he'd changed without noticing. Accepted her again as part of this life.

Her sake. But that was her business. Not his.

"Don't go," he said gruffly. "Stay a bit longer."

"23"
Ant Dry

'Number sixteen' called Jennifer.

Grant did not look up, 'May I help you?' he asked the vague shape on the other side of the counter.

'One hundred grams of salami, please'

Reach, grab, measure, jiggle, fold, print label, stick label down, hand-over, 'Anything else?'

'Some chicken legs please'

Grant didn't exactly hate his job, but it was a bit boring. He had wanted to become a mathematician when he left school. His Dad had laughed at him.

"Mathematicians are sharp, my boy. You're too much of a dozy bugger. Always dreaming. Anyways, there's no jobs in maths. Better off to get a real job. I'll speak to George at Woolies for you.'

Grant sighed.

'Excuse, me? Some chicken legs please?'

Grant recovered with a start. That was the worst thing about this stupid job, people kept interrupting his train of thought.

'What?'

'Chicken legs'

'Right, okay.'

Reach, grab measure, jiggled, fold, print label stick down, hand over, 'Anything else?'

'No thanks'

'Number seventeen' called Jennifer.

Bloody hell, that Jennifer was a bossy cow. He could see the numbers light up, why did she have to call all the time? Did she think he was stupid? He sighed again. How far off was tea?

'Number eighteen' Jennifer called. Grant was relieved to see Brianna rush off to sort out number eighteen.

Why couldn't he get a job with maths? He loved numbers, they made sense. They had a certain magical quality to them, they fell into place.

'Number nineteen'

Oh, bugger better do some work.

'Yes ma'am, may I help?'

As he fished around to serve the customer Grant realised with a little shiver of anticipation that the numbers were coming around to twenty three again. Of all the numbers, he loved twenty-three the most. It had no real beauty mathematically speaking, it didn't fall into any magical sequence, but there was something about it. He had been born on 23 July. His mother had been married at twenty three, and had been married to his Dad for twenty-three years. His brother had finally left home at twenty-three. 'Life begins at twenty-three" his brother had said. Good things seemed to happen to him every 23rd of the month. It was on that date that he had met Carol. And Marri-Anne. It was on the 23rd of last month that he'd had his first kiss.

He waited for number twenty-three to come around, which it did about four times a day. He always wanted to serve customer number twenty-three, and his day was made or broken on how many times he could do it. He had made no secret of his foible and the others usually humoured him. Except Jennifer. She always tried to beat him to customer twenty-three. Just to annoy him. The cow.

'Number twenty-one'. He had not even noticed that a few numbers had passed by. Must stop daydreaming. He looked up to see if anyone had noticed that twenty-three was imminent. Everyone was ignoring him. Except Jennifer, she looked straight at him, and she wasn't smiling.

'Grant', called Jennifer, 'number twenty-two'. She was pointing deliberately at a blur on the other side of the counter. 'Serve number twenty-two'.

Grant ignored her.

'I got it' said Brianna, and Grant slumped in relief.

The buzzer went. Jennifer did not call out any number. Grant looked up at the number machine.

'Number twenty-three' he called, and looked over the counter, bringing the blur there into focus. There, standing holding a scrap of paper was a girl of about eighteen.

'That's me' she said with a huge grin. Emblazoned across her tee-shirt was the number "23". 'Look, I'm number twenty-three and I picked number twenty-three.' And she laughed. It was a wonderful laugh, with a gurgle beneath. Grant was stunned.

'Guh .' he said.

'Isn't that cool?' she asked and laughed again.

Grant peeled himself off the back wall where he seemed to have become stuck, and fumbled his way to the counter. Mechanically he served the girl, trying not to stare, willing himself to keep his mouth from gaping. She didn't want much and left quickly. Grant leaned over the counter and watched her until she disappeared down isle two.

It was a sign. It was meant to be. A divine intervention, whatever that was. There could be no other explanation. He couldn't let her go.

He took off his apron, placed his cap on the counter and stepped away.

"Grant, where you going?' called Jennifer.

Grant took no notice and ran to isle two. What colour was her tee-shirt? How tall was she? What did she look like? He had been too stunned to even look properly. Where was she?

No one in isle two. He turned up isle three. No one. Isle four. Where was she? Isle five. Six. Seven. Eight. Nine. Oh, no she wasn't still there. Granted rushed to the check-out counter.

'Grant, please report to the deli immediately' called the intercom.

Shut up Jennifer.

Bloody hell, where was she?

Grant ran outside, looking wildly from side to side. No one, nothing.

There was a touch on his elbow, 'Grant' . It was Brianna.

'Huh? What?'

'What's the matter with you? Better come back. You'll get fired.'

'Did you see her?'

'Who?'

'That girl. She had twenty-three on her shirt.'

'What girl? Are you twenty three-ing again? There was no twenty three, that nasty cow Jennifer double clicked on twenty two. Just to tease you. Come back in you daft bugger. There was no twenty three.'

The Inheritance
Andrea McMahon

No sex. That's what Jim had said. They were not his exact words, but that was the message. Companionship. That was what he was after. Not that he used that word either. Jim had asked her to accompany him on a short holiday. A sojourn, he called it. Over the water to Tasmania...it will be an adventure.

Adventure...the word exists in Annie's memory as the aroma of exotic spices, the warm/cool currents of the Mediterranean, the silken touch of shifting desert sands, the brittle blue brilliance of glacial ice. For a moment, a fleeting moment, she is back in a distant land, wild and free...

But as it turns out Annie has never been to Tasmania. It had been too close to home to compete with the lure of faraway places. She has not yet given Jim an answer to his offer. But she knows what it is going to be. Beggars can't be choosers, she mumbles aloud, recalling the humiliation, the shame, of attempting to foist herself upon an old boyfriend in London. Divorced, living in a townhouse, she thought that perhaps she could stay with him for a while, a few months even, while she found work in another London pub. But ever so gently, kindly, he explained that it had been lovely seeing her again, but she must leave. There were children visiting on weekends. There was someone else.

So after many years abroad Annie finally returned to Melbourne, emptied her bank account paying the bond and one month's rent on a soulless unit in a suburban cul-de-sac. She had considered a share house, but pride stopped her. She was a fifty-two-year-old hospitality worker. Single, childless, parentless. Appearances were everything.

That had been two years ago. Don't spend too long at the fair. On one of her infrequent trips back to Australia her mother had quoted Joan Didion at her, waving a paperback in her general direction. Joan's words not mine. Joan—and her mother—had been right. The fair was well and truly over. She found the book, the quote marked in the margin, at the bottom of an overladen box of her mother's belongings. The words were burned into her memory...it was a very long time indeed before I stopped believing in new faces and began to understand the lesson in that story, which was that it is distinctly possible to stay too long at the Fair.

She found work in hospitality easily enough. No-one could argue she didn't have the experience. But that was until the back injury. Acquired in her own home as she went about changing a light bulb. It had just been a tiny tumble with a twist onto her bed. But it was enough. Not crippling enough to get her a disability pension. Too crippling to land her a job. Walking was difficult. It did not make for a favourable first impression.

Jim had noticed. Perhaps. Or perhaps he simply noticed the overgrown nature strip. He offered to mow both it and her tiny pocket of lawn. I can mow your lawns for you, easy for me, he'd said. Jim lives in the tidy weatherboard house opposite Annie. He is a sweet man. Not so smart, she decided, but sweet. In return she feeds his cat, Silky, when he goes away for the weekend to his block outside of Bendigo. Sulky would've been a better name, he'd said on more than one occasion. Sulky Silky had been his mother's cat. Jim himself is more of a dog man, his dog, Ranger, his constant companion. After a weekend away the two of them would pop over to thank her upon their return, offering up one or two highlights of the trip: a detour to a railway museum, a top-notch pub meal; for Ranger, a rabbit or two. She never invited him in.

It was the conversation over mobile phone plans that led to a recalibration of their relationship. Jim had been waiting for her to leave the house that day, corralling her as she slowly made her way up the footpath to the bus stop. He had a bundle of computer printouts in his hand and a harried look on his face. I need a new phone plan, he said. Boss reckons I'm being robbed. Bunch of crooks! Jim's brow was furrowed. His hands clenched the paper. His pleading was palpable. Annie held out her arm to receive the printouts. A committed act, which in hindsight seemed to her to have been as binding as the signing of a marriage certificate, the wearing of a ring.

Annie sorted out an affordable plan for Jim. If there was one thing she was good at, it was living on the smell of an oily rag. One of her mother's favourite expressions. Remember Anna-Maree, you can't live on the smell of an oily rag forever. Just watch me, my darling mother, just watch me, she thinks now. It still shocks her how much she misses her mother. Since she left Melbourne at the age of twenty, she had been back for a total of eighteen months, three of which had been to settle the estate after her mother's passing. It had been a quick succumbing to leukaemia. Annie hadn't returned to care for her mother because her mother hadn't told her that she was sick. That she had only months to live.

Her mother hadn't told her.

Why didn't she send for me? she had murmured to her mother's friends at the funeral. She would've, if she'd been sure you would've come. That had been Ruth, her mother's oldest friend. Blunt, but not unkind. Ruth had laid her hand on Annie's arm firmly, so Annie knew she was not to protest that she would've been there, would've jumped on the first plane from Frankfurt. Instead Annie whispered, I might've been there. But she had at least been able to take comfort in knowing that Eileen had not died alone. Ruth had travelled down from the Sunshine Coast in her mobile home, visited Eileen in the hospice every day.

I would've been there. Annie whispers these words aloud, hearing the lie. She knows her mother was right. She might have been there. She might not. Her mother hadn't wanted to know. It was part of the protective coating she had adopted so her nomadic daughter could do her no harm. There had always been excuses for not returning home. Jobs, travel plans, boyfriends. So many beginnings. There was always something beginning, something glittering on the horizon that pulled her away like a rip tide. When it came to endings with their accompanying tedium or turbulence, she had adopted a policy of avoidance, turning a bad ending into a glorious beginning. A relationship breakdown quickly became the hunt for a new romance, a job coming to an end an excuse to travel. She has travelled all around the globe, from the Arctic tundra to the Tierra del Fuego archipelago, covering too many destinations in between to recall. But she has never visited Tasmania.

Annie feels her heart flutter with excitement, a constrained, muted excitement, at the thought of a holiday. "I'm taking the car over on the ferry," Jim had said. "You can fly if you want. I can meet you at the airport if you don't want to share a cabin. No strings attached, as I've said. If Mum was still alive, it'd be Mum coming with me. I'd have to listen to her snoring all night. Never seemed to be a problem her being kept awake listening to me snoring…I miss my mum," he added, smiling to himself, "but I guess you'd know all about that."

Annie misses her mother but cannot remember if she snored or not. In the early days Eileen travelled to Europe every couple of years, spending three or even four weeks with her daughter on each occasion, ostensibly sight-seeing, but in reality eating pastries and drinking endless cups of coffee together in sidewalk cafes. And then her mother was gone. Annie had been working at a ski resort in Banff when the inheritance came through. Her nest egg proved very useful less than two years later when a skiing accident in Chamonix led to a compound fracture of her tibia and fibula. It had been the first time, but not the last time, that Annie felt so terribly, terribly alone.

But she has not felt alone lately. Jim, she has begun to realise, has become a friend. A friend with no strings attached. She has begun little by little to understand Jim. The word eccentric keeps fluttering through her head. At first she thought he must always have lived at home, one of those pitifully dependant adult children who had never really grown up, lived in the shadow of an over-protective or overbearing parent. The complete antithesis to herself. But Jim has land out of Bendigo, has built his own eco-friendly off-the-grid cabin with funds saved from fly-in fly-out work over in the West, or the Territory, or anywhere else an expert fitter and turner is needed. Jim told her that before his mum passed away, just a few months before Annie moved in, she had looked after Ranger while he was out of town and that neither Ranger nor Sulky Silky cared much for the arrangement. He'd been staying put for the past couple of years but reckons now it's time to get back out and about. "The FIFO life suits me, confirmed bachelor that I am," he'd joked. "he ole feet are starting to get itchy."

Annie, who had never mentioned her peripatetic past to Jim, felt her own feet itching in solidarity.

Jim had invited her over to his house so they could sit at a table to look over the mobile phone plans. They had entered the house by the back door, Jim guiding her to a table in a sunroom that had been built onto what appeared to be a recently renovated kitchen, French doors opening up onto a large deck. Jim offered her a coffee from a state-of-the-art machine that looked as if it would've been more at home in an inner-city café than a tidy suburban weatherboard. The coffee, strong and aromatic, had been excellent.

After they sorted out the plan and Jim had made the requisite phone calls, he stood, thanked her formally, and asked if she would like to look around the house. He had turned and exited the kitchen before she had time to reply. She followed him through to a formal lounge room. What she saw took her breath away. Took her away. The sensation was first and foremost olfactory. She was back in the grand bazaar; she was wandering through winding alleyways, lost, losing herself, breathing in exotic spices, stagnant sewers…breathing life into herself once again…

This is our Egyptian room, Jim was saying, his attention turned to a framed papyrus scroll depicting a scene from the Egyptian Book of Dead. "My great-grandmother and great-aunt were nurses during the First World War. Served in Cairo. Brought some artefacts home. Then my grandmother served in the second world war. Brought home a few more. Then Mum, also a nurse, went on a tour of Egypt, down the Nile, to Aswan and Luxor. Rosemary, my sister went with her. The collection got even bigger. This was all meant to go to Rosemary, but we lost her a couple of years before Mum. Breast cancer…" Jim's voice trailed away. Annie murmured words of condolence, but her attention was fixed on the mantel piece. Brass plates and bowls, wooden trinket boxes inlaid with mother-of-pearl; figurines of gods, Ra-Harakti the sun god, Anubis, god of the dead and afterlife, others she did not recognise. She couldn't see a speck of dust. A large skylight in the roof ensured all that was gold glittered.

"And through here we have the family room. It's the dining room but we call it the family room. You'll see why." Jim beckoned her through. Annie crossed a short hallway into a formal dining room, where six chairs surrounded a large mahogany dining table. Crystal decanters and glassware glittered on a sideboard, sunlight filtered through fine lace curtains and another large skylight. The room was decorated with framed family portraits, artwork in gilded frames, four filled-to-bursting china cabinets inlaid with art deco stained glass.

Annie felt the eyes of five generations boring down upon her and understood then, why Jim hadn't been able to sell the house, move back up to his eco-friendly block in Bendigo. And furthermore, she also understood—with complete clarity and conviction—what it was that Jim wanted. What Jim wanted from her, for her.

He wanted her to inherit the house. Keep his mother's, grandmother's, great-grandmother's legacy alive. When he broached the subject he had not couched it in those terms, of course. It had been a conversation about house-sitting and pet-sitting. Until he put the place on the market, arranged for all his mother's belongings to be cleared out at some undetermined future date.

The realization, so rich with possibility, had cast her afloat on a sea of relief.

She is waiting for Jim to return home now. The sound of his Holden Rodeo entering the driveway has become familiar, comforting. She is anxious to give him an answer to his offer of a Tasmanian holiday. She thinks perhaps he may invite her in for a pre-dinner drink over which they will discuss their travel plans. The evening is warm. She thinks she may be offered a glass of iced tea, served in gold-leaf Egyptian glassware out on the deck, bathed in the golden glow of a singular summer evening.

Being Grateful
Donna-Marie Koopman

I am very grateful for what I have in life.
My limbs are free to walk and run
not bound by any ties.
I can clearly see around me
all the beauty to be found.
And I have never known what it's
like not to hear a sound.
I can tell you often
I take for granted all these gifts.
Though if of these gifts I lost but one,
too late I'd treasure it.

Winter, Then Spring
Ant Dry

She left in the winter
My darling, my wife
The cold came and took her
And ended my life.

*****

We'd had no idea of the evil inside
Of the savage disease that tossed her aside
We'd lived our whole lives without a concern
Not thinking, not once, that we'd have to learn
That nothing, no nothing, could ever be firm.
How were we to know that our dreams would collide
With horror and blood and with Lucifer's bride?
Those glorious days when we used to sit
And gaze upon life as if "this was it"
Our visions, our dreams our infinite goal
What use to us now, that we are not whole?
The coldness of winter crept into my soul
I could never forgive my God.
He'd ended my life, my wonderful dreams
He'd taken my wife from me.
How so these rumoured "mysterious ways"
What rubbish what absolute cant.
Be gone you wretched most fallible God.
Turn your treacherous face from me.
I have no use for your meaningless love
I turn my shoulder on thee.

*****

In the middle of winter, In the deepest of drifts
I struggled to stay alive
I lived but barely, I struggled to breathe
I could hardly but carry the cost.

*****

Then spring arrived like a tentative fawn,

Peeking her head through the gloom
It came in the form of my daughter
Who arrived on the scene like a bloom.
She'd been away in some troublesome place
And hadn't been able to flee.
Her mother, now passed, had raked her heart
She felt just as wretched as me.
She took my hand and held it a while
The more to comfort me
And then, there it was, that infinite warmth
And my heart began its thaw
My love once withered, now started to grow
The season was winter no more
Spring had appeared in the form of a girl
Who chased the cold away
Who showed that love's seasons are more than that
That they carry their strength within
Such that winter, then spring, both pass away
And leave us on gossamer wing.

A Word is a Word
Donna-Marie Koopman

A word is a word and many I've heard
but does everyone hear what you say?
Now a well-meaning word when wrongly heard
is very often misplaced.
A loving word when it is heard
can make many hearts want to sing.
But a word is a thing, easily lost on the wind,
so listen, you may not hear it again.
A word is a word and I've often heard
to people you cannot relate.
But a word is a word, and cannot be heard,
if you don't hear what that word has to say.
So you see my friend,
if you don't listen in,
a word is an empty thing.

Evolution ???
Kathleen Bentley

The river of nature flows moving pebbles out of its way,
Gurgling around boulders, but moving them over time
When the water rises, due to rain or high tide somewhere
Such is the river of life, moving with our emotions.
Pushing life's problems aside just like pebbles.
Ruminating while tears flow until solutions are found.
Similarities are startling, and understanding
The ebb and flow of the river is vital.

So too is the ebb and flow of life,
And the continuance of its inevitability
Of this movement, from source to extinction.
The river moves slowly or swiftly,
Small streams or turbulent waters
Ending with its emergence with lakes, lochs or seas,
While the river of life emerges with death,
Waiting to claim new arrivals.

For those who believe in the afterlife
This emergence can be a new way of living,
Or not – just a void of nothingness.
Perhaps it's a melding of one body with another.
Is it too much to accept that the two bodies meet?
That death converges into nature's river
So the ebb and flow of both are entwined?
Is this merger the same as water into a lake?

   And human death?
   Do we return to earth through water?
      Think. Question.

The Secret
Tatiana Petrovsky

There is a secret box hidden
in the recesses of his mind.
Caution abandoned
fortified by spirituous liquor
he prises open the lid –

Weevils are weaving forlorn
webs in the discarded
breadcrumbs of desire
left overs from one-time
sumptuous delicious banquets –

Silverfish are masticating
holes in the forgotten love letters
shredding them into paper doilies
exposing his foibles
with razor sharp precision.

Wasps are swarming over
the last drops of honey-laced
words –'how sweet they
sounded ' the malevolent
buzz drones out resistance.

He shuts the lid
on past indiscretions
impeded by indecision
hope stutters away on
smudged moth's wings.

My Dad's Story
Pete Stratford

"Will you go and see where Dad is...'is tea's getting cold."

"Aww, I've just took me boots off."

"Just go and get 'im!"

Mum's voice had an edge of weary frustration, so reluctantly pulling my boots back on I headed off the back porch towards the stables. He should have already taken the plough horse from there out to the overnight paddock, but sometimes he took a bit longer, usually due to refilling chaff troughs or mending harness. Or just having a quiet smoke and resting from a day of trudging behind the horse between endless rows of spuds. How I hated that job too.

Dad wasn't in the stables, so I wandered out to the paddock where I could see him, back on to me, leaning awkwardly over the paling fence. Even when I yelled out a second time he didn't seem to hear me, so I walked across towards him and spoke again. But there was to be no response.

They had said it was probably a heart attack had killed him, although that was the least of our concerns with a funeral to prepare for. Meanwhile his body was laid out in an open casket set up on a couple of trestles in our parlour, where the undertaker had delivered it a couple of days earlier.

Although I was the second youngest of us five boys, my older brothers had already found work away from home, leaving me as the eldest still at home. Another brother and then our only sister were younger than me. Having just turned seventeen, I had long been expected to take on adult responsibilities in return for bed and food only. My school days had ended abruptly the day Dad had said to me, "you're big enough to walk behind the plough now, so you're stayin' home to help me," just before my thirteenth birthday.

Glancing at his waxen looking corpse as I passed through the parlour I was rather aghast at a change taking place. Having quickly found the phone number of the undertaker and then requesting the exchange operator connect me through to it, I waited for a response, which seemed to take forever. Finally I heard, "Smudge's Funeral Parlour, how can we help you?" in an unemotional – too frequently repeated – manner.

"Me Dad's got blood seeping out his mouth!" I blurted out over the phone.

"Well then screw the bloody lid on the coffin!" came back in an angry tone.

So that's what I did.

That was an era when one grew up fast, I guess, for there weren't really any alternatives on offer back then. Perhaps nowadays one would be sent off for a series of counselling sessions to alleviate the grief and trauma, and probably rightly so. But that benefit was still well into the future, while we still had the horrendous world war and the fall-out from that to deal with, before any type of emotional care was eventually introduced. Meanwhile, many of us youngsters were suddenly thrust into rapidly "growing up", very, very quickly.

A Matter of Perspective
Angela Bischof-Joseph

Everyone had gathered at a beauty spot along the river at the local park to share a BBQ after the church service. A long queue had formed. The food had been cooked and was ready to serve. Designated cooks were asked to cook, and a large variety of food was laid out. Tantalising aromas of sausages, meat patties, chicken, and minute steaks tempted the hungry crowd. A large selection of salads and bread was laid out on another table. As the queue passed each cook who served them, one young mother, Jane, stopped at Sumi's food tray.

Jane looked at the food, looked at Sumi, and looked at the food again and again at Sumi. Jane continued this surveillance for a good fifteen seconds or so. Next to her, the queue had stalled, making some people annoyed. Finally, she said with a worried look on her face,

"Oh, that will be hot." She exclaimed with a voice of concern. Sumi smiled.

"I promise it is not. Let's give you a piece to try. I will catch up with you later and ask you how it tastes. Jane nodded and accepted Sumi's offering. When everyone had been served, Sumi and the cooks took a break to have their lunch. With all the picnic gear cleared, Sumi looked for Jane and found her sitting under the shade of a tree with her family.

"Jane, how was the food I gave you? Was it chilli hot?" Sumi asked.

Jane did not utter a word but nodded to indicate it was not. She had a broad smile on her face.

Sumi smiled.

"I promised you it won't be hot. That was Honey, Soya Sauce chicken wings. The honey makes it look dark when cooked on the BBQ" Sumi informed her and left Jane to enjoy the rest of the afternoon with her family.

Officer, what do I do? Sumi asked the local police officer at the station.

She and her husband were moving from the mainland to Tasmania permanently. Sumi had trained and taken over her husband's gun licence to help run the farm. She was responsible for safely transporting the firearm, a twenty-two rimfire rifle.

"Pack the rifle into the bottom of the boot, making sure it is well out of sight. You will have to surrender it to Security for safekeeping on board the ferry before you board the ferry. When you get to Tasmania, as soon as you collect it from Security, you must again pack it out of sight. You will have to find a dealer or a licensed friend to store your rifle until your storage facility is available. You are not permitted to drive around with it in your boot. You will incur heavy fines and the confiscation of the firearm if the police stop you and find it in your vehicle," the officer advised.

Sumi followed the officer's instructions. On reaching the ferry for the crossing to Tasmania, Sumi was pointed toward the security officers to surrender her rifle. She walked her rifle to the security guard and asked.

"Where do I hand my rifle for safekeeping?"

The Indian security guard looked at her with a look of alarm on his face.

"That one yours?" he asked with a strong Indian accent

"Yes," Sumi replied.

"Go there." He pointed to another security guard standing just outside a large door on the ship's side.

Sumi walked her rifle to the following security guard, also of Indian ethnicity. He watched Sumi approach him with the gun. He looked at her with wide eyes.

"That yours?" he asked her again with his heavy Indian accent. "Licence, please." He asked with authority and aggression.

Sumi was prepared with her licence at hand and gave it to him. The security guard looked at the licence with Sumi's photo and then up at her face twice. He turned it around and checked her name on it.

"Papers, please." He asked again with aggression. Sumi handed the forms she had filled out at the police station to the guard. He checked them over and handed them back to her.

"Follow me, please." He said and turned to enter the security vault on board the ship.

"Put it there, please." He instructed, pointing to a space on a shelf. Sumi did as instructed and followed the guard outside the ship. The security guard's stern facial expression never wavered.

Sumi returned to her car and her waiting husband, glad the exercise was over!

The day crossing over the Bass Strait was uneventful. On disembarking, Sumi went to retrieve her gun. Her husband stopped outside a port perimeter fence where another Caucasian security guard stood beside a security container. As Sumi approached the guard, she noticed only two articles in the container. A gas aerosol can and Sumi's gun, which she recognised in a fabric casing that Sumi had made. The guard reached for the aerosol can and held it out to Sumi.

"That's not mine." She said and handed her papers to the guard. He looked at the documents, placed the aerosol can back into the container, reached for Sumi's gun and gave it to her.

"Thank you," Sumi said and walked back to her car. The security guard did not utter a word.

"How shall we get to know people? Sumi asked her husband, John.

"Why don't you invite them for a meal?" John suggested.

Sumi had a gut feeling about what to expect when she invited someone to eat at their home. The reaction would be one of joy or distress. Joy for anticipating a meal they can't produce in their own home or distress that they will be fed food so hot with chilli that they would be sick afterwards. Sumi always gave them a choice of cuisines based mainly on her husband and her own cultural background. Chinese, Malay, Indian or Western cuisines were offered as a choice. Usually, Asian cooking is chosen, and typically Indian, which Sumi suspected was because of her Indian ethnicity.

"Would you like to come to lunch?" Sumi asked Daniel.

"Thank you for the invitation. I will have to speak to my wife." He replied.

A while later, Daniel's wife, Jojo, came hurrying to Sumi, looking very distressed.

"Sumi" she said anxiously, "Daniel says that you have invited us to your home for a meal?"

"Yes," Sumi replied.

" Oh, but we eat only plain food," Jojo informed Sumi.

" Not to worry, I can cook plain food. What would you like to eat, Chinese, Malay, Indian or Western?" Sumi replied.
Jojo thought momentarily and said, "How about Chinese, as long as it is not spicy." Jojo requested.

"I must tell you something about the term "Spicy." Most people have mistaken spice for the heat of the chilli herb. A spice is a strongly flavoured or aromatic plant-based condiment used to flavour food. Spices come from aromatic roots, bark, berries, buds and seeds. The Tasmanian Pepper berry is a spice, but it is not hot. So are Cinnamon, Cloves, Mace, Ginger and Nutmeg that you would use in your cooking, especially in fruit cake. The word spice is from Latin, and it means "Species" regarding a particular kind of merchandise." Sumi informed Jojo. "I will cook a Chinese meal for you and your family. I don't normally make food chilli hot for my guests unless they request it. How many would I expect to cook for? How many children do you have in your household?" Sumi asked.

"I have two young daughters living at home and one who has just married. So there will be eight of us altogether." Jojo counted out.

Sumi did not intend for the married daughter to be included, but since Jojo had included her and her husband in her numbers, Sumi did not say anything. And so it was that there would be eight for lunch. A date was fixed.

Sumi prepared the meal of Chicken and Noodles. Jojo provided the dessert of a platter of fresh fruit. The family brought their own Coke and Pop drinks which Sumi and John did not drink because of the high sugar content and chemicals used in the production. They did not want any alcohol.

The family seemed to enjoy the meal. Sumi put a chilli condiment on the table, informing them that she and John used the real McCoy of Chilli. It was left untouched by the family. John and Sumi indulged in it.

When the family left, waving their goodbyes and thanks for the meal, John said,

"What did you do that for? It is the worst insipid meal you have ever cooked in the time I have known you!"

"Well, that is what Jojo asked," Sumi replied, laughing. "I think she must have thought that I was going to send her family up in smoke with chilli when she spoke to me about the meal choice she wanted!"

Daniel and his family's relationship never really jelled with Sumi and John. They sometimes did not acknowledge them when meeting Sumi and John at functions. Their children certainly did not.

Daniel, however, did come to their home several times as he was a plumber and was employed to work at their home. Each time Sumi would invite him to have lunch with them, she would prepare an Indian meal, no holding back on the spices, chilli included but within a reasonable amount. Daniel enjoyed every meal with no comments about the chilli heat. John had said to Sumi not to hold back on the spice department.

Sometime later, Sumi attended a ladies' lunch and was seated a chair away from Jojo. The conversation turned to food and cooking.

"I cooked a Thai Green Curry last night," Jojo said.

Sumi thought to herself. You said that you and your family only ate plain food. Well, another one bites the dust! Sometime later, Sumi was advised by another friend not to include the family in an invitation, or she might find fifty people at her doorstep!

Caucasian John wanted to please his new Asian wife, so he grew as much of her ethnic foods as possible in his farm vegetable plot. There were garlic, eggplant, lemongrass, kaffier lime, snake beans, mustard leaves and many more. But most important was the chilli. There were several varieties of chilli. Short, long, mild and hot. When the time came for harvest, chilli galore were dried on hot tin plates in the summer sun so much that they became self-sufficient in their stock.

Sumi decided to indulge and make a Malay chilli condiment called "Sambal Blachan", used by die-hard chilli-crazy Malaysian and Singaporeans in their diet. For a 100ml bottle of Sambal Blachan, the recipe called for as many as thirty dried chillies and twenty fresh ones. Along with other ingredients that are ground together and cooked till a fragrance is released. A bottle of which will be found on the table of every Malay hawker stall and eating house across Malaysia and Singapore.

Sumi and John enjoyed their evening meal with Sambal. John had gotten used to Asian cuisine, and Sumi was liberal in her helping of it. She had not had it for many years, living away from her native home of Singapore.

One a.m.. Sumi wakes up. "I am going to die!" her stomach burned so severely that she could not get comfortable. Not wanting to wake John, she goes to the fridge and gulps a glass of milk. Sitting on the sofa in the living room, Sumi waits for the burning to abate. It does somewhat. Sumi returns to the fridge and looks for something else to help her stomach; an hour later, she finds some cream she consumes. It works, and she goes back to bed—at three a.m.. Sleep ensues. John remains asleep, unaware of his wife's night escapade.

In the morning, Sumi told John what had happened.

"Why didn't you wake me up?" He chided

"And what on earth would you do? A stomach transplant?" Sumi replied. They both crack up in laughter. But it was not the end for Sumi; she remembered her meal for the rest of her day. Sumi went easy on the condiment from then on. Lesson learned!

The Inevitable
Pete Stratford

Evidence of death surrounded us on all sides, even from the ceiling. Exterior views of this building are unpretentious and would attract no particular attention from a passerby, but upon entering a sense of the macabre immediately assaults the senses. Bones, human bones, are stacked like wine bottles against walls to well above head height in places, while skulls create a facade covering entire wall surfaces. Adding to the hellish scene are skeletal remains standing clad in dusty chocolate brown robes with only hand and foot bones showing. Framed by their cassock hoods, skulls sightless eye sockets and with teeth bared by the desiccated flesh shrinking back from them, stare back at you with a gruesome grin.

Passing beneath a sign reading: "As you are now, we used to be. What we are now, so you will be," we had entered the Monumental cemetery of the Franciscan Capuchins, in Italy. Here the mortal remains of over four thousand monks of that Order have been kept since 1528 up until as late as 1870. Also the bodies of three children, nephews of Pope Urban V111, along with some Princes and Nobles are here, although not identified amongst the uncountable thousands of skeletal remnants that are to be seen.

Considerable care and even artistic flair have been employed to display many of the bones, some having been wired together to create candelabra, wall decor, even single finger bones in use as light switches! Even given that being devoid of flesh makes for a smaller stature, those bodies that are mummified intact are of very small build, indicative of a much less nutritious diet than we enjoy today.

It is said that the purpose of this rather morbid display was to cause viewers to be aware of their mortality and consider that there is a need to give thought to what may follow when they die.

Perhaps some of the many tourists that purchase tickets to wander through this house full of dry bones may give some thought along those lines, although no doubt many perceive it as just another tourist attraction designed to lighten the wallets of those with a morbid interest in those now long dead.

Certainly a number of people who passed through this building with us were rather keen to remove the dust from their footwear almost immediately they exited the gloomy and rather stuffy corridors and rooms of that building, having safely emerged again into a much more welcoming land of the living.

A Death
Kathleen Bentley

He leaned on the rail and watched the bundle sink slowly under the surface. He sighed. He was satisfied that he had attached the weights, a couple of bricks and a piece of iron rod, securely.

It had been a nasty business – quite unusual really, but every occasion had its idiosyncrasies, some problem that had to be overcome. Well, this situation really had taken the cake! Who would have thought this perfect union, perfect partners, would end up on the sea bottom. Regrets? Of course he had them, but he found it easier to see her once dead, as an empty shell. Well, there wasn't really anything left of her as she once was, so easy to dispose of the body without any emotional connection. He frowned and checked his watch. Time to go. One last look to ensure nothing floated then he turned and walked towards his car.

The estuary was almost full, helped by the late summer rain and high tide was imminent. The sun was rising, the sky coloured red and yellow promising the day would contain wind and rain – perhaps the storm that was forecast? There was a chill in the air and a few trees were already shedding their leaves, so autumn was just around the corner.

He eased the shift into reverse and backed out of his parking space then, putting it into drive, he slowly left the parking area and drove towards Pacific Highway. This would take him directly into Marketbay where he had taken a motel room. He knew this town like the back of his hand, although he hadn't been here for at least 20 odd years, but he had been born here, grew up here, married here. He shook the memories from his head. That was his old life, way back.

He pulled over to the verge and stepped from the car. The Chevrolet ticked over with hardly a flicker. He loved the car, bought when he had left town over 20 years ago and it had served him well. He particularly liked the deep, wide boot. Great for carrying all sorts of oversized packages.

With the rising of the sun came the early morning warmth. Jake shivered. His thoughts turned to that bundle he had thrown into the sea. Nothing much different about that, except their relationship had lasted almost 10 years.

"She's gone. She had to. I need a drink to wash away the memories. No regrets, remember?" he chastised himself.

Reaching his motel, he parked and entered his room. The half drank glass from last night stood where he'd left it, next to the washbasin in the bathroom. He took it through to the day room and filled it with scotch from the bottle on the table. The remains of his evening meal turned his stomach. He turned his back on it and switched on the television. The news was just the usual: politicians promising everything and delivery nothing, gas prices raising – again – garbage men striking for an increase in pay, and so on. Oh! and a bloody great storm with high winds and damaging rain, well what's new!

He stripped off and stood under the hot shower. He could feel the water relaxing the tight muscles in his shoulders and back. Eventually, he stepped out of the shower, dried himself and picked out clean clothing from his suitcase. Combing his hair the man in the mirror looked no different from many men going on 50 years old, except for the eyes. His looked old and tired. He turned away from his reflection and picked up his diary. Flicking onto today, he read the solitary name printed there WILTON CHESTER KNOWLES next to the time, 11 am.

He lay the diary down and switched on the electric jug. He opened the curtains while it boiled, then made very strong black coffee. He quaffed what was left of the scotch then the coffee, filling the cup again. He took this over to the couch and watched television for a while – a current affairs program due to finish at 9 am. He relaxed. Plenty of time.

What would he say to Wilton? Jake knew he wasn't good at words. How should he explain about the death and … about her disposal. He shuddered. Even though Wilton would be in his 30's now – no longer a boy – this death would be close to his heart. Jake ruminated on how he could explain what had happened. Over the last few months she had been getting unpredictable, especially when he went out in the evenings. Yapping about being left on her own, Why didn't he take her? Who was he seeing? Jake sighed. That last night he had met her eyes. She knew what was coming. She was quiet as she watched him fill the hypodermic syringe. She also wanted an ending.

Living in an upstairs apartment, with no garden, was fraught with difficulties. How could he tell Wilton that after her death he had to take her to the estuary, weigh her down and throw her in. He knew that Wilton had loved her as much as he had but, Wilton must be a man and look forward. No regrets remember. What's done is done.

Wilton would just have bite the bullet, and get himself another dog.

A new beginning?
Anne Layton-Bennett

can we start again
d'you think
wipe the world clean
of violence, hate, and anger
invoke some muggle magic
to tamper with the timing
and to reset the clock

maybe we could employ
a wand or two
to spread some witchery
infused with tolerance
understanding, peace
and love
both for people
and for animals
and this planet that is our home

Fenced in, Fenced out. I Walk
Jennie Herrera

"The new part looks a picture, doesn't it, so green,
and the roses blooming—whereas down here it has a neglected air.
They *really* should do something … "

The flaunting hybrids,
between mown fed watered grass,
the neat plaques in rows.

There is something about the garden part, that order,
that unnatural green, signals something without a soul, wars
with overheard conversations; this well-kept garden has
overwhelmed all sense of memory in its resting place,
its inns along an endless journey.

The chipped and cracked, tat,
broken jars and dead flowers,
white angels askew.

The old struggling with the new, as history flakes and crumbles,
with its weathered sandstone faces struggling for recognition,
its right to memory; it isn't surprising no one begs a plot
in this neglected spot, not any more.

By the post and rail
fennel bursts through, warm scented,
and blackberries drowse.

The straggling gums, with bark to lift and flutter helpless hands
in haphazard signings, seem so untidy, shabby dare I say it,
when seen against neat clipped mono-green enclosing
each new section with its plumply oblong beds.

The sun is warmer
on these granite slabs, and love
engraves itself here.

The higgledy-piggledyness of this neglected place still
embodies something of the mystery of life and growth,
the ambivalence which hangs round death and dying …
and remembering.

The river breeze catches
sagg grass and she-oak needles,
flirts with old-man's-beard.

The wind is always fresh along the outer boundary where a
decrepit fence runs atop the cliffs; setting the bush aflutter and
tapping canes against lichened wood, but it is tied and tamed by
niche-pocked walls, neat signs, bisecting hedges.
A pity, as its place is here, rushing where the spirit beckons,
finding meaning, absolution, as the clay turns, dries and pales.

Soul mingles with weeds
and flowers; to gather unseen,
and taunt stone's solidity.

Here the land's been leveled out for careful sowing, back there
the monumental markers crest the slopes, collect in dips,
entice the paths, to jog, angle, listen to the rustle of head-high
thistles.

The mason's art meets
and measures out nature's whims,
like links in rusty chains.

"These tidy paths, raked smooth, make walking easier, a boon
as you get older … yet, I think, if they'd take me, I'd prefer a
place down there, unkempt, out-at-elbows, whitened by birds.

More natural. I think then I'd feel as if I belong."

Maverick Maestro
Anne Layton-Bennett

you are the conductor
of this macabre musical
and its deadly warlike score
while we are the reluctant audience
of your brutal piece of theatre
a play whose episodes spool
across our screens each night
as we sit transfixed
repelled by a nation and
a leader who shows no remorse

and yet you're a man who knows
must surely know
exactly what you've unleashed
even as you continue this crazy conflict
as dramaturge and architect of a performance
that scythes lives
cripples futures
fractures families and
deepens malignant roots of
hatred among a people
and a planet
weakened by a constant need
to combat humanity
and a foolish belief she will always recuperate
regenerate
bounce back
and survive.

But will she?

A Beautiful Memory
Angela Bischof-Joseph

In the birthing unit, all midwives receive a handover of the women in various stages of labour from the midwives of the previous shift. The senior midwife of the oncoming shift then hands the cases to each midwife according to their skill level or if they had had prior contact with a woman.

I was given a first-time woman who had been in labour all morning and was in the second stage of her birth. The woman is given an hour if it is her first baby and half an hour for her second or more deliveries to push her baby out. Betty had been pushing for half an hour, so she had another half hour, failing which the doctors would reassess and consider a forceps or a Caesarean Section delivery. I had my work cut out for me.

'Hello Betty, I am Jan. I am taking over from the earlier shift.' I said to her, going to the head of the bed to greet her. Betty's eyes were glazed from happy gas and narcotics for pain relief. She was tired and at the end of her tether. Betty just nodded. Her husband by her side looked worried and tired too. The room was charged with expectant emotions.

Getting gowned up for the delivery, I had to make a decision about how I was going to help her. But first, I had to watch her push a couple of times and observe what was happening to the baby's head as it descended down the vagina.

'Push Betty, give it all you've got.' I encouraged her as I watched her baby's head come up further. But as soon as she stopped, it receded! This would not do at all. I have to put my plan into action.

'Betty, I will have to make a cut to help you.' I told her between contractions.

'I don't care what you do. Just get it out!' She screamed.

It was all action from then on. Assisted by another midwife, we positioned her bottom at the bottom edge of the bed and put her legs into stirrups to support them. I infiltrated her tail end with local anaesthetics and waited for the next contraction positioning special scissors just for this purpose in the required position. At the next contraction, she pushed, and I cut. Setting the scissors down quickly on the trolley, I applied pressure to the cut as it began bleeding. The baby's head came up further and fixed itself in position. Betty was screaming in pain.

'Betty, you have done well. The baby's head has progressed further. A few more good pushes, and you will be able to hold baby.' I called out to her. Betty and her husband did not want to know the sex of their baby antenatally. They had picked names for their baby; Liam for a boy and Clare for a girl. With the baby's head fixed in position, the bleeding from the cut was reduced. Two more pushes and the head was born, followed swiftly by the body that Betty "flew out" at me; a term commonly used by midwives when a baby is pushed out so fast that the normal mechanisms of birth are omitted

'Hello, Liam, say hello to your mum and dad.' I held baby up to Betty, and her husband, who were both in tears, and Betty's husband started showering her with kisses. Liam, in the meantime, told us that he had a robust set of lungs and a voice as I cut the cord and gave him to my supporting midwife to bundle up warmly and give him to his joyful parents. Betty's effort to push out the afterbirth was minimal, and I progressed to repair the cut I had made having been trained recently in the procedure.

The proud parents were engrossed in their new baby and, when mother and baby were freshened up, sent to the postnatal ward to rest for the next few days. I waved to them as they exited the birthing unit, already caring for my next mother-to-be.

A day or so later, as I was rushing to get home after a shift, I caught Betty's eye in the postnatal ward as I went by. She was bent over Liam's cot, attending to him. I waved at her and made a mental note to stop by the following day to ask her how she was progressing with being a new mother.

The next day after my shift, I went to see her and was met with an empty cot and bed freshly made up for the next mum and baby. I missed her; she had gone home. A few days later, I was handed a beautifully wrapped gift when I walked into the unit at the start of my shift – a white swan with a gold beak. His body, hollow at the top, was filled with gourmet handmade chocolates. It was wrapped in clear cellophane paper with a large blue bow and a thank you card.

The white swan has graced the back of my kitchen sink for the last thirty years. It has travelled with me from England to

Australia and is a constant reminder of a job well done and appreciated and of Betty's gratitude.

The chocolates have long gone, but the memory remains. The swan holds my scrubbing pad at the sink. I wonder what Liam is doing.

Memories
Kathleen Bentley

Memories are funny things.
It depends on the perception of the individual.
We all have different memories
Of the same experience.

Why is this? Are we so consumed
By our own understanding of the world, of people,
Of events, that we mentally block out
Other possibilities?

As sudden as a cloud blocks the sun
Then releases it to shine brightly again
So does the memory change
To be replaced by another.

When our memory of recent events fail,
How wonderful it is to remember past events–
Past relationships and long forgotten
Places we have visited.

Perhaps what we had for breakfast
Doesn't matter. Perhaps being young again does.
We can relish the warmth of such memories–
Like dancing with a dark stranger.

Now, what was his name? I laugh,
Of course I remember this
For I married him.
I hold a photograph and remember.

Fifty-one years together.
Now I am alone – with my memories–

A box full of photographs,
A drawer full of letters.

Kept just to jog the memory,
But not really necessary for I remember
Every moment spent together
And they are all happy.

Yes, memories are funny things.

Advice to a Domestic Virgo
Marilyn Arnold

Just for today, toss logic aside, along with the housework.
Splash out on the power bill – on icy mornings when your husband is at work,
Use the oven to warm your feet,
And, before he returns at night, put garlic and onion in the grill …
Let him think you have been cooking all day.
Appear co-operative at all times – wait till he is asleep before you pour
his beer down the sink, and flush his ciggies down the toilet.

Your calm, rational exterior means he must never suspect your anger,
Never fear your revenge, never expect that high-heel shoe
to come down on his forehead while sleeping….
Do not drink alcohol yourself if you want to remain unknown.
Beware of the Irish banshee in your soul, anxious to wail and wring hands.
eager to criticize. Remain stubborn and mysterious.
Never be satisfied with the way things are

Be wise.
Stay undercover.
Maintain the lies.

The Web
Kathleen Bentley

The web sparkles in the early morning sun,
Dew drops hang like pearls from its threads
As they stretch from branch to branch.
Watchful eyes keep vigil for visitors,
As hunger is always present.

A bumble bee clumsily crashes into it
In an eruption of splattered dew drops,
The bee shakes itself free
Before the watcher has time to move.
But damage control is necessary.

The day is warm, the dew evaporates.
Lunch caught, other tangled visitors wrapped for later feasts.
Dusk descends. The breeze is cool and the night dark.
But the vigil continues.

The watcher investigates movement on the web
And is drawn into its centre.
The visitor feels large, the watcher is hopeful.
The bird is quick, the spider gone, a good meal.
Nature's eternal quest for food continues …

The Cow Who Wanted to Sing
Edith Speers

Once upon a time there was a cow who wanted to sing. Her name was Daisy. She was a Poll Hereford heifer.

Poll means that she was born without horns on her head and she never grew any. Hereford means she had a beautiful red coat and curly white hair on top of her head. Most of her body was red but her face was white, her breast and neck were white, and she had white on her legs which made her look like she was wearing white stockings. Hereford also means that she was a beef cow and not a milk cow. People keep milk cows so they can get milk from them but they keep beef cows so they can eat them.

Daisy was a Poll Hereford heifer which means that she lived in a paddock on a farm. She and the farm were owned by some people. Heifer means that she was a young cow who had never had a baby calf. This didn't last for long.

As she grew up on the farm among other cows Daisy heard the birds sing in the trees. She heard the skylark sing as it rose in circles higher and higher up into the sky. She heard the farmer whistle a song as he went to work. She heard singing come out of the radio that the farmer sometimes carried with him. Then when all the heifers were moved into a paddock close to the house Daisy looked through a window of the house and saw tiny people singing in the television. Tiny women were inside the television singing.

These women had beautiful red coats. They had curly white hair on their heads. They had white faces and white breasts and white necks and they had white stockings on their legs. They did not have horns on their heads. From what Daisy could see these women looked like herself only they were much smaller. When Daisy saw this she wanted more and more to sing. One day she sang.

It felt wonderful. She had never felt like this before. She lifted her face up to the sky where the skylark flew higher and higher in circles. She opened her mouth and she sang with all her heart. The other heifers copied her. Then the farmer put the bull in the paddock with therm. The bull fell in love with Daisy and Daisy fell in love with the bull. Then Daisy stopped singing. Also she began to grow a baby calf inside her.

Daisy gave birth to the calf. It hurt to give birth so Daisy sang a song about being hurt. Daisy loved her calf and took good care of him. When the farmer took him away from her, Daisy felt lonely so she sang a song about feeling lonely.

After a while Daisy thought about what it was like to be in love. Then she lifted her face to the sky where the skylark flew higher and higher in circles. She opened her mouth and she sang with all her heart about love. Again the other cows copied her. Again the farmer put the bull in the paddock with them. Again the same things happened the same way as before. This went on for several years.

Then one day the farmer sent Daisy away. She was killed and cut up for meat. The meat was put into sausages and sausages were put in the window of a butcher shop to be sold. A woman walked by the butcher shop. She had curly white hair on her head. She stopped. She looked at the meat in the window. She bought some sausage and took it home and ate it.

Later she went to a television studio. She put on a beautiful red dress that was cut very low in front to show off her white neck and her white breasts. The dress had a slit up each side to show off the woman's beautiful legs in white stockings. The woman stood up in front of a lot of people and television cameras. She lifted her face to the ceiling where bright lights shone down on her. She opened her mouth and she sang with all her heart about being in love and getting hurt and feeling lonely.

The Maze
Kathleen Bentley

The road through life has many twists and turns
When we find out about ourselves.
We understand the way we think, and why we think thus,
And why the road ahead may be full of brambles or may be
clear.

We follow our conscience, we are told. Or do we?
Or are we led, manipulated by unseen forces?
Is there such a thing as self-will? And if so,
Shall we make the right decision?

Can we cast aside long held beliefs, rituals and lifestyles?
Can we break new ground with new ideas?
Will our eyes be open to new possibilities–
New ways of operating every day?

Can we go forward without looking backward?
Can we grasp the light just beyond our reach?
Can we find true contentment, discounting envy, malice and
hate?
Can we live life quietly?
Can we unburden our souls to those who will listen?

To those who will guide us through the maze,
And welcome us home?

Those Terrible Too's
Pete Stratford

For those who've raised children
it wasn't great news
when each reached the age
called the "terrible two's."
But what many don't know
since it's not quite as plain
when we all become older
it can happen again!
For it's not only youngsters
who have terrible too's
for we hear it too often
from us older ones too.
When grocery shopping
their comments we hear;
this checkout's too slow
and the items too dear!
Those trolleys too heavy
to steer through the crowd
the staff are too busy
and the music too loud.
All drivers too fast
out there on the streets
yelling too many words
that ought to be bleeped!
Everyone's too impatient
all in far too much haste
and with too many choices
there's far too much waste.
The weather's too hot
or too cold, or too dry.
Not like in our days
we hear their outcry.
But the years go too fast
at a pace we can't keep
and there's too many tablets
to take before sleep.

Then the food nowadays
the meat's far too tough
food's served too cold
and meal times too rushed.
It's too far to the toilets
and the shower is too small
they'd take too long to find me
if perhaps I should fall.
I can't hear what they're saying
'cos they speak far too soft
they're too quick to complain
if I just fart or cough!
They're all too patronising
treating me like I'm two!
What right have these youngsters
telling me what to do?
There's too much I can't stand
it's all too much for me
so tonight I'll have two drinks
then again...maybe three!

Travelogue: A Trip to Central Asia
Ant Dry

In 2012, my brother and I, accompanied by a friend, took a three-week trip to Central Asia. These are a few of my notes on that trip.

KAZAKHSTAN – home of Borat

A very brief history

Kazakhstan, as a nation with its own identity only came into existence in 1991 at the breakup of the Soviet Union. Prior to that it had only ever been "part of" other realms because, being very flat and semi desert, it was not easily settled and thereafter not easily defended from invasion.

The first people there were nomads, on their way to other places. By 500 B.C. it was part of the Scythian Culture. From about 550 AD to 750 AD it was part of the Chinese Empire. From about 850AD it was part of the Samanid Dynasty based in neighbouring Uzbekistan. In 1220s Genghis Khan swept through and annexed the area. In 1380 or so Timur from Samarkand conquered the southern part of the country. From about 1730 the Russians began to take an interest, an interest that waned only on the breakup of the USSR. The Russians established the Kazak Soviet Socialist Republic in 1920.

Borat

Most people only know of Kazakhstan through *"Borat,"* (a satirical mockumentary film). Sacha Baron Cohen, also known as Ali G. is "Borat" a Kazak journalist who travels to USA to see "the greatest country in the world." In doing this he shows America up as definitely NOT the greatest country in the world.

One would expect Kazakhstan to be deeply offended by the film, as Borat is portrayed as a gross and insensitive fool. On the contrary the Kazaks have a sense of humour and are delighted that as a result of the film, tourism has increased twenty-fold. One of the Kazak tabloids in reviewing the film described it as "The best film of the year. It is not anti-Kazak, but cruelly anti-American – amazingly funny and a bit sad."

On a trip we took with a taxi driver, we asked what he thought of Borat. He immediately burst into song, singing, as Borat did in the film, to the tune of *The Star-Spangled Banner*, "Kazakhstan is the greatest country in the world" He knew the whole song, and sang it through with great relish, waving his arms around in time with the music, much to our alarm as passengers.

Current politics.

The country is run by President Nazarbaev, whose election, like so many others in so many other less developed countries in the world, was marred by vote rigging and the banning of opponents.

The citizens are aware that he is a despot, but as they are doing all right and as they all have jobs, they don't mind too much. Our cab driver was quick to say though that should the President try to take the country to war, he would be on his own as the Kazaks would not regard his war as theirs. The cabby said that the President had relocated the capital from Almaty to Astana not only to keep the Russians out, but also (and mainly) because he wanted to avoid an uprising against him. Glasnost and Perestroika started in Almaty, and he has no wish to see a repetition. The army and all his loyal civil servants are based with him in his new capital.

Why did we go to Kazakhstan at all?

In looking at a tourist destination any sensible person has to ask, "Why Kazakhstan?" since it has very few tourist attractions and, before Borat, was a country, whose name was so difficult to pronounce than no one was interested in it anyway. The reason we went there was pretty prosaic. Almaty, the largest city in Kazakhstan, is the regional transportation hub. Most flights into the area fly into Almaty. Were it not for that fact and had we had not been curious about Borat we may well not have gone to the country at all.

Almaty

This city until recently the capital is a crazy mixture of western and Muslim cultures. Almaty could easily be mistaken for any European city. Every road is tree lined. Residents and visitors make use of outdoor cafes for meals. The full range of cuisine is available. The girls dress as our girls do, jeans tee-shirts and short dresses – there is no hint that the predominant religion is Islam.

Despite its modern surface, however, the city does have a number of aspects that keep it in the bracket of a less developed Asian city.

• The hot water supply for the entire city comes from two central points (a hangover from the Soviets' need to control everything), so it takes about 15 minutes for the hot water to arrive once you turn on the tap.

• The streets are swept by hand by ladies using grass brooms. They sweep everything into the gutters which are then only cleared by heavy rain.

• Meat and other fresh produce is sold from stalls on the street, subject to no health requirements.

Again, as a complete contrast, there are a large number of very expensive motor vehicles, in fact Almaty is the only place in the world I have seen, in one day, on the city streets, a Porsche, numerous Mercedes Benz's, innumerable BMWs, two Lamborghinis, and (a first-time ever) a Maybach (the Merc that is to Merc what Lexus is to Toyota).

The Apple

Of especial interest to residents of the Apple Isle, Almaty is the genetic source of the apple. To quote from Wikipedia; *"There is great genetic diversity among the wild apples in the region surrounding Almaty; the region is thought to be the ancestral home of the apple, and the wild Malus sieversii is considered a likely candidate for the ancestor of the modern domestic apple, which explains the "Alma Ata" name. The area is often visited by researchers and scientists from around the world in order to learn more about the complex systems of genetics, and also to discover the true beginnings of the domestic apple."*

We saw a number of wild apple trees growing at various sites, and none of them looked like the apple we see in Tasmania.

Kok-Tobe

A smooth ride in a Soviet era cable car takes you to the top of the mountain behind the city. From there you have spectacular views of the city and the areas around it.

Incongruously, in walking around the top you come across a set of life size bronze statues of the Beatles, placed there in 2007. Playing in the area around the statues is an endless loop of Beatles music. We heard the Beatles singing "My bonnie lies over the Ocean" which they recorded before they were famous. It was a cover version of the traditional song, sung with Tony Sheridan. Obviously the authorities in Almaty had gone a long way out of their way to make sure they had all of the fab four's songs!

The Great Almaty Lake

This natural lake, turquoise in colour, is situated some 2,500m above sea level. Set amongst a majestic mountain range, it is very beautiful. It supplies Almaty with fresh water. The Soviets increased its capacity by building a wall and concreting the sides. Despite this brutal approach the lake remains ethereally lovely.

Tian Shan Astronomical Observatory

Just above the great Almaty Lake is the old Russian Tian Shan Astronomical Observatory, which still houses what was the second largest Soviet telescope, with magnification of 1000.

Since the withdrawal of the Russians, the place has been abandoned. There is one Astronomer who visits over the weekends to check that the equipment is still working. On site, there are still staff who provide service to the few stray tourists who wander that far. We used the canteen and were served by the classic grumpy old woman, a caricature, wizened and bent. She would not have been out of place in a horror movie.

The setting was James Bond-esque. Snow piled up against the side of unloved badly maintained scarred derelict unfriendly but still imposing buildings, with a stunning background of snow-covered mountains. There were dodgy looking guards slouching all over the place looking decidedly bored. The corridors were long and cold and the bedrooms awful. The toilet was a squat pan that was so filthy I couldn't even go inside, let alone use it. Outside was a bank of solar panels, all broken, the steel frame rusted, power now supplied through the mains from Almaty. Once a proud symbol of Russian advancement and leadership in the field, this is now a monument to waste and to what could have been.

Kosmostantsia

Above both the Lake and the Observatory is an old Soviet Nuclear Research Station known as Kosmostantsia. Here Soviet scientists battled for years to discover the beta particle (or something) in their quest to best the Americans. The site was abandoned immediately the USSR ended and appears to remain abandoned, the only resident we saw being a dog tethered to a post. Quaintly one finds three World War Two air-raid spotlights abandoned in the middle of the site. Why were they there? So that the scientists could ski at night! True story.

This was another wonderful setting for a Bond movie; stark, beautiful, lonely and abandoned. Littered with electrical and unfathomable gear. It must have cost the Soviets millions to run. All for nothing. You have to wonder at the futility of hostilities, and at what real benefits those scientists could have wrought had they concentrated on useful research rather than on seeking a random particle whose existence is not confirmed and whose practical use is not known.

Growing up in the USSR

Our cabby was a bit of a character. He shared the following with us: –

• Old Soviet joke—when an atom bomb is dropped on you, you should hold your rifle at arm's length. Why? Coz it will melt, and you don't want to spoil your boots

• Russian proverb: It's nice to live nice. It's better to live better than nice

• When our cabby was at school, all the kids had to have their name tags sewn on to their shirts. Why? So that in the event of a nuclear attack, the bodies could be easily identified

• The Russians only foreign policy ever was to be better than the Germans and the Americans. The measure was quantity not quality. They made 100 tanks for every 10 the Americans had; it didn't matter if half of them broke down, they still had more than the Americans

• Toilet = white horse

• George Orwell was better with his predictions than Muhammad.

UZBEKISTAN – my favourite of the Stans

Of the three countries we visited in Central Asia, Uzbekistan was my favourite by far. As Central Asia's "cradle of culture" it is home to three of the most spectacular and ancient cities in the region, Samarkand, Bukhara, and Khiva.

It is also home to the most wonderful people. The youth, in particular were warm, friendly, and welcoming. We had a number of memorable encounters with the youth, which I detail below.

Money

Our first requirement in Uzbekistan was to find some local money. The official exchange rate is US$1 = Som 1800. The black-market rate is US$1 = Som 2800. We took a taxi and drove around until the driver saw some dodgy looking guy lurking under a tree with a large plastic bag in his hand. The driver waved his hand and the dodgy guy sidled across. There were a few words in Uzbek, and we swapped $100 for Som 280,000, a considerable amount of cash as the biggest denomination is Som 1000.

Encounter with youth 1

At the top of a tower we climbed to get an overview of Tashkent (our first port of call), we had our first encounter with the Uzbek youth. There was a party of about six 14-year-old girls on the top of the tower when we arrived. They took a fancy to my brother Dave, and all wanted their photo taken with him.

They asked him if he knew Harry Potter. They were very chatty, and their English was not at all bad. After they and Dave had been chatting for some five minutes, a group of Uzbek boys aged about

16 arrived. The girls shut up like clams and disappeared like mist in the night.

Samarkand
Probably founded in the 5th Century BC Samarkand sits on the crossroads of the Silk Road, although the city that stands today only dates back to 1370.

We took a train from Tashkent to Samarkand. The train was comfortable. There were handmade Persian carpets on the floor! To keep us entertained there was a soapie running. In Uzbek.

Encounter with youth 2
On the train a young man of 25, by the name of Jumaev Shahzod came up to me to chat. He was studying English and wanted to practice. We swapped Facebook addresses. I asked him if he was married. He said he was in love, but that his beloved's parents had not considered him good enough for their daughter, and with her being a good Muslim girl, she had had to marry another man. She now had two children by her husband. They still spoke to each other on the phone regularly and "their love was strong." He said, "Heartache is my destiny."

The Registan

In Samarkand we came across what has to be one of the sightseeing highlights of my life, the Registan. This is a collection of three mosques and madrassas (Muslim schools attached to mosques), grouped around a square about the size of a footy field.

There are not sufficient superlatives to describe the Registan. That it is beautiful is beyond doubt. That it was built to impress is obvious. It was more than both of these though. It was Old Testament biblical in its magnificence.

A policeman sidled up to us as we arrived and offered to allow us to the top of a minaret for $5. We took him up on his offer. The view was exceptional, but my legs felt like jelly for the rest of the day.

Bargaining with the locals

On our first night in Samarkand we went out to a restaurant that promised local food (which was awful) and belly dancing (there wasn't any). The taxi afterwards was interesting though. Dave did the bargaining, and it went like this:

Dave: Grand Samarkand Hotel, 6000 Som, OK?

Taxi-driver: (driving a hard bargain): No, no no no no no, 4000 Som

Dave: Okay.

Laundry

At our hotel they did all the laundry but refused to do underpants!!

The Silk Carpet Factory

Another highlight of the trip! We were given a guided tour. A single cocoon of silk yields a 1,200m strand of silk. The silk thread used to make silk carpets is made from 600 strands of silk, so each cocoon yields 2 meters of usable silk. Only natural dies are used to colour the carpets. The red comes from the root of the madder plant (growing in abundance in the grounds of the factory), yellow from asparagus, blue from indigo, green from mixing the yellow and blue.

(human right activists should skip to the next paragraph)

Only women make the carpets in Samarkand and the finest carpets are made by younger girls as they have smaller hands to handle the looms. The factory guide boasted that the best carpets took two 14 year old girls two years to make. Considering that these carpets were then sold for $5,000, it shows how little the girls are paid.

(OK, human rights activists can tune back in now)

After the factory tour, we were treated to tea and lollies to soften us up for the kill. The salespeople showed us an array of about 50 carpets, carefully explaining the difference between each one. Paying for the carpets was a problem as the salesman wanted me to pay his sister in New York. It sounded too shonky for me, so I said we couldn't do that and started to walk away. The salesman then suggested that he send the carpets to us anyway and that we need only pay his sister after the carpets arrived. All very odd, but then how else do you do business with a non-functioning banking sector and a black market?

Bukhara

We took another train to Bukhara where we stayed on the Lyabi-Hauz, a plaza built in 1620 around a pool. The plaza is sublimely beautiful, despite the fact that the water in the pool is green, thick, and glutinous to the extent that we decided we would be unlikely to survive if we fell in. The pool is surrounded by mulberry trees, the oldest of which was planted in 1377 and is still alive!!!!

Encounter with youth 3

In Bukhara, we went into a curio stall and met a young lady by the name of Parvina Rustamova (at right, with her Mum).

She was 19 and studying English. She wanted to travel, to go to university and to become a journalist. The evening we met her, she enlisted our assistance with an English assignment she was doing.

We met her later outside an internet café and stood for hours chatting in the twilight. She revealed that as a Muslim girl she would marry whoever her parents selected for her. Our chats with her were continually interrupted by a wanna-be boyfriend, who kept trying to drag her away. We asked if this was her boyfriend and while he nodded vigorously, she told us that her parents would not accept him as they would not like him. Despite this, she eventually gave in, and we watched as the boy led her to the edge of the pool and proceeded to take photographs of her. She was definitely up to this and posed quite readily, enjoying herself. So much for our preconceived ideas of shy Muslim girls dressed in Burkas. She offered to spend the next day showing us the sights. She was an excellent guide and absolutely delightful company, mature, funny, and up to date with world affairs.

We asked her how her mother would feel about her spending all day with three (supposedly) Christian men, and she said, completely without guile; "But you are old!"

Local Politics
In the local museum we saw the complete works of President Karimov (still in power since 1990). We were told that school children had to study them at school. It was intimated that they were very long and that no one really understood them.

Old politics
We were shown the local gaol, where two British officers had been incarcerated for three years before being beheaded in public in 1842. Their crime? They had been foolish enough, when appearing in Bukhara, on the Queen's business, not to bring a present. Additionally their letter of introduction was from the Governor of India and not Queen Victoria (whom the leader regarded as his equal).

The British, in an incredible show of support for their loyal subjects, did nothing in retaliation.

Khiva
We drove from Bukhara to Khiva, a trip I would not recommend to anyone. The driver drove as if he was pursued by demons, but the road was so bad that despite this, we averaged only 34 km/hour!

Khiva is an ancient city supposedly founded by Noah's son Shem. It certainly existed in the eighth century, but the city we saw was built between the 10th and 14th centuries. It is perfectly preserved, complete with city walls. If you ever wanted to get a feel for what life was like 800 to 900 years ago in Central Asia, you would benefit from a visit to Khiva. Hot and blindingly bright, the walls are dry and dusty, the roads unpaved and baked hard. Mosques, minarets, and palaces of the powerful dominate, richly decorated, and built to intimidate. The poorer members of society must have led a grim life of poverty, fear and hardship.

National food
The National food of Uzbekistan is plov. This comprises rice in cotton seed oil mixed with yellow peppers and/or carrots, with shaved mutton sprinkled on the top. It sounds unappetising, but it was very filling and quite delicious. I loved it.

TURKMENISTAN & the politics of repression
Of the three Central Asian countries we visited, Turkmenistan was the most stressed. The country has been ruled by despots throughout its entire existence, initially by the nomadic tribes, then by the Russians and now by their own home-grown despots (since independence from the USSR in 1992). The evidence of repression and unease with the outside world is palpable. Curiously, despite this (or because of it?) the Turkmen are fairly polite too.

At the border coming in – we took three hours to get through border control – the staff were excruciatingly slow in processing documents, partly due to there being only one window at which to process these. Phil, our travelling companion, and I were both called into a small room for "questioning." The sole purpose of this was to determine how our experience at the border had been. The senior officer doing the "questioning" was very polite and apologised for the delay stating that the border staff were all new and afraid to make errors. So frightened to make a mistake that we were delayed by three hours????? Must have a pretty scary boss.

In Ashgabat, the city, we went for a walk. We came across the Presidential Palace. It was unrealistically spectacular, with gold domes, marble walls and paving, a huge completely empty parade ground in the front and gold tipped railings. Gross and vulgar. The first President must have thought he was God. We decided to take some photos. This was a very bad idea.

The Presidential Palace;
© Alexey Averiyanov/Shutterstock.com

Immediately a military guy on the other side of the road started shouting and waving at me furiously. He beckoned me to come to him. My heart sank to my boots, but I crossed the road anyway. Wrong plan! The minute I did that there was an even louder and angrier shout from a policeman standing further away. The Policeman obviously outranked the military dude because as I approached the military one, I was shooed away. All three of us were summoned by the policeman, and I had visions of us spending time behind bars. All he said however was a very polite "Salaam" and to tell us in not bad English that we must not go near the Palace or take photos of it. No one bothers about anyone taking photos of Kirribilli House or the Lodge or of Buckingham Palace or the White House and you can get guided tours of the last two, but the same thinking does not apply in Turkmenistan.

At the airport on departure, we went through four x-ray checkpoints (on initial entry to the airport, on entry to the international departure area, on entry to customs and then for our hand luggage only on entry to the departure lounge). Our passports were examined six times, at each of the places mentioned above, and then also at immigration and at a point mid-way between passport control and the departure lounge. At each of these passport checks, the documents were examined long and hard, sometimes even the blank pages. One of the officials even turned my passport upside down. They all looked from the photo page to me a number of times, thrown perhaps by the fact that my photo page showed me without a beard and there in front of them I had one. This seemed to cause immense confusion. On initial entry to the airport an official asked me to open my bag. They examined everything as if I were carrying moon rocks. My camera (a very basic one) caused great worry. It was examined closely. All the buttons were pushed and what could be pulled was pulled. The official looked completely baffled, but asked nothing, and simply handed it back to me, the worried look on her face never relaxing.

Control of the population

On driving through Ashgabat and outlying villages we noticed that every dwelling seemed to have at least two satellite dishes. Our guide Oleg told us the satellite TV was free in Turkmenistan. There were three satellites that they could tune into. The first showed Russian TV, the second Turkish and the third all the other channels. Oleg told us he had over 300 channels he could watch, even a Muslim pornographic channel, on which he said there was an occasional kiss.

The government also provides power almost free. Oleg said that he had forgotten to pay his power bill for four years, so he had been fined. The total cost of four years power plus a fine was $70.

Conclusion on politics – The regime is repressive. It is still in power as the people are looked after very well. I doubt if the majority of people regard themselves as repressed, as they have been repressed for so long that it's just their way of life. Interestingly our guide Oleg, who has done some international travelling, would not talk politics, no matter how we tried.

It was all very reminiscent of Africa and reminded me why I left.

DESPITE all that, there were some fascinating things to see in Turkmenistan.

Konya-Urgench

This was our first tourism point of call. This had once been the capital of the area, but was completely destroyed by Timur, a mogul invader, back in 1388. From a high vantage point we saw that once it must have been impressive, but all that is left standing are a few half-re-built ruins.

Appeals to Allah

At Konye-Urgench, for the first time we came across what we were to see frequently in Turkmenistan. Wherever there was a mausoleum, a place of rest for the dead we found a number of physical manifestations of indirect requests to Allah.

Apparently, Muslins cannot directly ask Allah for anything, they have to ask a deceased person to make the request to Allah on their behalf. In such places we came across sticks onto which people had tied pieces of cloth. This was a general request for good luck. There were also strategically placed keys. These were a request for new apartments. Dolls and toy cots were requests for fertility. Piles of rocks were requests for homes and good things in life.

Burning crater

Turkmenistan is the world's largest exporter of natural gas. Gas is so prevalent there, that it leaks out of the ground. Some decades ago some men were laying a pipeline across the desert. They were unaware that they were doing so over the top of a gas bubble. As one of them stuck his pickaxe into the ground he broke the bubble, and the earth started to fall in around him. He scrambled to safety, but a crater appeared in front of him, about the size of a small footy field, with sheer sides to about 30 metres tapering down to a point in the middle. Sometime later a passing shepherd flicked a cigarette butt into the hole and the gas lit and has been burning ever since.

We arrived in the early evening and sat and watched as night fell. There is something magical and mesmerising about fire. Seeing it on such a grand scale increased the feeling of awe. We walked right to the edge of the crater and could see the very bottom (well-lit by gas light!!). There was no sign of a safety barrier, and no indication anywhere that we were dicing with death by venturing too close to the edge.

That night we slept on the edge of the burning crater. We ate a typical Turkman meal of chicken cooked on skewers over an open fire, with eggplant and tomato relish and local bread. We drank too much Vodka and listened to awful Turkman music (which became more palatable as the level of vodka in the bottle lowered), courtesy of Oleg's car stereo. We watched the crater from afar and from close by. We sang songs in the moonlight.

Sounds romantic, but the reality was that the ground was bloody hard, and the food had sand in it. We all felt filthy as the desert dust got everywhere and into everything. There was no toilet, just a roll of loo paper. No spade was required as Oleg said the dung beetles would clean up anything we left within two hours.

Gonur Depe
Gonur Depe is one of the most significant archaeological finds of the last 50 years. The archaeological world thinks, and it has been confirmed internationally, that they have found a new civilisation, one that moved away from Mesopotamia once that civilisation became too crowded. The findings date back to 3000 B.C.

Knowing that, and knowing that the Chief Archaeologist, Victor Sarianidi, who had turned the first sod and had been involved there ever since would be there, left us with great expectations of what we would see.

Like Pip in *Great Expectations*, we were disappointed. The site was extremely grubby and unromantic (as one would expect from a desert dig). Sarianidi looked like an aged Greek peasant with a not very high IQ. His shirt was covered with food stains. He was as interested in us as any one of us would have been in the state of our next-door neighbour's toenails. I took a photo of this famous man and shook his hand, but he couldn't have cared less. To be fair to him, it was very hot, and he was very involved in a game of backgammon, but I did feel he could have made a bit of an effort. We spent some time looking around and when Dave, exhausted by the heat came back early and sat in the shade with Sarianidi, he was told that he would have to move somewhere else, as lunch was about to be served. Altogether not too welcoming! I suppose once you get to 83, and it's hot and you are the world expert in your field, and everyone bows and scrapes to you, you do lose sight of the niceties of life.

The site was, however, fascinating. 5000 years ago they made ceramics there. We saw some pieces and the quality is superb, easily better than anything we get today. Not sure how they would fare in a dishwasher though!

This was believed to have been the birthplace of Zoroastrianism, the first monotheist religion. They worshiped only one God, but fire, water air and the earth were sacred. One of each of the city's four gates was dedicated to one each of these elements, and at certain times of the year there were celebrations in honour of the elements, celebrated at the relevant gate. One of the things the priests used to control the masses was a drink made out of hashish, poppies, and ephedra. It no doubt kicked like a mule, gave them a trip to heaven and back and kept them coming for more. Interestingly there were a number of sites that none of the archaeologists could explain. There was a water system that seemed to have no purpose. There was a selection of graves, in honour it would seem, of animals.

Merv

Destroyed by Genghis Khan, Merv used to stand alongside Baghdad, Cairo, and Damascus as one of the great cities of the Islamic world. Now it is an archaeological site. The earliest parts of the city were built in the 6th century BC. It is full of fascinating old ruins, which really have to be seen to be appreciated,

One of the more interesting places was the ice houses. Here, the residents used to collect the snow when it fell and make it into ice. This would then be kept, in specially designed buildings with good ventilation (I couldn't see how they were different from any other building or how the ventilation was better, but I bow to superior knowledge) for up to three years if required. The ice was kept and sold to the populace when required to assist in the preservation of foods and to make iced drinks.

RETURN TO AUSTRALIA

Travel is wonderful and great fun. It is described by the wise as mind expanding. This may well be the case, but, nothing beats coming home to Australia for solidity, security and welcoming warmth.

Mud and Monsters
Jake O'Mara

"Don't worry, I'll rearrange your flights." The boss says on the phone. But I do worry. She considers herself to be the World's Best Travel Agent, and I fear she will have me going from Alice Springs to Melbourne via Vladivostok. Something like it has happened before. That's the trouble with overly positive people; they have too much self-belief.

Here in the most remote community in remote Australia I have been on-call 24/7 for twelve weeks and I'm stuffed. Now that I'm due for leave, they want me to drive 700 km south to look at a couple of sick kids.

"Why can't Sally do it?" I ask.

Sally is the resident nurse where the sick children are.

"She resigned suddenly a week ago."

Bugger, she's only been in the job a few months, but they don't last long here. Some have lasted only one day.

The day before I am to leave to check the ailing kids, the tail of a big tropical low sweeps in, dumping a heap of rain on an area the size of Victoria. All roads turn to slush, but I must try to get through. Saying the roads are impassable never enters my stupid head. The first 200 k's are formed up a bit and slippery, but not boggy. Still, I keep the Daihatsu in 4WD all the way.

When I turn south onto the Sandy Blight Road, my worst fears are realised. The track was punched through by the famous "Gunbarrel Road Construction Crew" in 1956 and has had nil maintenance since. Most of the 250 km from the turn-off to my overnight stop is through an ocean of scrubby sand ridges. They are only five to eight metres high but very steep, and the gullies between them are natural if temporary receptacles for rainwater. That gully water is now deeper in the wheel tracks which are worn well below the surrounds. Forward progress is a constant battle in very slow motion, now that goanna looks the same as the one way back near Mt Liesler. The little bugger has overtaken me!

Just when I build up some speed, I crest another rise and am faced with yet another fifty yards of water. I check the steepness of the sandhills, the density of the scrub, and how many 'fridge-sized boulders are loitering around the numerous rocky outcrops. Any of the above might make water of unknown depth a better option. I could get bogged, but I'm less likely to stake a tyre or rip the sump out on a rock. I grind slowly through water up to the tops of the tyres, but every few kilometres there's a gully that's too risky. I launch off the road, but the sand and scrub make for even slower going. I make around a thousand gear changes in two hundred kilometres and see not one other vehicle. Only idiots and nurses travel after a big rain. Obviously, I am both.

This morning I went straight home from the madness of the clinic, threw my stuff in the car and took off, ramming biscuits into my mouth like a demented hay baler as I drove. It's now late afternoon, and I need rest. I stop to boil the billy at a desolate pile of black boulders known locally as Lupul. There are petroglyphs on these stones, markings so old the Ngaanyatjarra people have no cultural memory of them. Here, a human lifespan is not even a comma in the encyclopaedia of prehistory.

So, I sit on the ancient rocks, sweating and trying to keep the hordes of bush flies out of my tea. I'm OK with them crapping on my food, it could only improve the flavour. If only the little buggers were illegal drugs, I'd be a bloody millionaire. Or in prison. But even being a millionaire couldn't help me now. I'm still more than a hundred kilometres from my overnight stop, and the time spent on revitalizing my body means that darkness is upon me well out of Yiwala.

If the road and environs was a bit fraught in daylight, it is ten times more so in the yellow glow of the Daihatsu's headlights. I become more and more desperate, driving well beyond the limits of the feeble lights and my even more feeble brain. Near the turn-off to Yiwala the country flattens out into saltbush-covered flats, allowing me to drive further beyond sanity. I fly around a corner and have no chance of slowing enough for the wide expanse of water ahead. I brake hard, slew sideways in a spray of red soup and crash into a deep hole. Blackness and silence. One headlight is under and the motor has stalled. After the bump and rattle of the past eight hours it is strangely peaceful.

Bastard! Water everywhere. I restart the motor, but it only produces wheelspin and there is nowhere dry to put a swag. I check the odometer and hope Yiwala is less than twenty kilometres away. I open the door and red water rushes into the footwell. Double bastard and no option but to walk, with the added joy of wet feet. I have a tiny torch, no use at more than three metres and it soon expires as they always do, except in the movies. The night is as black as the inside of a cow, but I can just make out the lighter wheel tracks through the vegetation. It is very quiet, and occasionally I hear the soft churring of nightjars in the distance. I am in "kurrturturturr (nightjar) dreaming" country and as I trudge along, I marvel at how closely the Aboriginal name mimics their call.

Suddenly the night is split by an awful coughing bellow, very loud and close by. It sounds as if it has come from the bowels of hell. I remember stories of a huge spirit snake or Warnampi that is supposed to inhabit a sacred waterhole near here. Could it be real? I stand and listen, scared shitless, but in a silence so profound a fly's fart would sound like a gunshot, I hear nothing.

Maybe I imagined it. I continue walking, but only get a few yards. The hellish roar happens again, this time much louder and closer, maybe thirty metres or less. I feel the fear rising, but over the bellow there is the distinctive slap of a huge tongue. A bloody camel!

This is not good news. It means that somewhere in the darkness a bull is warning me off his harem. He needn't worry, the ladies are a bit too ugly, or maybe they are only too tall. But bull camels have been known to knock people down and crush them with that massive callused and tough brisket. This one has obviously come well toward me already, and the herd will be watching from a safe distance. "F%#* off!" I shout impotently into the blackness, as though the expletive would make the huge beast think I am one tough sod, best left alone.

I try to stroll nonchalantly off, whistling like Popeye, lest my fear and flight provide him with the courage to attack. I can't see where I am going and won't see him until he hits, and I could be walking toward the harem. He evidently decides I'm not worth the effort, and I pick my way along in the blackness for another couple of hours, hoping like fury there are no more frights to be had. Eventually Yiwala's dim pinpricks of light wink through the scrub and a bit after midnight I wake the resident nurse, who utters a couple of expletives.

"…Yeah, yeah, I can hear you!" She thinks it's a medical callout. Standing there in the porchlight I must look a strange sight, bleary-eyed from tiredness and liberally smeared with red mud.

"Shit Jake, you've been mud wrestling again!"

"Well, you know how it is, the girls just won't take no for an answer."

"Yeah right, – what happened?"

"Got bogged out near the turnoff."

And Lena Danced the Limbo
Meg McLaren

The fragile wooden walls of 'Zeb's Tropical Tattoos' shook beneath the attack and woke Lena from a deep sleep. Rain pounded and the wind howled. Clouds loaded with thunder turned the world dark around her. She stretched out along a straw mattress laid on the floor and looked over at Zebedee, still asleep and unaware of the chaos outside. Lean and supple from head to toe, her skin, the colour of ebony, shone like the polished keys of a piano. Her eyes were obsidian, glass like and deep healing. One glance from their magical properties and past traumas disappeared and new horizons opened. Her hair was cut close to her scalp like steel wool, tight curls and kinks revealing flat features and high cheekbones.

They were married at Blue Basin. Found a travelling preacher who agreed to 'tie the knot' and a picnic was organised. The bus, filled to capacity, wound its way up the crumpled folds of the Northern Range. It entered without warning into the gloomy light of the rainforest revealing shadowy shapes of branches and vines, dense and tangled. Eventually they arrived at a clearing where there was a high, grey rock face with a waterfall unravelling down into a deep pool of water, clear as crystal. A jumble of flat rocks surrounded the swimming hole and small sandy coves were set between the rocks giving easy access to the turquoise water. A cloth was spread over the warm stone and cushions scattered about. It was a splendid day.

Taking hold of a branch pulled from the Almond tree outside, Lena pushed open a wooden shutter letting in the smell of wet wood and dusty soil, soaked through. Flies simmered and swarmed. The dark cul-de-sac, moist and steaming from the heat, was filled with the faint odour of urine.

"Wake up Zebedee, today de day! I'se hopin' dis rain goin' ease up by lunchtime, oderwise we'se all caput!"

Zebedee moaned and curled up under the sheet.

"ZE-BE-DEE!! Get up!"

He leapt up from the floor, tousled and bewildered, shaking his head, dislodging that dreamy, tentative region of sleep from his brain. When Lena shouted in that manner it was best to do as she said. His skin, black as the sky on a winter's night, was damp from the hot moist air, his hair in tight plaits stood straight up around his head. He smiled revealing a flash of perfect white teeth and began to make himself an open sandwich of bread and butter sprinkled liberally with raw cane sugar.

"Dat sugar go rot yo' teeth Zebedee." Lena steupsed, sucking her teeth, her mouth puckered.

"Wha' time de plane arrivin'?"

"T'ree o'clock dis afternoon."

"No time to waste den."

The limbo was deeply entrenched in Lena's blood, as it had been in her mother's and grandmother's. Inherited from the days when slaves entered the hold of those coffin ships, bending backwards as low as possible, to get past the bodies crowded together. Today, though, was a celebration. Christmas was in the air. Parang music could be heard everywhere, maracas, steel drums and mandolins. Parranderos going from house to house singing Christmas songs; the smell of ginger beer fermenting and rum punch, sorrel and eggnog. In every kitchen a bowl of fruit soaking in rum stood covered on the dresser ready to go into the 'black cake.'

"Hurry yo'self, Zebedee! De bus comin'! We ain't gonna get a seat."

Lena, dressed in leggings and a swing top thickly embroidered with sequins and shiny beads stood outside holding a long pole wrapped around with ribbons. Her arms from wrist to elbow tinkled with the sound of thin gold and silver bangles packed tightly together. Around her ankles coloured beads. Zebedee stood inside the doorway and a piercing whistle rang through the air.

"Zebedee!!! Watch yo'self! Ain't I tell you sooooo many times. Don't embarrass me! Is an insult!"

"But you is so beautiful Lena. I jus' can't help myself."

I'se more dan jus' a body! Do dat one more time and I'se leavin'!"

Lena turned her back on him and made her way to the crossroads where people were gathering. Large hats of plaited palm leaves with frangipani and hibiscus flowers stuck into the wide brims, bobbed and nodded; children ran rampant; men squatted wherever they could find some shade.

The bus could be heard approaching from a distance. The sound of people banging on the sides, in time to the calypso music reverberating from the interior, was deafening. As soon as it came to a standstill, the waiting group rushed, pushing and shoving, to get on board. Lena sat down and saved a seat beside her for Zebedee. Then they were off…lurching, the horn blowing and no intention of stopping again until they reached their destination.

CHAPTER TWO

Piarco was looking its Christmas best this year of our Lord nineteen hundred and sixty three. People bustling around the airport had one thing on their minds. The arrival of fifteen hundred Scotch pine trees from Canada. After many mishaps these elegant pines had been stranded in Barbados and had remained there until BWIA were persuaded to save the day and fly them to Port of Spain. Today they were being loaded onto a Vickers Viscount for the last leg of the journey. The seats had been removed and two enterprising young men, casually called Bob and Bing, were to accompany them on the flight to Trinidad.

Dressed in short pants and sandals, with a bottle of VAT19 sneaked aboard, the two were excited.

"I never fly in a plane before, Bing. I ain't even got a passport!"

"Bee-Wee done come to de party. Dat's why dey is OUR Airline."

"Good t'ings happen when you dream big!"

A roar went up as the plane circled the runway preparing to land and came to a standstill in front of the Airport building. Then a larger than life figure made his way onto the tarmac and stood arms outstretched. A hush fell over the crowd. Fred Marsden was known throughout the island for his rendering of the Tarzan call and he didn't disappoint now. The loud, haunting call of the jungle ululated through the air as the hatch opened and Bob and Bing appeared carrying the first tree.

"He better 'dan Johnny Weissmuller!" The crowd were enthralled.

Then the steel drums and maracas were heard pounding out a calypso beat and Lena and the troupe began setting up for the dancing. For one minute she thought she heard a whistle coming from the direction of a group of onlookers that had travelled on the bus with her and Zebedee...but then silence. "He would never dare!" she thought and smiled to herself as she prepared to slide under the pole, the way her ancestors had done so long ago.

Finally, after much singing, dancing and cheering, the trees were loaded onto a truck to begin their final journey to Port of Spain where they would be sold, a dollar a foot.

The journey home was noisy, everyone 'catchin up' with the day's events, all talking at once. Alighting from the bus, Lena and Zebedee walked home together, her hand warm in his. The sun, blood orange, melted into the mountains, and a mist rose from the jungle like smoke. Later, the kerosene lamp casting a soft glow and shadows playing on wooden slats, they sat on the porch and sipped on glasses of icy sorrel.

"You done great today Lena. I'se not able to take my eyes off you."

NOTES: This story is purely fictional, but based on a true event. Before this, at Christmas, the people of the island used branches cut from a guava tree or whatever was at hand and decorated it with cotton wool and coloured baubles.

BWIA........   British West Indian Airways.

Bee-Wee... The local name for the airline.

VAT19........ A local Rum.

The Venus of Hay Street
Jake O'Mara

Late afternoon in Kalgoorlie at the end of three weeks leave. I wander the dusty streets, perhaps trying to soak up that last bit of Australian country town normality before tomorrow. Tomorrow I depart for the republic of lofty ideals and earthbound damnation in the Gibson Desert, where I am a lone nurse in a community of 180 souls. I have already lasted longer than ninety-five percent of my colleagues in similar situations, but it is gradually tearing me apart. How can a job provide such satisfaction while slowly killing you? Is that what masochism is?

I wander over street and park, as did *"The Man from Ironbark"* in Banjo Paterson's excellent poem, "…till I am like to drop, until at last in sheer despair, I seek a knocking shop." Well, it was a barber's shop in the poem, but this is a mining town, an antipodean version of the wild west.

The "knock shops" in Kalgoorlie's red-light district are well known to me, as they are to many males in Kalgoorlie, but for slightly different reasons. A lot of the men of Kalgoorlie are young, randy and single, in the well-paid employ of gold-mining companies. Single females are relatively scarce, so the cashed-up male presence drives a subsidiary sex-worker economy.

They are not allowed in the town centre except between certain prescribed daylight hours. Their unfenced prison is well away from the CBD in a short section of Hay Street, to protect upright citizens from being confronted by what human need creates.

I cannot afford the services in Hay Street, and if I could afford them, my better knowledge of sexually transmitted diseases would counsel against such risky extravagances. The other limiting factor is my strict, guilt-laden Methodist upbringing. Methodists are against sex while standing up, as it could lead to dancing. I go to Hay Street, believe it or not, for female company and conversation.

I am aware that this sounds like buying Playboy for the stories; unfortunately, it is true. My self-esteem has sunk so low, and I ache for female company so much, that it is a balm to just be in the presence of women, sex workers included. I also have both sympathy and empathy for those on the fringes of, or invisible to mainstream society, like prostitutes and remote indigenous people.

Hay Street is long and narrow, lined with old weatherboard miner's cottages, most of which are in a less-than-perfect state of repair. The footpath consists of cracked and broken bitumen except where it crosses driveways and narrow lanes, where it becomes dusty and potholed gravel. On the southern side, within a few metres of the road, are two or three sets of conjoined rooms, each group like a miniature motel in sagging weatherboard and corrugated iron. The rooms themselves are no bigger than the bathing boxes on Melbourne's expensive eastern beaches. They are from the times when a girl could make enough in six months to buy a house. Those days are gone forever, but the dilapidated rooms have recently been painted a variety of bright colours. Maybe the owners want to disguise the numbing dullness brought on by the business of doing pleasure.

The girls sometimes come outside and lean on the fence to attract customers, so I stroll along, looking for a bored or friendly face, someone willing to pass the time of day with a man who believes that he is unworthy of their attention. But the tiny front yards are deserted, it's too early. Hay Street comes alive after nightfall.

Suddenly, a sailor's dream steps from a doorway. She is in her mid-twenties and pretty, but with an overlay of world-weariness or despair. Most of the girls are fully dressed when outside their rooms, but this one does not believe in leaving the best until last. Tall, wildly curvaceous and blonde, she is clad only in brief lacy knickers and an equally skimpy lace bra, which is stretched over large, impossibly pneumatic breasts. Dazzled by what I know to be artifice, I try not to stare. I rest my arm on the fence and adopt my best nonchalant pose, as though I am unfazed by this amazon in lingerie. The truth is I can hardly speak.

"Hello Sir!" The tone is non-committal, and I reply somewhat nervously,

"Good afternoon to you."

She flashes a practised half-smile and says,

"I'm Candy, what's your name?"

"It's Jake. Is Candy short for Candice?" I'm remembering Candice Bergen.

"Er… yes." Too late I guess that it's a working name and I'm stupid for asking. She wants to keep the conversation away from herself and says,

"Are you from around here?"

"No, I'm a nurse and work in an Aboriginal community way up north. Where are you from?"

"Sydney."

Just then a car carrying four young men rolls to a halt at the kerb. Candy looks at me; back-on to them, I mouth "go ahead." The car's engine is left idling as she swings the rusty front gate and approaches the car's open passenger-side window. With her hands on the car's roof she leans forward, suggestively jiggles those amazing breasts and says,

"Can I help you fellas?" From inside the car there is nervous laughter. Someone says something unintelligible, and there is another burst of laughter. The engine is revved, and they speed off as if from a gun-toting madman. The girl is left standing on the dusty footpath in her underwear. The incongruity staggers me, but if she is surprised at their response, she doesn't show it. Instead she invites me inside. I follow her into a room no bigger than an average bathroom. It contains a single bed, a small table and one chair.

She motions me to sit on the bed and shifts the chair. In doing so she winces, and I notice her left pinkie finger is swollen and angled slightly outwards.

"That finger looks sore, want me to have a look at it?"

"Nah, it's OK, a customer did it yesterday, it'll come good."

"What! Some bloke hurt you?"

"Yeah, they do that sometimes." She seems off-hand, inured to such things.

"You should get it looked at. At the very least strap it to the next finger. Otherwise the joint could be permanently damaged."

"I might, but it's OK." She has no intention, I'm sure.

I'm dismayed by the injury and her response to it, but it's clear she wants to get laid and paid as quickly as possible, while I am embarrassed by my fears and moralism. She seems nice at heart but clearly inhabits a harsh and sometimes cruel world. Candy opens a drawer under the table-top and extracts a condom.

But her injury has caused me to convert her into a patient. I want her so much, but know that it will be a quick, empty and ultimately sad experience. Avoiding eye contact, I mumble,

"...Look, I'm sorry for wasting your time." I extract money from my wallet and give her about half of what "full service" would cost. The notes are accepted, and as I go out the gate she calls out from the doorway,

"You're a really nice man, Jake!"

I walk slowly back to my motel, wondering what will become of her. The hopeless romantic in me wants to somehow rescue her from all this, but I know that is impossible. I also know two more things; I need friendship and intimacy more than sex, and I have just seen both sides of the paradox of being female.

Where there's Smoke...
Pete Stratford

It was back in the early 1980's, an era before the powers that be brought in occupational health and safety rules that made it illegal to kill or maim oneself in the workplace. Of course, none of us were intelligent enough to be responsible for our own safety and consequently many now bear the scars to prove it. So it was that during this era another fellow, "Rusty" and I were standing on a scaffold plank, either end of which was supported by a trestle so that we were able to reach through a hole that had been opened up in the ceiling of a commercial building. That the plank was elevated above the floor about three metres, and it was only about twenty centimetres wide, was not an issue of concern because the concrete floor below was not going to sustain any damage should either of us happen to step sideways or lose our balance and fall down onto it. That really comforting thought increased our confidence.

The purpose of being elevated in this manner was to make it possible for my companion to use an oxyacetylene torch and cut through a fabricated steel truss crossing through the ceiling space. Years of accumulated lint, dust, and other readily flammable debris was very evident in that large cavity beneath the roofing iron, and sparks were going to be an inevitable by-product of the operation, so my role was to be at the ready with a small extinguisher and endeavour to prevent the entire building becoming our funeral pyre. Not exactly an unimportant role in the overall scheme of things, but rather difficult to carry out with my gas torch wielding companion standing right in front of me making it quite impossible for me to move past him, should I be required to attend to any fire.

Of course there was one, and I began smelling smoke at the same time as panicked cries of "Oh! Oh! were coming from Rusty as smoke began curling up around him, but I was unable to discern the source.

Now every Boy Scout worth his badge knows that teased out cotton fabric makes a very good fire starter and Rusty's old worn out overalls were very frayed indeed, especially around the crutch area. With smoke curling up past his face, and now wide eyed with alarm, Rusty turned to face me, as we balanced precariously on the plank. Like a sparkling circle of fairy lights, the ever enlarging ring of burning fabric around his groin was evidently providing more thermal increase than he felt was needed, so I leaned back from him as best as the situation allowed and directed a long blast from the extinguisher at the source of his concern. Had it been a dry powder extinguisher he may have been more appreciative, but the wet chemical spray saturated the area and then quickly formed sparkling ice crystals over his now well exposed underpants. This caused his repeated cries of "Oh!" to rise in crescendo even more, as his pride and joy which had been in grave danger of incineration, was then becoming snap frozen. You just can't please some people!

The Vote
Ant Dry

I marked my ballot paper with a flourish. The choice for Mayor was easy, I simply gave my number one vote to the person I liked most and who I actually knew, and my number six vote to the man I detested and considered a little squirt. The numbers in between I numbered randomly, not caring one way or the other.

The votes for the Councillors were a bit harder, but still laughably easy. I numbered them fairly randomly, giving my low numbers to those who I had heard of and marking only as many boxes as I needed to make my vote valid.

Five minutes. Job done. No hassle.

All a bit of fun, and really a harmless waste of time – I am completely indifferent to who makes up the City Council. They won't affect my life much at all.

All in all a pretty mundane exercise for the average Australian.

As I dropped the ballot paper into the mailbox, I reflected on the last time I had voted in the country of my birth.

I had woken up early in the morning, before the sun had risen, to get a good place in the queue. My wife, a South African citizen and therefore ineligible to vote, took me down and dropped me off with a hat and a tube of sunscreen.

I joined the back of the queue, which was so long I could only just make out the front. There must have been a few thousand of us already. My fellow queuers were delighted to see me, a solitary white man in a sea of black.

The polling booth was at the local primary school, which was, as were most schools in Zimbabwe, secured by a ten-foot fence, with a sturdy, heavily locked gate in a wasted effort to protect them from theft and vandalism.

The queue grew very fast. We were a cheerful lot, smiling and laughing. We were here to vote. We were going to change the government. We were going to change the world. Nothing could stop us. We were invincible.

"We are together!" had been the battle cry for the last few weeks. "We" encompassed not only black and white, but tribe and tribe, sex and sex, everyone was included. We were united in removing the President.

"It's time the old man went" was the cry.

A few more white people turned up. They were welcomed with cheers, "We are together!"

Much laughter, smiling faces. High fives.

The gates were supposed to open at 8.00 a.m. By 8.45 they were still firmly locked.

The crowd was now very large. The queue, very orderly and well controlled, if somewhat boisterous, was so long it disappeared around the corner and up the next road.

A truck load of policemen arrived. The crowd quietened noticeably. There were a few sullen looks.

The policemen debussed and walked up and down the queue, slapping their batons in their hands. The crowd turned their backs, refusing to engage.

Another truck arrived. This truckload drove to the gate, opened it, went inside, and re-locked the gate behind them.

There were a few murmurs from the crowd.

Some three quarters of an hour later, at close to ten o'clock, and a mere two hours after the gates were supposed to have opened, the police began to let people through, one at a time.

The crowd cheered up.

The sun was hot, I was grateful for my hat and sunscreen. I felt thirsty. I phoned my wife, and she appeared shortly thereafter with a crate of Coca-Cola, which was greeted with much delight by my new friends in the queue. She disappeared and returned with another two cases. Everyone was thirsty it would seem. She was cheered lustily and thanked profusely. Everyone was in a good mood again. We were going to vote.

By four o'clock it was apparent that the queue was not moving fast enough. One of my new lady friends, Bethaline by name, who had told me that her children were pupils at the school, suggested to me that it would take less time to vote if we left the queue, and sneaked into the school grounds through a hole in the fence that she knew, joining the queue again inside.

At that stage I had been in the line for eight hours. I was up for anything. She and I asked the others to keep our places (which they happily agreed to do), and we snuck off around the corner.

There was no hole in the fence. It may have been a simple hole earlier in the morning, but now it was more of a thoroughfare – we were not the only people with Bethaline's idea. We all joined the shorter queue inside. No wonder the queue was moving so slowly outside.

Polling was supposed to end at six in the evening. At five o'clock, as we were within sight of the school hall, the actual polling booth, the police closed and locked the gate.

What happened next seems to have happened in slow motion, as if I were dreaming.

The crowd outside the gate moved as a single unit. It swelled and swirled, moving closer and closer to the fence. Faces and body parts were pressed into the wire. The crowd murmured, almost groaning as one, pressing closer and closer. The fence shook and swayed and then, slowly, and silently, bent over and gave way to the crowd. There was a huge shout of triumph, and the crowd surged over the fence and rushed the polling booth.

The hall doors were slammed shut, too quick for the crowd, who then proceeded to beat on the doors and scream in rage.

Bethaline and I stood rigid, awestruck. It had happened so fast.

I looked around for the police. They were nowhere to be seen.

The crowd had settled down a bit, but they were going nowhere. They wanted to vote, and they were going to vote, no matter what it took. They stood and started to chant, keeping up a continuous banging on the hall door.

A police siren sounded a few minutes later, and then a single police Land Rover appeared.

The crowd went silent as the sole occupant, a young policeman climbed out of the Land Rover, clambered onto the roof, and addressed the crowd. He spoke in Shona and did not speak for long. The crowd cheered. The policeman climbed down off the roof and banged on the hall door. He spoke for a while and the door was opened a crack and he went inside.

"What was that about?" I asked Bethaline.

"The policeman, he told us to quieten down, he would make sure we all got to vote" she replied, grinning.

I felt a sense of wonderment and disbelief. This guy was one brave man, to make such a bold statement. The booth was legally supposed to close at six. He must have been mad. Or maybe he was stupid. He would have had no authority to ensure that promise; in fact he would be deliberately defying the authorities. He would lose his job.

Sure enough, the door re-opened, and the crowd, as orderly as they had been for most of the day filed in, but now it moved quickly. When I walked through the door some two hours later, now well past the booth closing time, the single policeman was directing affairs, bustling around getting people into the right places, chivvying the officials along, and keeping the crowd in a good mood.

When my wife eventually arrived to collect me, she asked.
"How did it go?"
"It was an interesting day" I said.

Filmed
Jennie Herrera

The location people found the ideal house. The props manager excelled himself inside it. The actors and directors and film crew were carefully picked and asked to sign a statement: 'I am not afraid of spiders. I have no problem working with spiders. Signed .... '

Several people hesitated, then signed. They felt themselves caught in a dilemma. They weren't precisely afraid of spiders but neither did they feel particularly comfortable with them. And they all had the secret fear that should a spider actually run across their skin or become entangled in their hair they might forget themselves enough to let out a gasp.

Normally this would not be a problem. Most films which include spiders require people to gasp and scream and try to brush the spiders away from their faces or off their chests. This film was scripted rather differently. It was based on a close study of the habits of spiders and was classed as a psychological thriller.

The spiders themselves were never blatant. No huge swathes of spider-web in the tumble-down house. No spiders the span of a man's hand. No large groping hairy feelers. No gleaming evil eyes. These spiders lurked in their corners and gaps and hidden spaces, only emerging from their untidy swags of web at the sight or sound of prey. Invisible much of the time. Protruding as a couple of legs, as a sudden dart when their web felt the blundering tug of a fly or moth

The problem for all the cast was that the film was using real spiders in real webs with real insects. Much of the filming of 'Spideery' occurred with no cast present at all.

It was all the waiting around, all the sense of deliberately heightened tension, all the mystery of what was actually going on inside the house and the other makeshift sets when no actors were permitted to be present or to see the rushes, which made everyone edgy and a little queasy. Even the scripts came in two sets: one literally for the spiders and one for the actors and which simply filled in the other segments as 'spiders on stage'

"If they'd filmed our parts first," one actor complained strongly, "so we could've got the bulk of it over and done with ...

and then they could mess around with their spiders to their hearts' content … "

"Yes … or if the plot was clearer. We know our lines. But we don't know how exactly they fit into the overall story-line … we're as much in the dark as …"

"As the spiders," someone said tartly.

"It's even worse than that," someone else sighed. "It's as though we're the artificial props. We go out and say our lines and put on our emotions, but we're like dummies playing a part. We don't know any more than what we're programmed to do."

"That's true," another cast-member nodded. "Normally the spiders are plastic or rubber props … or computer animations, these days, maybe … but we might as well be clockwork toys for all we know of the climax and outcome …"

"Maybe that's the intention. Maybe that's why they made us sign that statement. Now we have all this time to sit around wondering if we were honest when we said we weren't afraid of spiders."

"At least we're being paid to sit around—"

"Yes, but I don't like to have time to think about real spiders—I just want to get stuck into it and do my piece and know for sure I can take spiders in my stride."

"And they didn't really explain that they wouldn't be artificial spiders—I just assumed that."

"Well, we haven't got an out now—because a lawyer would argue that a spider is a spider, not a lump of plastic."

"More coffee anyone? I think we'd be better just to forget about what they're doing up there and get on with other things."

Several people nodded. They had other scripts to consider. And there were always card games, gossip, knitting, or a good book to while away the time. But the spiders had acquired an intrusive life of their own and the cast sat round, waiting, and trying futilely to banish them from their thoughts.

*

By the time two weeks had passed the actors were getting definitely mutinous. They had tried pumping camera-men, set designers, lighting people, even the directors, without getting anything more specific than a heartfelt "It's more than my life would be worth!"

or the plain "We signed an agreement to keep the story under wraps."

"Well, it's their money," one actor with a very small part said philosophically, "so I suppose we shouldn't complain."

"That's all very well for you," was the sour rejoinder. "You're only going to be on for ten minutes. If you find yourself getting queasy you know you'll soon be finished. But I sit here wondering how I'm going to manage hour after hour with … well, who knows what? Do you know they've even got a security firm in there that usually specializes in intelligence material—"

"How do you know that?"

"I'd never heard of them so I looked them up."

"Oh! That's getting a bit drastic, isn't it?"

"That's what I thought. It makes us seem like suspects not professionals."

"Maybe we are suspects—"

"How could we be suspects? We haven't done anything! Isn't that the problem?"

"Yes, we have. We've all signed to say we aren't afraid of spiders."

"Well, there aren't any surveillance cameras in here—"

"How do you know?"

"Look around you. Bare walls. Not a camera in sight."

"Not a spider in sight either." Then, unaccountably, the speaker shuddered. To go from here with its clean bright walls and smell of coffee and donuts into … but suddenly she didn't want to envisage what that old house might be like inside.

*

People who prided themselves on their professionalism began to feel a little uneasy. It was one thing to know a part back to front and inside out, another to go on to an unknown set …

And people who had been friendly and enthusiastic and supportive began to get on each other's nerves. At first they shared something of their lives and experiences. Then they exchanged all their memories and ideas on movies which included spiders. They talked of personal moments of fear and distress and surprise. They dredged up family anecdotes which included spiders. They expressed shock, surprise, annoyance, criticism of the script and everyone involved with the film.

By the third week they had begun to hunt through their parts for evidence of what was going on. They played them out, at first casually, then going over and over every line for the smallest clue, for what might be hidden between the lines or contained in gestures and required emotions.

"We don't even know if the spiders will actually be on stage with us at any time. I can't find anywhere where we are required to actually respond to the creatures. No moments of fear or surprise or apprehension."

"Perhaps that's the point. We don't get any prior warning? If you had a line which said; 'Spiders Enter Left' you'd be prepared. But here, where it tells you to move towards the door … what if just as you get there—"

"No, don't! If I thought I had to face a spider suddenly running across the door handle or dropping on a thread I think I'd find myself rooted to the spot!"

"No, you wouldn't. You've said you don't suffer from arachnophobia. You wouldn't be able to explain your fear away."

"It isn't a phobia exactly. It's the element of surprise. If you had to do a film with wolves and they never told you when the wolves would be on the set and when they'd only be on the soundtrack howling in the distance it would be two different things—"

"But maybe it would be more frightening to sit for three weeks knowing exactly when the wolves were going to be released on to the set?"

"But at least wolves would have professional animal trainers with them. I doubt if they've got any special spider trainers over there."

"Don't say that! It conjures up images of spiders being tempted out on cue with a bit of dead blowfly or something … uuugggh … I don't think I can bear the thought of having lunch now."

"And it isn't clear from my lines whether I'm supposed to have any contact with the spiders or not. Listen to this—" And he began to read his first lines over again.

*

"They've been there long enough to film a thousand spiders in their nests," one of the cast complained as they went into their fourth week of waiting.

"And I find myself getting up each morning with this horrible sort of black fear over me … of coming in here … of sitting waiting … of never knowing when someone might come in that door and say 'we're ready for you' … " And suiting the action to the word he went over and glanced out. "Nothing. Absolutely nothing."

"We could gatecrash them."

"No, we couldn't. Didn't you read the small print on your contract?"

"No. What does it say?"

"That we wait until we're called for filming."

"That's a strange thing to put in a contract. You assume that's what you do … but I've never seen it put down in black and white … "

"Don't say black. I can't even bear the thought of black spiders."

"Maybe they aren't black? Maybe they're redbacks or funnel-webs—"

"Don't say it! It gives me a horrible shiver up my spine. It doesn't take much to stir up a funnel-web and get them ready to attack."

"You mean—but there's nothing in the script to suggest the spiders are actually going to attack us!"

"You don't know that. You haven't seen the parts they didn't give us."

"But here, where it tells me to come downstairs … and the rooms are dark and I'm supposed to grope for the light-switch … Holy-Moly! You don't think … do funnel-webs go upstairs in houses?"

"Who knows? These are movie spiders—they probably get to do whatever the script demands—"

"Don't say that! I won't be able to sleep tonight, thinking of a funnel-web creeping upstairs and getting on my bed."

"They say they like to go in bathrooms—"

"Isn't it redbacks that get under toilet seats?"

"My mum always said the black house spiders seemed to have a thing about laundries ... Is there a scene where someone has to go into the laundry?"

"I don't think so ... but there's one in the kitchen. Spiders like kitchens because of all the flies that come in ... "

"I've got a daddy-long-legs in my kitchen—"

"They say they're the most poisonous species of all. It's just that they have difficulty piercing your skin ... "

"But isn't the point of the story that the spiders gain access to something in the house, some chemical or odour or spice or something that makes them start to grow bigger?"

"God! I hope not! The only reason I can cope with spiders is that they're small and easy to squash!"

*

By the fifth week no one in the cast regarded coming to work with equanimity, let alone enthusiasm. They had begun to talk almost obsessively on spiders and what was happening in the spiders' house ... because it had ceased to be a movie set and become a place filled with ever-increasing spiders ... They had begun to dread the hours cooped up in one room, no matter how bright and pleasant and well-supplied with food and coffee and magazines. They knew every line of everyone's part. They had dissected and explored every exchange, every look, every movement, every likely part where spiders might intrude. They had ceased to feel comfortable with each other. They had ceased to enjoy coming to work. They had begun to doubt their vocation as actors. They had started to wonder if they could do justice to the movie when they finally got in front of a camera. They had begun to debate whether they really had signed on for a genuine movie. They had, one by one, come to believe they could not face a spider, real or plastic, and they all felt they'd been fools to sign a contract with a stipulation about fear ...

Early in the sixth week they were all paid off, thanked for their patience, and told the movie was finished and they would receive their invitation for the premiere. For a moment relief and bewilderment warred in every face. Then they all took their pay and left, half-expecting to receive a call a day or two later.

"I honestly don't know what was going on there," one actor told his girlfriend. "I think they decided it just wasn't going to work and they couldn't bring themselves to admit they had a dud script."

He didn't tell her he wasn't sure whether he could bring himself to go back again if the producer decided to give the script another go; what girl would want a man who couldn't face a spider on a movie set?

And now, with a couple of days in which spiders never intruded, he began to wonder what had taken them over, day after day there, when it was just a movie, when every actor knows waiting is a part of the life …

*

The premiere was billed as 'The Most Terrifying Movie of the Year'. All the unused cast gave in to their curiosity, spiders notwithstanding, and went along to the first showing of 'Spideery'. Several of them could not remain till the end.

Their voices, their fears, their growing sense of unease and apprehension came it seemed from some mysterious echoing space in the house. Sometimes the spiders appeared to be listening, to be going towards the voices, to be puzzling over their never-seen human prisoners. Once a spider darted towards an apparent voice and appeared to push something into its untidy grey ball of web, below which small flakes of hard shell and detritus lay in dismal heaps. One of the cast screamed in sudden horror. Several people followed suit. Her voice there, echoing and muffled. Then she fell back into her seat in the dim theatre and wiped her sweating palms with a tissue …

There must be … easier ways to make a living …

Tasmania – Day One (and beyond)
Laurence Harrould

If you're normal in a psychotic society then you're psychotic.

I didn't realise how true that statement was until my wife and I migrated to Tasmania from the North Island.

I'd lived in Sydney for most of my life and she'd lived there all of hers. Traffic, road rage, pollution and high costs (and more) were all considered normal.

The day we arrived in Tasmania was a shock for both of us.

We drove from the ferry to an AirBnB on Middle Road, Devonport. We'd booked this as somewhere to arrive which would allow us time to find somewhere to rent for a year, during which time we'd find a house to buy. We'd done a very quick reconnaissance trip earlier that year and decided that we didn't want to be in Devonport. Our options were limited though, and that gave us somewhere that would work as a base for one month – that's how long we expected it would take to find a rental property somewhere that wasn't Devonport.

First item of the day was to take our dog for a walk. He'd been locked in a cage for 12 hours and really needed to check out some greenery.

A big shock was being greeted by complete strangers who said hello and smiled at us. In Sydney, a basic rule of survival is: don't make eye contact with ANYONE in a public place and in private, only if you know them well. So, having people being friendly was strange, and we were quickly exhausted by having to return greetings.

While walking down Middle Road a woman drove into a driveway immediately in front of us and got out of her car, clearly intending to speak to us. I'd had a similar experience in Melbourne and prepared myself for the conflict I knew was coming.

Let me explain: one night, while living in Melbourne, I was walking home on the main road of the suburb I lived in. As it was late and there was no traffic I crossed the road in the middle of the block, not walking the rest of the block to reach the traffic lights. I'd crossed at that point because it was directly opposite the side road I needed to go down to get home – this seemed to me a sensible choice. As I walked down this road, a car pulled into the driveway in front of me and the woman driver started to shout abuse at me, for not crossing at the lights (gender is relevant as it relates back to the Tasmanian experience).

So, when the woman pulled in front of us in Tassie it brought back my previous experience and my fight or flight instincts kicked in and I was gearing up for the fight.

What happened was unthinkable: she got out, smiled and started chatting to us. Something had happened on the street the night before and she asked if we'd heard or seen anything. I really had no way to deal with that and was dumbstruck. My wife explained that we'd just arrived and the lady was lovely and welcoming.

The other thing I remember about that day was our visit to The Harbourmaster Café. The dog had sorted out his introduction to Devonport and it was our turn to address ours – coffee was in order. On the menu was a drink I'd never seen before; a Dirty Hippy. I asked the waiter what that was and he replied; "if you ask my brother, it's me". We really felt we'd landed on another planet.

After that introduction, we found we had been sadly mistaken in our first impressions and now love living in East Devonport (OK, not technically Devonport but still in the general vicinity. And, Devonport has changed a lot since we arrived – paranaple centre and surrounds, Hill St… Not at all like it was on our earlier drive-through.)

I realised I had acclimatised when we went for our first trip to Hobart a few months after our arrival. I had a mild panic attack as a result of all the traffic – I just couldn't cope. Even though I had lived with Sydney traffic for decades I couldn't handle Hobart traffic after having settled in Devonport. Sanity had started to appear.

We talk to friends back in Sydney and wonder how we ever managed. One friend, who lived on a main road in the Eastern Suburbs, pointed out that it took her half an hour each day to get out of her driveway, due to the traffic.

My wife had an experience where she had to go into the Sydney CBD for a client. She was parked for 15 minutes and it cost her $85. We now resent paying $1.50 to park in Devonport CBD.

One of the conditions I had agreed to with my wife when I proposed moving to Tasmania, was that we would go for a trip each weekend to see new places. This worked out and she'd post photos of the places we went on her Facebook page. One person posted the comment; "where are all the people?" Someone else responded; "I think that's the point."

I used to read a columnist who would always finish her articles with "Be nice". I don't remember her name but I suspect she was either Tasmanian or aspired to be one.

A Walk in the Park
Ant Dry

I went for a walk in the park today.

I know you'll think that's a bit boring, and in a way I suppose it was, after all, a park is just a park no matter where it may be.

The difference this time was that on my way there, I was joined by a lady who introduced herself as Emma. We met at the traffic lights on the way across the highway.

"Our lot remember walking across the Bass Strait, you know" she started, "We've been here for forty thousand years."

We walked through the gate and into the park.

"Are you Aboriginal then?" I asked.

"From the Tommeginer tribe" she replied

In silence we walked to the War Memorial.

"You know, a lot of black fellas went to that war" she said, pointing at the obelisk, "No one would employ black fellas in them days, so they went to war. We're very proud of our lot that went to war."

We turned our backs to the War Memorial and looked out over the water.

"It's very beautiful" I remarked. Over the top of the blown roses, the Bass Strait, blue and turquoise and still, stretched out seemingly for ever, the tiny waves breaking on rocks on the side of the highway.

Emma fondled a rose. "We have a way of looking at these." She said; "We want to know three things. Can we eat it? Can we use if for medicine? Can we burn it? If we can't do any of those it's useless to us."

I smiled at her. "Her lot" would have had no use for a lot of the European imports.

"Our lot probably camped here at one time" she mused. "They probably set up a camp here. The women would go fishing for crayfish and the men would hunt for meat. The women would keep their hair short. Long hair's no good for fishing. We women would supply the basic tucker, and the men would provide the tucker for feast."

"Do you eat much bush tucker now?" I asked expecting to be told that this had been replaced by KFC and Maccers.

"When we come across it," she said, "on the side of the road and stuff. When we were growing up, we were very poor, very poor. So poor. All we ever had to eat was bread and crayfish."

I Went a Travelling One Day
Donna-Marie Koopman

I went a travelling one day
To find in this world I may
Some beauty left to see
And I saw a mountain high
I saw an eagle fly,
And I saw a mother rock her babe to sleep.
I went a travelling one day
To find in this world I may
Some beauty left to hear
And I heard a bluebird sing
I heard a rippling spring
And I heard children playing in the street.
And as I journeyed on and on
My hope was not all gone
Because in my search I found
Beauty and truth will right the wrong
And I just saw the sunrise where I stood.
And my hope lived on, for a world of good.

St Helens And St Marys (What's in a name?)
Graeme Hetherington

St Helens and St Marys, towns
I know well, close together on
Tasmania's sunrise, weather-blessed

Most cheerful side, by virtue of
Traditional, famed names endow
With evocations of the good,

The spiritual and civilized,
Distilling in six syllables
My European heritage,

The strongest antidote I know
To negativity my child-
Hood on the Hell's Gates' prison-cursed

Culturally deprived West Coast gave.
The only two such havens in
The island's verbal wilderness

Of aboriginal words used
For places to recall a folk
We showed such scant respect for when

Alive we all but wiped them out,
The first has the bonus of streets
Surprisingly, classically called

Jason, Medea, Perseus,
Circe, Atlas where I live and dub
Homer sometimes to suit my mood.

A Moment in Time
Kathleen Bentley

The air is clear and still,
Cries of cicadas shatter the silence.
The river gums tower over us.
    As we sit on the bench holding hands.
    The sun caresses my cheek,
Your eyes are closed
A smile plays around your mouth.
A pleasant thought, I muse.

The stream chatters and gurgles
As it falls over rocks
And moves pebbles out of its way.
A lazy breeze rustles leaves,
One or two fall into the creek.
My heart swells with joy
To sit here with you.
Sharing time together.

Every day is heaven with you.
You fill my soul.
You share my hopes, my fears
And my life without judgement,
But with understanding and love.
You are a beautiful person.
And this is such a perfect, perfect
Moment in time.

LOVE
Ant Dry

Everybody knows what love is.

Pick up a book, and there will be a love story. Listen to the radio and you will hear a love song.

We are saturated with love. We are all experts.

You can't tell the average citizen about love, because he or she knows it all.

I also thought I knew everything about love. I was brought up in a household where I was loved. My parents were wonderful. They loved me. I knew it and I loved them back.

I met my wife when we were both students. We fell in love, and I love her to this day.

Love is easy, love really is as the song goes, "all around".

All good so far.

These are the types of love, for your parents, or for a life partner, that you know about, that the books and songs teach you about. These are the types of love that our lives prepare us for.

But there was another type of love that I had no preparation for at all.

I had no idea about love until I had children.

My wife fell pregnant as I was writing my final exams as a Chartered Accountant. I had written major exams every year for 13 years (apart from one year when on National Service), so I was heartily sick of exams, and having to be studious and careful.

I wanted to party for a few years after qualifying, but my wife had different ideas. We'd been married for four years, she was 27 and according to the thinking in those days, getting close to being too old to have children. What rubbish we thought back then. She'd also been told it took a few months for her body to get back to normal after years of contraception, so she went off the pill so that her body would be back to normal by the time I was ready to have kids.

She fell pregnant the first month she went off the pill. She was both delighted with the fact and horrified at my prospective response.

I was aghast to say the least, and as the pregnancy progressed, so I became more depressed at the thought. I was not going to be able to party after all – thirteen years of study and I wasn't to party. I wasn't a very happy puppy.

My wife worked for a gynaecologist. She mentioned my dismay to him, and he said there would be no problem. All she had to do was ensure I was at the delivery.

My wife tells everyone that as she grew bigger, so my face grew longer. This was not much of an exaggeration.

The day of the birth arrived, and we duly drove to the hospital.

In the delivery room, my first concern was where I could faint and not get in the way. I'm not good with blood. I had visited a friend of mine in hospital once, when he was recovering from a gunshot wound, and I had had to leave his bedside and find an open window, as the sight of the blood and the tubes made me feel very unwell. I fully expected the same reaction in the delivery room.

My wife, as a practiced gynaecological nurse, had no such concerns. Her gynaecologist believed in administering epidurals, so she knew there was to be no pain involved. This allowed her to effectively enjoy a cup of tea as she pushed!

The labour was not long or complicated, and very soon the baby was crowning.

As our baby's head appeared, the gynaecologist turned to me and said,

"Here, take your baby's hands"

I was horrified, but carried away by the event, I reached over and took my baby's hands.

But I didn't take her hands at all. My beautiful daughter clutched my fingers like her life depended upon it. She was alive and wanted ME to deliver her.

That was me done. I pulled her out and the theatre nurse had to struggle with me to get my daughter away from me so she could be washed.

As far as I was concerned, that was MY baby and I had delivered it. My wife was lucky to be there.

That Gynaecologist knew a thing or two about psychology.

We took her home and settled in. I had thought my life had been perfect. I had been wrong.

NOW my life was perfect.

I was slightly jealous of the time my wife got to spend with my daughter, so to make up for that, I, ever an early riser, used to wake up as soon as she cried. I'd get her up, I'd change her bum, feed her a bottle, chat to her for a bit, and then I'd wrap her up and leave her sleeping in our bed with my wife, before getting ready for work.

I remember how I felt in those days driving to work. I would turn right out of our gate and as I drove past the length of our yard, I would watch as the fence passed by, and I would think to myself that at last I knew what love was all about.

All of the things I loved most in the world were right there behind that fence.

It was a thought that would keep me buoyed all day.

Grey
(What's in a name?)
Graeme Hetherington

Self-portrait Dorian-Gray poems
Written to transfer hate to them,
That otherwise would poison me,

Are now beginning to backfire.
Baptised 'Graeme', I only heard it
In Aussie style shortened to 'Grey'

Till seeping in as surely as
The West Coast of Tasmania rain,
I quickly became as sad as

The sodden paling fences of
That hue, as the drenched garb
Of Hell's Gates' chain-gang convicts, or

The winter fires I sat round with
Mean gloomy parents watching die
Rather than putting more wood on,

It turns to ash the colour of
My name, though soul was darker still,
Evolving to the deepest shade,

And overloaded I began
To fail to 'bear it all within'
As James McAuley has advised,

The cancer of my inner life
Verse bursting at the rotting seams,
Pustules erupting on my face.

Hell's Terminal
Allan Jamieson

*Allan has flown into or out of 250 different airports
around the world*

It must surely be true that nobody plans to end their journey at Hell, however, if one is not paying sufficient attention in planning a journey from "A" to "B", it is possible to find oneself with an intermediate landing at Hell, experiencing thereby the pleasures of Hell's Terminal, such as the five I will now point out.

The first pleasure happens before you have reached the terminal building. Planes are required to park some distance away in order to refuel and passengers must deplane while this takes place. In your case, you deplane because you will catch a different plane to get to "B". On descending the steps of the mobile gangway, you come face to face with Hell's welcoming committee – each man lined up with his sub-machine gun to ensure that you will walk in a straight line away from the plane towards the building. As a result, you walk in a straight line.

Of course, you will have had a long time in the air before arriving at Hell, so it is likely that upon entering the building, you will seek out a toilet. A true pleasure of Hell's Terminal then awaits you. There are corridors leading in several directions, but no signs to indicate the location of a toilet. You choose one corridor and commence walking. The space between ceiling lights lengthens and darkness gradually deepens. When you are about to turn around, unsure if you should have ventured this far, you detect a characteristic smell emanating from an open door. Through the dimness you can see a large room. Desperate now, you enter, noting that it is deserted and empty, except for a rope hanging down over a hole in the floor in the centre of the room, which is at the low point of the floor. Ah hah! You have found the toilet. You are supposed to suspend yourself over the hole by holding the rope, blackened as it is by decades of use. You add your own layer of filth to the rope.

There will always be a long wait in Hell's Terminal in any event and this means that you can experience the next of Hell Terminal's pleasures. Contrary to what you might imagine, Hell's

Terminal has shops and things are on sale. You decide that bringing home a fridge magnet or some other trinket from Hell would be amusing. The currency in Hell is the Diabolus, which no other country wants – or is permitted – to hold. Thus, you do not have any Diablos to use. You begin looking for a money exchange, and a smiling man wearing a beret and sporting a revolver at his hip comes to you. He beckons you to follow. You follow, of course.

It is curious, you realise later, that though you entered the building on the ground floor of International Arrivals, the only money exchange is located on the third floor of the building next door – the Domestic Departures Hall – hence the prevalence of helpful men with revolvers. The Departure Hall is a place where you do not want to be, as all planes parked here go deeper into Hell. You are worried that your guide, with his revolver, will not allow you to return to your Terminal. Trapped! If you are lucky, all the planes to Hell's destinations are full and so you get a reprieve and are permitted to return to your building – a fact that you decide should now be seen as a true pleasure.

At last, your plane is boarding. You walk out of the Terminal at ground level, only to find that there are five or six planes parked there. Which one is the one you want? There are no signs and no guide – with or without a gun – to help you decide, so you end up choosing the plane toward which the greater number of passengers is heading. On board things seem to be normal, though you are a trifle disappointed to be leaving Hell's Terminal and all its pleasures, of course. After all, it isn't every day that you can claim to have come back from Hell. Little do you realise though that two more of Hell Terminal's pleasures still await you.

Your plane takes off, climbs and then the Captain's voice comes over the PA system. He announces that the flight to "C" will take three hours. Wait a moment: YOU ARE SUPPOSED TO BE ON YOUR WAY TO "B". There is nothing to do but to settle back and ponder how to recover from this latest pleasure.

Eventually, you arrive at "C", not knowing too clearly where it is in relation to "B", but you will have to collect your bags and then set to work to find out. The last of the pleasures of Hell's Terminal now happens. On the baggage carousel, you sight the luggage starting to arrive from your plane. Something is amiss. Every case is empty – its sides sliced open by a sharp knife or its locks or hinges ruptured by brute force. Every bag on board the plane has been gutted.

Do you want to know where Hell's Terminal is? I can vouch that it moves around, but at certain times, it has been located at Moscow's Sheremetyevo Airport, at Istanbul's Ataturk Airport, at Rio de Janeiro's International Airport, at Stockholm's Bromma Flygplats and at London's Heathrow Airport.

You have been warned!

Desperate Haste
Anne Layton-Bennett

so what would you take
if forced to evacuate
suddenly and unexpectedly
because of invasion
or bombs
or floods
or bushfires

there's no time to think
have to be nimble
dash to the drawers
the wardrobes
the desk, the cabinet
and the cupboards
and grab passports, cash, ID docs
photo albums, phone, laptop
and a change of clothes

because in a matter of seconds
your life is crammed into a suitcase
and a backpack
you're a displaced person
a refugee
and running for your life

Offspring of an Empire
Meg McLaren

The sun is blood orange.
The air hot and heavy.
A brown-skinned man with twisted legs,
All skin and bone,
Pushes his barrow beneath the creeping heat,
Tormented by flies.
He feels splinters deep in his palms.
A block of frozen water fills the cart,
Melting into a rough, hessian sack.
Jugs of flavoured syrup, balance precariously,
Cherry Ripe, Orange and Mango.
"Ice! Ice! Shave' Ice!" He calls out.
Offspring of the Empire.

Luli shuffles down placid, tree shaded streets,
Lined with the booths of hucksters and peddlers.
Past gloomy doorways covered by sticky plastic strips
Gathering dust and flies.
Past Our Lady of Lourdes,
Angels hanging out over the street.
Past the docks, where slaves once stood,
Heads bowed, picked over at auction.
Past the grand, ceremonial route
To the Governor's throne.
Laundered gardens filled with colour.
Stone lions at the gate,
Embody the might of Britain.

A glimmer of daylight left in the sky,
As the mottled night spreads her canopy.
Luli trundles home along a track choked with banana trees.
Mosquitos pricking at his wrists.
The mother country has not nourished him.
The aims of colonialism
Have let him down,
Lost in the pursuit of an Empire.

Outposts established by force and violence.
Like a medieval parade.
A bleak story tainted with darkness.
At the crossing between heaven and earth
Luli was forgotten.

Overland track
Susan Arthur

early start
dozing
to the car's hum

chomping sounds beneath the boardwalk
wombats

cradle mountain
seconds spent admiring
everlasting daisies

echidna
snuffling through a mound of ants
wearing them

undulating hills, he called them
muscles ache

quartz and schist
grind underfoot
goose-bumps

march flies find us
every break

purple trigger plants
floral columns
snap pollen

one step
thousands of cushion plants

buttongrass shadows
waltz with me
along the track

scoparia
fields of dead flowers
remnants of summer's colour

the hut at last
sun down
feet up

My Old Man
Graeme Hetherington

My old man was an outgrowth of
The West Coast's murky tangled scrub
And Hell's Gates' past, a background that

Also explains the Devil as
A fitting emblem for the isle.
Horses and greyhounds, carnivals

Where booze-deadened indigenes
Could be punched drunker still by whites
Who'd step into the ring with them

For a share in the loose change thrown,
Where 'chops', 'gifts', 'wheels' and beauty queen
Competitions were held, defined

His interests as opposed to those
His sherry-sipping schoolmarm of
A brother-in-law, whom he loathed,

Preferred instead of beer and bets,
Such as mounting insects to be
Studied beneath a microscope.

And artfully he spread the tale
That this 'ciss of a man', in league,
Truth be known, with Old Nick, would push

His father, unable to stop
Because of Parkinson's disease,
Towards the fireplace, roaring on

A winter's day like the one folk
Still feared below, rescuing him
Only at the eleventh hour.

The Waiting Room
Meg McLaren

Framed within the window of room one ten,
clipped autumn hedges, naked trees,
lamplight shining on winter puddles.
Two dogs, keepers of the Home,
chasing magpies across a cool lawn,
golden shadows in the soft mist.
  "A dirty 'oul day."
  Sean from next door
  wheels past in his chair.

In the darkening hours,
Sheila prepares for the loneliest journey.
It will take her over snowy ramparts
into the outback and beyond.
She lingers in a nest of plastic tubes,
hands pecked and bruised by the beak of time.
Narratives buzz behind opaque lens
like a tinnitus, barely discernible.
  And she smiles
  in my father's arms,
  dancing the *Tennessee Waltz*.

My mother dissolves like birdsong at sunset,
like droplets of water from a mountain stream.
A garland of beads, heavy with medals,
twists around slow fingers.
And under the gentle gaze of the prophet,
His heart pierced and bleeding with love for her,
she draws the dark blinds,
and closes this house.
  And she sleeps quietly,
  as all that she has been
  comes to an end.

Then, as the long night approaches,
A single star beckons.

"I can see the star" she sighs.
I bend to kiss grey temples
and whisper
"I love you."

When the Worm Turned
Pete Stratford

It was essential that hundreds of casual labourers were employed in the harvesting of what was then, a thriving tobacco growing industry in New Zealand. Hence each season would see a great influx of holiday makers, drifters, *etc.*, from far and wide, arrive to earn quite good money and perhaps have enjoyable leisure activities also. Australians were well represented in the group employed on the farm where I was employed, including one very bright well informed lad whom I shall call "Keith".

While out in working in a paddock of tobacco, along with half a dozen or so other workers, Keith came upon a small burrow going down into the soil. The entrance was perhaps thirty or forty millimetres across and he asked me what would have made that burrow. I knew that it had been a field mouse, but answered; "earthworms!" Others there were very quick to ridicule the idea that a worm could have created such a large hole, however Keith was adamant that back in Gippsland there were worms capable of doing so. That brought various responses of ridicule along the lines of "we've - got - bigger - and - better - than - you" banter. Even though I had read about such creatures and was aware that they existed, I also joined in with the entertainment provided by some considerably amusing and good natured refusal to accept the unbelievable story he was telling about such gigantic worms.

In the chemical spray shed I came upon a very large rubber "O" ring from a drum which was about a metre long when cut, then I added a cork head, with pearl headed pins pierced through to create eyes and fangs. Carefully parcelled up, it was addressed to Keith, plus a used Australian stamp attached, then was included with the Mail delivery for the seasonal staff. Upon opening it he found an accompanying letter from the "Mayor of Gippsland. Mr. R. Sole-Brown" who sympathised with Keith over the incredible ignorance that Kiwis had about Australia's amazing creatures, plus apologising that the worm enclosed was merely a baby one, because even with the aid of hunting dogs it had proven quite impossible for them to capture a fully grown adult one without endangering the dogs!

Over the following weeks Keith used a process of elimination until he finally accused me of being the perpetrator, which despite my denial, was not believed by him. During the intervening days he had enjoyed plenty of laughs as well as some free beers at the local pub by displaying his "genuine Gippsland worm" along with letter from their "Mayor," to others drinking there. There ended what had been a successful and amusing practical joke ... or so I thought. Several months after the seasonal workers had departed the district, there arrived in my mail box a letter and photographs from a fellow in Gippsland who had been forwarded "my" letter seeking information regarding those enormous earthworms.

So thus the worm had surely "turned" and to this day I have retained that correspondence.

If We Can't Live Together
Donna-Marie Koopman

If I speak to you softly will you listen and stay?
For I am your brother, I am of your own.
But the way we've been treated
you'd never have known.
So take hold of my hand and listen to me.
There's not enough love in the world don't you see?
So, though you don't know me, show that you care.
Fighting and hating gets us nowhere.
So give a little of you, before it's too late.
If we can't live together; then what of our fate?

===///===

Donna-Marie Koopman

When you are so far down
and you feel God has left us.
Just remember He never leaves us;
we leave Him.

Thanks for Visiting
Anne Collins

The young man in the office at the heritage museum
is so neatly groomed.
His hair, short-back-and-sides with a wave across the top,
is precisely combed into place.
His round, fresh face, his open smile,
his well-mannered helpfulness in explaining to us,
map-in-hand, how to find our way
through the maze of rooms and exhibits:
it's as if he's emerged
from one of the hundreds of black-and-white photos to be
found here.
He's like those clean-cut young men from the 1940s,
or a character from *The Sullivans*,
someone my grandmother would have liked.

The museum, a former School of Mines and Metallurgy,
displays rocks, minerals and machinery
from a time when all this was newly discovered
and newly invented technology -
like the carbon arc Blue Printing machine
built in the early 1900s.
The museum's office is partitioned
by the elegance of hand-blown Victorian glass
windows with wavy reflections
framed in polished wood. I imagine
long-ago employees with bowties and round spectacles
stamping the paperwork.
Now the office houses a 21st century computer system.
It seems like a haven for the young people
who work in this building full of relics,
frozen in time like a movie set.
But I'm a brief visitor
and there's a limit to first impressions.

Nearby the once-lively Gaiety Theatre seated a thousand.
Now its faded grandeur and yawning emptiness

echo our footsteps
as we try to think of the town Silver City
booming for decades before it went bust.
There's only so much that can be dug up and sold.

Outside the small stretch of footpath
laid with hope and 1990s pink-pavers,
looks naked in its relative newness
against a backdrop of abandoned buildings
stretching into the mist.
It's raining the day we visit. The only cafe is closed.
Tucked into the museum's portico
is a caravan
where a few locals line up to buy pies and coffee.

In the 1890s this was a town of nearly ten thousand people.
About seven hundred live here now.
There's still money to be made from mining
but home is elsewhere. On-shift workers
live on the town's edge in new Colorbond clad units.
Along Main Street
older fibro houses sit squat, scruffy and vacant.
Still in the back streets
there are people who've lived here for decades
with mountain views. This far west
you can afford to buy a house and garden.
You can go glamping in the summer too
or join a bicycle tour and bring your own party.
After the boom then bust,
there's the lingering effort to continue,
like a long-distance cyclist never quite ready to give up.

A light comes through the clouds and shines on
the young man from the office
who is walking straight and tall
through the centre of town.
Perhaps he's returning to work after lunch.
My heart leaps at the sight of him,
his sense of purpose.
I wish for the place to grow again, brighter and smarter.

Home
Ant Dry

The flight into Harare airport is always good. The air is clear and still and the aeroplane lands without fuss, and we gently move to the arrivals port and disembark.

The walk to customs and immigration is short and easy.

The bottleneck starts at the top of the ramp down towards the officials. The customs officials are not in a hurry. They never have been, they never will be. To them the arrivals are more of an irritant than anything else, interrupting their daily routine of drinking tea and gossiping. We see them sighing collectively at the sight of us as we gather in the queue waiting to be allowed into the country.

Eventually it is my turn.

He does not even glace at me.

"Passport." Taciturn, even rude.

I hand him the document. There is a twitch of interest as he sees my Zimbabwean passport, and he briefly raises his eyes in surprise.

He stands up and walks away. I see him chatting to a fellow officer, my passport open at the identifying page. They both laugh, look at the document and disappear from sight.

I breathe deeply, and the person behind me breathes deeper. Our eyes meet. Fleetingly, we smile, but there is no mirth in the smiles. It looks like it's going to be a long day.

About ten minutes later, the official re-appears, holding a dusty receipt book.

"You have to pay for a visa."

"No I don't, I am a returning resident."

"You live in Australia. You have not been here for more than six months. You have to pay for a visa."

This is getting tedious.

"No I do not have to pay for a visa. I'd like to speak to your supervisor."

"The visa is fifty dollars, but if you give me twenty, you can proceed"

"Ten."

He holds out his hand, I pass over a ten dollar note, my passport is stamped, and he waves me through.

I lean over and snatch the ten dollars out of his hand. He looks shocked.

"I don't need a visa," I remind him, and I move away, not looking back.

The baggage carousel is broken again. How is it broken? The airport is no more than five years old. I look down the chute at the loaders overseeing the baggage. They are sitting on top of the luggage, smoking, and chatting.

Then there is a flurry of activity, a voice raised, speaking Shona, loudly and aggressively. The workers jump to their feet and busy themselves with the luggage. The carousel lurches into life and the bags start to climb the conveyor belt to the top. I see my suitcase. It arrives, and I head down the "nothing to declare" route.

"Excuse me Suh."

I stop. It's another official.

"Come this way."

"Why?"

"Routine. I'd like to inspect your baggage."

I grit my teeth and follow the official, into an interview room.

I place my suitcase on the table and open it. I feign indifference as he starts to rummage through my things.

He picks up my toilet bag.

"Do you have any drugs?"

"Have a look if you like."

He tosses the toilet bag aside without looking at it.

"Wait here."

He disappears, and I remain standing. There is no chair. Five minutes go by. Then ten minutes. Eventually he returns.

He asks, "what are we going to do about it?"

I stare at him. "About what?"

He stares at me. I stare back.

"May I go?"

He leaves the room. I stuff my belongings back into my suitcase, close it and walk away.

The car hire desk is just outside the arrival's hall. I walk over to the desk and introduce myself. They are ready for me. The very charming lady behind the desk takes my details, smiling broadly at my Zimbabwean driver's license. She hands me a set of car keys and escorts me outside.

The car is a Datsun 1200. It looks about 30 years old.

"I asked for a Toyota Corolla," I say, "That's what I ordered."

She looks completely unflustered.

"We don't have any. You ordered a Corolla "OR EQIVALENT" This is the equivalent." There is not a trace of a smile. She is dead serious.

She walks away. She has done her job, and she is no longer interested in me.

I look around me, taking stock. The weather can only be described as glorious. The sun is shining. It's not hot. It's beautifully warm. The sun caresses my skin. I do love the Zimbabwean sun. The air smells good too. There is an energetic crackle to it. The flies buzz but don't intrude. My irritation begins to seep away.

I load my suitcase, open the car door, and slide in. It is not exactly filthy inside. Someone has tried to clean it, but the vehicle is so ancient, that the dirt has become fully ingrained.

The car starts fine. A strong trusty little engine. My mother used to have one of these. She bought it forty years ago. They stopped making them over twenty-five years ago.

On the road, I notice I have to pull the steering wheel to the left firmly, as the vehicle tends to move to the right, as if it knows where it wants to go. I recollect my daughter's horse used to do this too. I smile, remembering.

Fourth gear seems to be a problem too. I have to hold onto the gear lever to stop it shifting into neutral on its own.

I approach a traffic light. It is not working. I look to the left, and then to the right. There is nothing coming, so I go through the intersection.

A policeman jumps out from a bush on the side of the road and holds up his hand.

I stop.

"Driver's licence."

I hand it over.

"You went through a red traffic light."

"Rubbish, it's broken, it wasn't red. It wasn't working."

"Ah, but it is working. Look."

I crane my neck and see that indeed the lights are working. On this side. Not on the other.

"It's a fifty dollar fine."

"Look mate, you know very well the lights are broken on the other side. I'm not paying any fine."

He looks belligerent.

"Fifty dollars."

"Will you give me a receipt?"

"Ten dollars."

"I tell you what. Why don't we go together to the station, and I can explain to the officer in charge?"

He looks at me, long and hard. He dismisses me.

"You may proceed."

Nothing has changed.

I am home.

The "Logic" of Competition
Allan Jamieson

Picture a priest who is also a well-known photographer, but who now finds he is staying as a patient in a hospital on the campus of a famous women's university. In that one sentence, there would seem to be several incongruities, but – nevertheless – let us ignore these for the moment and discover what the priest experienced while he was in hospital.

The priest was in hospital for treatment against cancer. For a while he felt very near death and he began to seek ways of occupying his mind to help him master his experience. He asked for a couple of his favourite cameras to be brought to him and he began to document the life in the hospital.

As a priest, he was used to death; at least he thought he was. Eventually, he asked for permission to visit the room where recently-deceased patients were taken awaiting burial arrangements by their next-of-kin. A doctor said that it was not permissible for a "lay" person to go to that room, but the priest persisted and eventually he found someone in authority who accepted his request after being persuaded that the priest had a "professional" need to see the room.

However, he had his own private reason for wanting to see the room. He was near death and he wanted to understand what would happen if he died at the hospital.

A visit was arranged. Accompanied by a hospital orderly, he made his way downstairs. He was wearing pyjamas and had a camera slung around his neck. Being a priest, his head was shaven, though if this had not been the case, the cancer treatment would probably have made him go bald anyway. The two of them eventually stopped at a door. The orderly opened the door.

The priest went in to a small ante-room, off which were three other rooms. In one of these rooms a body was lying on a table. The priest, however, was surprised to find a man sitting on a chair in the room. "Who are you?" he enquired of this man.

The priest heard that the man was a salesman (a "tout") for a firm of morticians. He was waiting for the relatives of the dead person to arrive. He would express sympathy to the relatives and offer his assistance. Had they already thought of burial arrangements, he would ask. Apparently most people had not done any planning for the situation they were now in, so often they would turn to the man and invite him to help them. The man would immediately offer to drive the deceased to the place where the burial service would take place. In the country where this story happened, it was customary for a service to be held in the family home and the man would find out where that was.

The man's job was to sit in the basement rooms for up to twenty-four hours at a time, so that he (or an accomplice who would relieve him every other day) would have first chance to assist the relatives of deceased patients. The man was keen to talk – he didn't often get the opportunity to have a conversation – and he had brought in a small television set just to while away the time.

This "service" was big business! It was a large and famous hospital, with several hundred patients dying each year. The funeral parlour could expect to charge at least a thousand dollars each time it gained a corpse. It was such good business, in fact, that there was real competition between undertakers to gain the rights to have a representative sit in the basement rooms. The priest heard that the Manager of the hospital also benefited, as he was always under great pressure to appoint one funeral firm exclusively in preference to many other firms and he found his decision was made easier by his palm being greased generously.

Being a famous hospital, it sometimes happened that prominent persons went there for treatment and some died at the hospital. Thus, the man often had to deal with important and wealthy families. Of course, a wealthy family would want to spend lavishly on the funeral of one of their members. This gave the man an opportunity to make some money for himself. While driving the corpse to a designated house, he would stop at a telephone booth and ring around various undertakers to let them know that he had "a good one." Whoever conducted the burial ceremony would expect to receive a substantial fee, so the man would encourage bidding among the various firms, with a "finder's fee" to come to him, of course.

Given a certain workload at his own firm's premises, he might also try to off-load the body of a poor person too as – on average – it was better for his firm if their "clients" were from well-to-do families and some other undertaker might be a little short of work on the day and be happy to take over the body. Bodies would change hands somewhere on the road to the location of the burial service.

It was at about this time that the priest found himself in a predicament. He felt that he wanted to go to the toilet, but some relatives had just come into the ante-room and he was conscious of how it would look if they were suddenly confronted with a strange, bald man in pyjamas coming out of this temporary morgue and carrying a camera. His "friend", the tout, was able to arrange things so nobody was embarrassed and the priest left the basement.

He had thought that he knew about death, but he had learned that he had much to know still, especially about the industry that existed because of death. His experience had changed the way he thought about his own future. In fact he didn't die in that hospital, but survived to write this story.

A Living
Ant Dry

Giles brought the ute to a halt at the edge of the rubbish dump.

The track to the dump was well worn, and at the edge the dirt was baked hard by the African sun and beaten down by the traffic. In front of him stretched a sea of garbage, multi coloured and as rough as the ocean on a windy day. Plastic flapped in the light breeze. The smell was powerful and unpleasant. Crows wheeled above the site or sat on the piles of garbage, tearing at food morsels and unidentifiable lumps of rubbish.

There was a tap on the window.

'You want some help, boss?'

Giles looked through the window. An urchin of about 10 stood outside, bare footed and dressed in what looked like cast-offs he had found in the dump.

'What?' asked Giles.

'You want help? Unload your truck?'

Giles opened the door and looked down at the urchin.

'No. Go away,' he said

'Two dollars, I unload your truck.'

'I said no, now get lost.'

The urchin leapt onto the back of the ute and started to unload the garbage.

'I said get off and go away!'

The urchin just grinned at Giles, 'Okay' he said, 'one dollar.'

'I don't want your....' Giles didn't finish. It was obvious he wasn't going to win.

The urchin grunted and pulled and piled the garbage at the edge of the tip. He ripped open the first bag and pored over its contents. There was a mouldy pizza crust on top, and he took a bite. He chewed, clutching the rest in his hand for later. He scratched through to the bottom of the bag. Giles had spent the previous day going through his bookcase and had thrown away some of his less loved books. The urchin found a Jeffrey Archer book, dusted it off and carefully placed it on a dry spot on the ground. He squatted on the ground and went through the rest of the bag, carefully brushing the books clean and placing them next to Jeffrey Archer.

'Where you from?' the urchin asked.

"Australia" Giles replied.

'Why you throw these away?'

'Do you read?'

'Of course. I shall read these.' He took another bit of the pizza crust.

'Why aren't you at school? You can't be more than 10.'

The urchin shrugged and started on the next bag. He found one of Giles old shirts, ripped on the shoulder where he had been snagged climbing through a barbed wire fence. The urchin grunted with pleasure and put on the shirt. It was far too big. Once he'd rolled up the sleeves, it looked as if he were wearing a night shirt.

'I go to school. It finished at one o'clock. I'm 12. I am going to be a doctor.' He held out his hand. 'Where's my dollar?'

Giles took out a dollar and held it out of reach.

'If you go to school, what are you doing here? Does your mother know?'

'Just give me the dollar. I have no mother. '

'What about a father?'

'Give me my dollar. I unloaded your truck.'

'I'll give you the dollar, just tell me where your father is, and why you're here.'

'My father is dead. Give me my dollar.'

Giles handed over the cash.

'Where do you live?'

'With my brother'

'Ah' Giles had learned that "brother "could mean anything in Zimbabwe, from an actual blood brother to an acquaintance recently met.

'Why are you here then?'

The urchin looked at Giles. He shrugged. He shook out an empty plastic bag that had just fluttered over from the middle of the heap, and carefully packed the books into it. He tucked Giles old shirt more firmly around him.

'It's a living.' He said, and wandered off.

Where Dingoes Howl
Pete Stratford

Our torchlight seemed to be absorbed
into rough-hewn and fractured walls
as here and there bush timber stood
preventing death from loose rock falls
though long years of slow decaying
had robbed these logs of strength
so we were loath to linger there
to plumb that mine's full length.
Yet seen half buried in floor debris
a worn pick with splintered handle,
while protruding from rock walls
old rusted tins held stubs of candle.

With laboured breath and aching back
who had slaved on bravely there?
Soaked in sweat while choked with dust
what anguish did they bear
when each barrow yielded nothing
apart from more useless dirt,
without glint of shining nugget,
while more blisters burst and hurt?
They had laboured on to no avail,
down there no wealth for toil,
hard effort only earned more grief
from that tough gold-barren soil.

It was only as we trudged away
to leave this worthless mine
did we see the rows of rock
laid out neatly in straight line.
Then closer to and we could tell
that these stones still marked the spot
where someone who had perished
lay beneath this arid plot.
No timber cross bore witness
to whom, or when, or how

their mortal bones now rested
where desert winds still softly sough.

Did someone notice he'd gone missing
perhaps some parent, sibling, wife?
Or just another lonesome miner
who was anonymous in life
and tempted by the lure of riches
had sought hidden fortune deep below
in ground bereft of gleaming nuggets
though that fact he didn't know?
Devoid of friend to ease his pain
did he die down there alone,
no calming voice to offer comfort
or to ease his dying groans?

Had he collapsed from heat exhaustion
or was it venom from snake bite?
Perhaps he succumbed to bad air
entombed far below sunlight?
Was his body reverently interred
or lay desiccated, bleached,
before another mortal soul
this nowhere place had reached?
To now be mourned each daybreak
when, with each coming dawn,
dingoes howl to greet the day
with their dirge sad and forlorn.

Lament for a Long Summer
Marilyn Arnold

Sitting in a purple beanbag,
outside, crisp early morning air,
ignoring my attention-seeking cat.

In my lap, an old book of Tim Thorne's poems,
A virtuoso performance which makes me
shake my head (when I'm not shaking it
from my sad lack of understanding).
Who'd be a poet? All those loved words soon lost
that form an autobiography

I think of winter; there are diamonds in the grass
by moonlight; the frost can be dazzling.
Some days are diamonds....
Some days are frail, ...a bunch of twigs
Collected just in case... like memories
They could become all that is left

Too soon gone, this garden, this meagre sunshine,
Like the generation before me.
Like the butterfly wing lightly brushing the lavender
in the distance...and I hear,
shivering grey and indistinct: a subterranean howling,
an almost indiscernible moaning.

Like this, the net descends,
Capturing a sadness, holding within it
all kinds of sea creatures of memory,
tired creatures without names, with only feeble voices,
A grief which arises from nowhere,
Bringing behind it a tsunami...

The diamonds in the grass at midnight
are gone by morning. Like my mum,
like my poems, like that sobbing
that seems to come from somewhere near the Elm tree...

It will be a hard summer, unless the sun burns away
this sorrow interminable, seeming without cause.

Captive on an Island
Pete Stratford

Years ago they became marooned on an island, ever since being held captive by such dangerous conditions that any attempts to depart would likely be fatal. That is their plight, and yet they have grown accustomed to the limitations they find themselves governed by, and in fact they appear quite content with the situation. Granted they have no shortage of the essentials to sustain life there, since adequate food, water, and shelter are not a concern at all. Even an element of protection exists for them, because approaching this island would prove to be just as dangerous as trying to depart from it would be.

Quite a number of generations have now lived in this environment, spending their entire life there, all happily cohabiting within their social structure, where monogamy is no longer considered the norm. In fact it would be highly abnormal within their community after so many generations of what outsiders would deem to be incestuous relationships. Hence some of their physical characteristics are multi-generational, with distinctive coloured hair, facial features, and even a very distinctive gait as they move along. All symptomatic of a limited gene pool, yet apparently has not been as harmful as one may have expected, since there's no apparent evidence of diminished intellect. Nor sadly, of any high development in that department, though that seems to have had little impact of their expected life span, or their productivity during it.

Content simply to exist, pass on their genes as frequently as possible, as meanwhile the rest of the world passes them by. Political issues, world events, cost of living even, are meaningless to this isolated, close knit community, yet they all appear perfectly content. Would they be more so if they had some higher goals to strife for, such as a larger home, easy access to health benefits, even an opportunity to travel further afield? Surely not?

However, I tend to believe that their limited responsibility and ambition may well be the key to their contentment, since very contented they appear to be, despite the earth trembling caused by the outside world rushing by, the constant danger if they should attempt to leave, or even the risk of attack from the "outside". None of this seems to bother them as they go about their daily or nocturnal activities. But then perhaps this enviable situation isn't unusual for rabbits living on a grassed traffic island?

Blowies In Wartime Rosebery
Graeme Hetherington

Eating sultanas I dry-retched
Remembering Mother yelling out,
Stewed up one steamy summer Sun-

Day cooking the de rigueur Roast,
'The flies has smelt the cabbage, quick,
Make sure the screen door's kept shut tight.'

And slamming it closed I then sprayed,
The buzz insisting, building to
A loud collective hum as they

Swarmed, covering the rusty mesh,
And maddened by the scent, en masse
Squirmed trying to find a way through.

'Like Asian hordes', my father said,
Roused enough from lethargy to
Muster an interest, big-note with

Men's news from the pub of Japs in
Sydney Harbour, of Darwin bombed,
Returning to the seething with

The information that the tails
Of tiny yellow, densely packed
Maggots were dangerous to health

As carriers of polio,
Straight-faced remarking peril from
This colour had resulted in

The White Australia Policy,
Then deserting as on I fought,
Squirting, brushing in panic those

I saw and felt, could easily find,
From orifices, flesh, hair, clothes,
Into now quieter, stiller heaps

For sprinkling over garden beds
In shovelfuls, thinking of dried
Fruit sticking out of buns and cakes.

Memo to World Leaders
Anne Layton-Bennett

if only we could refresh the page
delete the anger, the violence
and the rage
start again, agree to sometimes disagree
to compromise
and value difference

we've used and abused
our planet home
and now she's struggling to cope
so before that fictious clock
strikes thirteen
and seals a doom
that will be all too real
can we please stop the wars
break out the peace
and learn to finally live
in harmony

He's Gone
Donna-Marie Koopman

The dawn will soon be breaking
on another lonely day.
The sun will raise its sleepy head
and chase the night away.
The old man lies there dreaming
of the days of long ago.
When the days were full and laughter rang,
but now who wants to know?
His children have forgotten,
the old man lying there.
Their days are filled with their own lives
to stop and even care.
He hangs his head and sheds a tear
for the youthful days gone by.
Just to share a yarn or two,
with some old friend in time.
He prays for death to take him,
before too many dawns.
The sun will raise its sleepy head,
but who will know he's gone.

Scrub Cutting
Pete Stratford

The very title seems to suggest a rather lowly task, and so it is. Literally clear felling scrubby trees growing on steep hillsides. Since tractors were unable to access such areas to clear the vegetation that gradually spread to cover over valuable grazing, this became winter work for those willing to undertake a hard physical task, often in unpleasant weather conditions. Back in the early 1960's my main income was as a freelance shearer, a well-paid but very seasonal task seeing me effectively unemployed during the winter months. When the opportunity to get some winter work arose I was eager to grasp it, despite not having had any previous experience working at that particular job. Although quite capable of rustling up myself a feed I certainly was not used to having to cook for myself on a daily basis.

One of the legal stipulations was that one could not cut scrub alone, due to the potential dangers of becoming injured while in very isolated areas when felling some larger trees and using chainsaw and axes on very steep hillsides, so it was essential that I find another chap willing to be involved in this too. Happily I soon located Joe, a good worker, who came with the bonus that his wife Lill was more than willing, and even happy to camp with us to be our cook, a task she was proficient at doing.

Our camp was situated about thirty miles up a rather barren valley and accommodation was a couple of three metre square "rooms" joined together. Constructed of weather boards on the outer with some thin plywood lining within, and a corrugated iron roof without the luxury of a ceiling, it could accurately be described as "basic." One room being our kitchen, contained a bench table, and we added stools, plus built a bunk bed from bush timber, beneath which was our total storage space. The second room became a bedroom for my partner and his wife, and was where our occasional half carcase of mutton, purchased from the owner, was hung from a rafter as we had no other place to keep our meat supply.

Without electric power our sole heating in this hut was the stove, which stood beside the entrance door and was a tiny cast iron stove reminiscent of what one may expect in a Hobbit dwelling. Intended to emit the smoke from that appliance was a chimney pipe of about arm's-length and too small to put a hand inside. As our only fuel was pine wood scrounged from beneath a small plantation across the paddocks, this chimney regularly blocked up with soot and we soon learned that very frequent cleaning was essential. After this filthy task one usually followed it with a quick wash down in the creek, itself an uninviting activity given the temperature of the water. We had no need for a fridge, the overnight temperature being sufficient to freeze water inside the hut. It was under such Spartan conditions that Lill managed to provide very adequate and mostly tasty meals for us two hungry blokes. Our only water supply was from the tiny creek nearby, which after rain ran turbid resulting in grey and gritty mashed potatoes being served up. "Roughage," became an interesting addition to our cuisine, even though Lill would try and let the grit settle out in a billy before using the water which remained grey.

Accompanied by the owner we two walked around an area of the hillside, a mile or two from our camp, where we were to clear away many isolated clumps of tea tree. Having pointed out visual boundaries such as the creek at the bottom, or the gap between two larger patches of scrub, Joe and I would then guesstimate how many days we thought it would take us to clear fell the vegetation within those parameters and then offer a quote to the owner. Sometimes he would quibble a bit, but usually we came to an agreed price quickly.

Once he had departed we both would get stuck in and fell the area as quickly as we could, usually in far fewer days than we had estimated, but we received the agreed price as was written on our contract. This was frequently just a scrap of paper on which was noted the boundaries of the area along with the agreed contract price and which then carried the signatures of all three parties. Once an area of scrub was completely cleared the process of establishing another area, and contract, would be repeated.

This seemed such an easy way to earn some very good "winter" money, and so it proved to be. However, we two new chums had not factored in that this was a region tucked in close to the Southern Alps and frequently snow-covered once winter weather arrived. We were soon to discover the dubious joys of working on steep slopes covered with knee deep snow. Of course we dressed appropriately to prevent an untimely and miserable death by freezing! One thing we learned very early in our snow experience was that wet, half frozen long trouser legs were by far more unpleasant to walk and work in than wearing shorts. Heavy boots and equally heavy socks kept the snow from getting down inside the boots, and our legs soon became accustomed to being bare, which also had the advantage that on days when the sun did come out and reflected off the snow, one felt the benefit immediately.

Although we worked in snow some of the time while climbing to slightly higher areas on the slopes, generally we were more fortunate to be below the snow line. However we were never below the frost line and regularly we would have an eye on the sun as it climbed above the ridges to eventually begin thawing the frozen grass that felt like razor blades against our equally chilled bare legs. Having very much shorter sunshine hours saw us begin chopping at about 9:00 am and then cease to head back to camp around 3:30pm or so. Our meal breaks were eleven-ish and then around one thirty, occasions for which we'd fell a sturdy bare trunked bit of scrub uphill, leaving the cut end resting on its high stump, creating a "bench" to sit on as we drank from our hot flasks, rather than planting one's bum down onto the snow. That could well cause one to get chilblains on parts where it's not at all pleasant to have chilblains!

As with any task, I suspect, there were incidents that could well have been rather serious, but fortunately proved to be far more hilarious instead. One such incident occurred during a tea break, as described above. Joe had sat a bowl on his lap and then poured very hot soup into it. Re-capping his flask he upended the bowl of scolding soup causing a very rapid reaction. Standing up and quickly shedding his pants he began packing hands full of snow around the burned areas. Certainly a practical thing to do under the circumstances, however to watch such an event without roaring with laughter, was something I found impossible to achieve. On another occasion, Joe had managed to push his way in underneath a solitary growing bush that was situated near the edge of a small bluff. There was maybe two or three metre drop to the steeply sloping hillside below it, and I was keeping an eye on him at the time, but when the bush rolled over the bank, to continue tumbling down the hill, only the chainsaw and a pall of smoke from it, were left beside the stump where the bush had been. Entangled within the bush, Joe had travelled unharmed but somewhat shaken, about twenty metres downhill before coming to a halt. His comments about my mirth were not suitable to record in print here!

While it didn't happen on site, as it were, one of my enduring memories that still brings a smile to my face occurred when we were seeking payment. Instead of paying us by cheque when each contract was completed, the owner would write us an "authority to pay" slip which we needed to present at a Farmer's Co-op office in the nearest township, about twenty miles away. There we would be paid in cash. Joe, Lill, and I all wore garments suitable for the climate and conditions we were living in. That was plaid woollen shirts, heavy boots, shorts or jeans, covered by heavy woollen jackets for "better" occasions. Joe and I also had grown quite bushy beards, which in that era were not very often seen around civilisation. Another part of the general psyche of the times was the fear of "Reds under the Beds", paranoia about Russian spies in the country. Given all of that, when we three walked into the large open space office, we attracted stares from behind every desk spread around the room until finally a pimply faced lad, whom I took to be the junior there, nervously approached to enquire what we wanted. Being the sensitive chap I am, putting on my deepest, gruffest voice I said; "Aghhhh, komarad! Ve ist lookink for ze Roshin embazzy!" Poor little bugger just stood there going scarlet faced and I thought he'd pee his pants, so promptly requested he cash our payslip, a sum larger than he earned in several weeks. On subsequent visits we received prompt and courteous attention.

Throughout our first day at the task I swung an axe, clearing smaller stuff that the chainsaw was unsuitable to cut. The following morning I fronted up to the patch to continue, but when I swung the axe it flew rather gracefully through the air and disappeared amongst the bushes. My hands, sore and swollen from the unaccustomed work, had been unable to grip the handle tightly enough to retain it! Seeing it happen, Joe made the rather laconic quip; "before you swing that bloody thing again, tell me so I can go home!" Fortunately we both quickly became proficient at the task in hand and during that winter we cleared an area which the owner had budgeted to have done over two winters, so he was very pleased and we had earned ourselves a very fat wad of notes. For me, the bounty was very beneficial as I was contemplating presenting a diamond ring to an attractive lass who had captured my attention.

However that's another very much longer story which may, or more likely will not, be told.

The Black Wok
Angela Bischof- Joseph

Chan was a pretty Singaporean Chinese woman still in the honeymoon period of marriage. Trained as a nurse, she was my colleague and professional mentor in my consolidation year as a qualified nurse. Chan was even-tempered and good at her job. Even though the shift may be one from hell, she always had time for me, and we often shared a laugh.

"What's the matter, Chan? I asked her one afternoon. "You don't look happy today?"

She looked at me and smiled a half-hearted smile.

"I'll tell you when we have some downtime." She replied. At the tea break, she poured her heart out to me.

"My mother in law, I can't wait to see the back of her." Chan's hands were fists.

"Why?" I asked her.

"She told me that I was lazy and needed to take more care of my pots and pans!"

Chan's mother-in-law had come for a short stay. She was an old-school Chinese woman from a village in middle China resettling in Singapore with her husband some thirty years ago. She is still dressed in traditional Chinese clothes, consisting of a samfoo which has black baggy trousers and a blue top with a high collar and fabric buttons running down the left. Chan's husband was born and bred in Singapore. His mother had been widowed recently and comes to stay with Chan and her son periodically. Her Mother-in-law had kept her Chinese traditional culture and was a fantastic cook. She spent most of her time in the kitchen preparing the day's meals and used all of Chan's kitchen equipment.

"She complained to my husband that the pan was so dirty that it was black in and out! She did not realise that it was a non-stick pan and my husband had only just bought it for my birthday. My husband did not say anything. He did not want to upset his mother, Chan moaned.

"I decided to do some cooking last night and could not find my new pan. When I asked her where it was, my Mother-in-law gave it to me from the backyard. She said she had cleaned it for me and looked very pleased with herself. I placed the pan on the stove and lifted the lid. To my horror, it was shining white inside. My Mother-in-law had scrubbed every bit of non-stick coating off the pan! It was down to the raw aluminium. I was lost for words," Chan said.

Chan looked like she was close to tears. We were in the 1980s, and non-stick pans were a new invention. Not many homes could boast of owning the still expensive item.

"What did you do?" I asked her.

"I complained to my husband and showed him the pan. He laughed, but I am raving mad!" she replied.

We returned to work when tea break was over, and nothing more was said about it. I asked Chan about it the next time I met her at work. She seemed like her old self.

"Well, hubby told his mother about the new invention of non-stick pans. She did not say anything and went back to her home the next day."

"And the pan?" I inquired.

"That went home with her too, and hubby bought a new one for me. I think it will be a while before she comes for a visit!"

Forgiveness
Tatiana Petrovsky

Headlights flaring through
cold glass walls, metallic clunking
of doors slamming shut.
Revving of motor, car drives off
she startles at the muted crunching of
footsteps on the white quartz gravel.

Door opens, ice-laced air
swirls in sneaking into
every warm corner.
Shoeless, shoulders hunched
wrapped in a dark coat,
he beseeches her with
black brigand eyes.
Rue and regret exudes
from his pores.

She opens her arms
'Dostoevsky man!'
Pleased with the epitaph he
embraces her longing.
His coat reeks of unspeakable
oppression and grief.
She touches the faint stubble
on his sunken cheeks,
tentative fingertips tracing
the gouges and gashes of
his self-imposed exile.

She knows not to question his crime
choice of punishment
or why he has appeared now-
tonight is for reliving.
No words are spoken -
forgiveness folds around them,
creating a comforting cacoon.

Together they dance
to tunes of remembrance
until the morning breaks.

Winter of the Heart
Kathleen Bentley

The four winds blow
    According to the season.
    Snow blankets the landscape,
    The rivers are frozen,
        As is my heart.

    Seasons change. The sun shines.
And now the snow melts,
    The rivers flow again.
    Soon we shall be together,
        I await that day.

The Nut
Pete Stratford

Volcanic rumblings marked your birth
as you erupt' from Mother Earth
with primal moans and sulphurous boom
emerging from within her womb.
While claiming land around your own
you raised a smoking, ashen cone
within your throat, still heated more
flowed molten magma - liquid core.
Did eyes witness your birth, or no
as night was lit with fire aglow?
And from above projectiles streamed
spewed up by belching gas and steam.
Eventually your anger quelled
then magma in your throat slow gelled
becoming rock – solidified
'neath ashen cone, but deep inside
aeons cooling, out of sight
forming dense, hard dolerite.
Before man's feet your slopes had roamed
assaulting waves had crashed and foamed
while against your flanks raged storm and squalls
in vain they battered your steep walls.
Harsh elements against you railed
as weather scorched, then froze, and flailed
eroding off your coat of ash
until against bare rock it thrashed.
Impervious you seem to be
to now stand proud 'gainst sky and sea.
Your crest of tussock and scrubby weed
covering sites where sea birds breed
their chicks providing man with meat
long before came white man's fleet.
On their arrival, they, with glee
built a village on your lee.
Far grander names may suit you, but
you're simply known as The Nut.

The Delivery
Kathleen Bentley

I quivered, my eyes devouring the carton.
Hands shaking I picked up the sharp knife.
I examined the knife.
I examined the carton.
Slashing through the tape which sealed it –
My anxiety knew no bounds.

My breathing was rapid. My heart pounded.
The moment of truth, the revelation.
I closed my eyes, drew breath.
Slowly I opened the box,
Folding back the cardboard flaps.
Crumpled brown paper slid to the floor.

My fingers shook. I reached into the carton.
Slowly I fingered the contents.
The colours were so bright.
The lettering blinding.
I pulled out the first one. I was amazed.

I was overcome with emotion. Was this real?
From scribbles to such professionalism?
Yes, it was *really* real!
Yes, it was the end product.
Of eighteen months toil, finished at last.
I emptied the carton revealing –   MY NOVEL IN PRINT!

The Poems Don't Love Us Anymore
Marilyn Arnold

• *Leonard Cohen (title plus other lines); Mary Oliver, Sylvia Plath, T.S. Eliot, Pablo Neruda, Helga Jermy (Tas).*

A person wants to stand in a happy place, in a poem.
My hours are married to shadow.
The moon has lost her memory, while
the sad wind goes slaughtering butterflies.
A poem should always have birds in it.

All the long-gone darlings, they
dissolve the floors of memory.
This is to inform you that I've already turned to clay.
One day we will visit the graves of the poets…
A poem should always have birds in it,

something with the wings of a bird,
something of anguish and oblivion.
The world is all forgetting, and the heart
is a rage of directions.
What branches grow out of this stony rubbish?
A poem should always have birds in it.

A Contorted Comedy
Anne Layton-Bennett

Am I the only one
in awe
and struggling to wrap
my mind
and my mouth
around names full of
'z's
and 'x's, 'v's, and 'y's
but hardly any vowels

I watch in admiration
as a man, an actor,
a stand-up comic
who, a short time ago,
trod the boards
for laughs

He now dominates
a larger stage
giving the performance
of his life
and that might cost him
his life
because this show's no comedy

it's tragic compelling theatre
that horrifies, thrills and inspires
a world and a population
too long starved
of heroes, leaders
and hope

The Aftermath
Jennie Herrera

The sudden swift and thrusting green;
Sun catching shining splashes,
Scudding rough and ragged cloud overhead,
    like a bed left rumpled.
A world of rain gauges
      and long discussions
                outside the local store,
And new hope for the coming season.
Did you? and How much? and
              Haven't seen the like
    and Don't know when we last …
There's nothing like rain to make neighbours talk.

Bridgewater
Adam Stokell

Froth,
milky swirls of you
hate to think what,
malingering Derwent's edge,
shallows, rocks.
A little early in the riverside
track to stop and sulk, a little rich –
your rusted-on frustration.
A Welcome Swallow's switchback
cuts between your standstill
and the water doing its level best:
read beyond the introduction.
Middle distance might become
your friend as you resume the track.
A bend hemmed by rushes, then
an epic Derwent
spreads wide as a year.
Weather all the time
novembering, estuarine.
The river you are could do
with a swig of rain,
a bite of wind. Look:
there must be hundreds
of black swans flecking
that slow bluegrey spread;
some float closer,
making nurseries of the rushes;
grey cygnets learning to game
this world of Derwent,
all its snakes and ladders,
all its spilt industrial milk.

Ecological Ramifications of Globalisation
Allan Jamieson

In 2001, I attended a pulp and paper conference in Japan, where I met a Japanese person who obviously delighted in playing around with words. This hobby might run in his family, as his son was about to go to England to further his education: The son already had a PhD in English Literature.

In conversation, however, the man mentioned that he was recently in London where he saw the Queen departing from Buckingham Palace on some ceremonial occasion and he was very bemused by the behaviour of the pigeons after she passed by the place where he had been standing.

As some sort of kindred spirit in the word arena, I took it upon myself to compose a short story on the subject and I said that I would send it to him. What follows was written over the space of the following two days as I travelled in Japan.

====== ====== ======

P1: I haven't slept for two nights, ever since I got a letter from my cousin in Australia.

P2: Ah, the ever-reliable Pigeon Post! Apart from that unfortunate bird that didn't get through the hail of bullets at the end of World War I, that is.

P1: You mean the pigeon that didn't get his message to a British regiment to tell them of the Armistice, so they fought on for three more days?

P2: None other. I always say they should erect a statue to commemorate that bird.

P1: Yeah, you're right; a statue of a pigeon that people could sit on. I hear that anthrax has stopped the U.S. Mail. So much for their much-vaunted slogan – "Neither snow nor rain nor heat nor gloom of night."

P2: Shit on, did you say?

P1: Sit on – shit on, whatever takes your fancy.

P2: Anyway, you were saying?

P1: My cousin wrote that, the other night while he was asleep on a branch of a big tree, the branch snapped off and crashed to the ground.

P2: You're kidding!

P1: No, I'm sure it happened. Eucalypt trees are well-known for dropping their branches. "You can imagine," he wrote, "the cacophonous noise that went on for several minutes while us twenty birds tried to disentangle ourselves from a mess of leaves and twigs in total darkness, still startled and only half awake." Apparently the cockatoos at the outer end had the easiest task, but you wouldn't know from the noise *they* made. Well, that gave me quite a stir that did. I couldn't sleep on the *Golden Hinde* like I normally do. I kept imagining what would happen if it suddenly sank.

P2: So?

P1: I've stayed on the ground the last two nights.

P2: What? And risk being pounced on by a cat or pissed on by a dog? No, I'd rather take the chance of Drake's ship capsizing. Besides, it wouldn't suddenly go under!

P1: Oh yeah? It's been known to happen.

P2: The *Golden Hinde*?

P1: No, I mean other so-called permanent structures.

P2: Name one.

P1: The Berlin Wall.

P2: That didn't come down over night!

P1: Tell that to the Germans. Part of it did!

P2: Well, anyway, your ship's mast is safe.

P1: I'm not so sure. I reckon only as long as Royalty survives.

P2: Explain!

P1: Australia.

P2: What?

P1: Thin end of the wedge, I reckon. My cousin wrote that Australians are gearing up for another referendum to become a republic. And what's Royalty without the Empire? Once Australia goes, can New Zealand, etc. be far behind? Soon there will be just us and India.

P2: I thought all the Indians were in London.

P1: They will be, they will be, but apparently there are still some buses in India.

P2: Anyway, what has all this to do with the imminent collapse of your roosting place?

P1: Simple! The Queen – or King Charlie – won't go without a fight, so there'll be a revolution. Old Drake was the darling of Queen Bess, so his ship will be a symbolic target that the masses will go for early on.

P2: Never mind. If Royalty goes, so do us pigeons. We have a hard enough time whenever the Queen goes to Balmoral, but with no Queen, there'll be no food.

P1: You're right! I hadn't thought of that. No Queen, no Horse Guards and no horses. And no horse shit – jam-packed with No. 1 grade corn for us pigeons to eat. We'll starve within days. We'll die.

P2: Bloody Australians!

Shackles of Conformity
Donna-Marie Koopman

My gypsy soul bids me break loose
the shackles of conformity.
Free me from my self-made prison
urged on me by society.
Then shall I mount the wild free spirit
lying long dormant in me,
and ride the forbidden plains of truth
that we are not to see.
I shall not harness my steed with rein or saddle,
for he goes where I too go.
Beyond the border of normality
seeking how and why,
the reason we would know.
I shall not wear your garments fine
or breathe in your breath of prejudice.
Nor close my eyes to your wars and dying
and accept it like the rest.
Though I will try and understand
and love you for all your frailties.
For you have not dreamt my dreams,
touched the stars,
or ridden the wind like me.
I shall ride the winds of question
even though I die.
Even though I die
I still may not find the answer to this life,
though I have tried.

In the Blink of an Eye
Allan Jamieson

In 2015, I was staying in a large hotel in Dafeng, a port city north of Shanghai. Having an hour to kill before finding the way to a banquet room for a business meeting and evening meal, I turned on the TV in my room and "channel surfed" among the dozens of stations.

At one point, the screen filled with the view of a large, open town square somewhere in China and the camera was in a fixed position upon a pole so it provided continuous monitoring of the goings-on in this area. People and cars and bicycles were going hither and yon. Near the right-hand edge of the screen, I could see a footpath and a couple of cars were parked alongside; the one closest to the camera was a large black SUV.

Two little girls suddenly ran across the footpath and onto the road, in front of the SUV. The older girl was leading; seemingly trying to get the smaller one to hurry up, but the small one stopped, turned and ran back, stooping down in front of the SUV to pick up whatever it was that she had dropped. At that very moment, the driver of the SUV chose to pull out from the kerb – over the little girl.

Shocked, I immediately changed channel.

Until now (25 May 2022), I had never revealed this scene in any form to anyone.

Tasmanian Symphony
Graeme Hetherington

Wind maddening the trees, by turn
Howling and sighing through for days,
Causes me to regress, relive

The horrors of Van Diemen's Land,
The bark flayed off the trunks like skin
From convicts' backs, and jigging limbs

Are they hanged, scurrying leaves lost,
Aimless, anathematized souls
With no resting place to be found,

Blacks keening for murdered kin, their
Dispossession, this symphony's
Fortissimo notes, crescendos,

Colonial leitmotif in
A composition I conduct,
Interpreted according to

A dismal English heritage
Scored ineradicably as
The haunting music of my mind.

Aunt Lucy's Final Wish
Andrea McMahon

Aunt Lucy had one final wish. By Christmas the sickness had spread through her bones so that she had to sit in a chair all day. This was not at all like Aunt Lucy, whose favourite thing was walking up mountains with a heavy pack on her back. And that's the reason we're on a holiday to Maria Island – because my mum says you can't deny a dying person their final wish, even if the business of carrying it out might kill you too. Aunt Lucy has been cremated, and what's left of her – her ashes – is in a jar in mum's backpack. Aunt Lucy wanted her ashes scattered from the top of the highest mountain on the island. It's a three-hour walk to the top, but Mum thinks I'll be able to do it.

My big sister Taylor says she's not going to do it, and that Aunt Lucy isn't going to care, or even know about it, for that matter. My brother Andy wanted to go up straight away, but Mum told him not to be ridiculous, we're going in the morning after we've had a good night's sleep. Taylor told Mum that she was being ridiculous if she thought any of us were going to get a good night's sleep in the old Penitentiary. The Penitentiary is where the convicts slept in the old days when Maria Island was a jail. Can't you hear them screaming? Taylor said to me. But I can't, and I'm not going to either. Because there's no such thing as ghosts.

My brother Andy is upset because he wanted to sleep in a tent. Andy is a nature freak, and I mean that. He loves everything about nature, especially birds. He's brought his binoculars and his guidebook and his notebook and his camera and we're all sick of hearing about the forty-spotted pardalote and the masked owl and the Cape Barren goose. Andy is under strict instructions not to wander off. This is because sometimes he wanders off and forgets to return, and then we have to send out a search party.

We went on a walk to the painted cliffs after lunch. Taylor refused to come. She lay on her bed and listened to music with her headphones on, which Dad reckons will end up getting fused to her ears. On the way we had to look out for the forty-spotted pardalote, which meant walking quietly a long way behind Andy. He found them, twittering in the bushes, and spent a lot of time staring at them through his binoculars. He was very excited, but I don't know why. It's just a small bird with spots. After that we got to climb over the painted cliffs which are all different coloured stripes and patterns. Now that was fun.

We went on another walk after tea, this time in the dark to search for the masked owl. We didn't see one though, and Andy threw a tantrum when Dad said we had to go back to get an early night for our big walk tomorrow. Dad said that in his own way Andy is as difficult as Taylor.

I can't get to sleep in the Penitentiary, not that I'm scared of ghosts or anything. So that's why I hear Andy get up. I ask him what he's doing and he says he's going for a pee. I say I'll come too and he gets annoyed and tells me to go back to bed. That's when I know he's going looking for the masked owl. I know Andy might forget to come back, so I'm going with him. Taylor doesn't wake up – she must've been tired from listening to music all day.

Outside there is a full moon and no wind at all. We walk down a rocky track, moonlight shining on our faces. Andy hears an owl and turns off up a hill. It's hard work keeping up. We're standing still, listening carefully, when the moon disappears behind a huge cloud. It's dark.

Very dark.

Andy searches for his torch, but it isn't in his backpack. In the bush at night there are noises.

Thumps, bumps, rustles, shrieks. Lots of shrieks.

'Where's the track?' I ask, but Andy doesn't reply. I scream and grab onto him as something thumps by close to us.

'It's only a wallaby,' says Andy. 'Be quiet or you'll scare off the owls.'

'I don't care about your stupid owls,' I say. I'm crying now. Just a little bit. I scream again when I see a light in the distance. I know it's coming our way. I think of all those convicts, all the robbers and murderers, and I know they're coming for me. I scream again as the light gets closer and closer.

But then I hear a familiar voice.

'You're so in trouble, nature freak.' Taylor has her arm around me now. I feel better. We walk slowly back to the Penitentiary. Taylor holds my hand all the way. We see torches as we approach. I hear Andy groan. He knows he's in big trouble.

'This is your fault, Will. If you hadn't followed me and then kept screaming everything would've been all right.'

'Except you would've probably fallen off a cliff,' Taylor says, squeezing my shoulder.

When we get back Taylor speaks first.

'We're feeling sick. You poisoned us with those disgusting sausages we had for tea,' she says. 'I won't be able to climb that stupid mountain tomorrow. We'll have to go home early.'

I could see Dad looking suspiciously at Andy's backpack.

'Get back to bed right now,' he says in his serious voice. 'We don't want to keep Aunt Lucy waiting tomorrow.'

As I enter the door of the Penitentiary I hear him say to Andy, 'I'll be having a word with you tomorrow, young man.'

As I'm drifting off to sleep I think about Aunt Lucy and I think about Taylor searching for us in the dark. Aunt Lucy would've been proud.

The Idol
Leigh Swinbourne

Dianne had often envisaged leaving Griff, when he thoughtlessly upset her or for some reason things weren't going right between them, although never seriously, it was just a kind of escape valve, one of many in dealing with a long-term relationship. But when he, right out of the blue, got up and left her, she was totally blindsided. Gobsmacked.

An 'unplanned leave' day manically scouring the house top to bottom—skirting boards, windowsills, kitchen pantry, never had it been this clean—she then wandered back out into her well-ordered well-bordered world in an uncomprehending daze, knocking against the furniture, tripping on the footpath, forgetting routine work duties. It was a kind of grief she realised, not grief like an actual death, but still, here was a metaphoric death, a genuine loss, and through that daze Dianne gradually began to see more clearly how she was mourning not so much for Griff and what they had had together, but more for what they might have had that never eventuated.

For, in truth, particularly recently, the relationship had become stale, threadbare, she couldn't even remember the last time they'd had sex, they hardly spoke to one another, even went separately to the cinema, once their big mutual passion. They had lost the knack of intimacy. But still, never she could have foreseen her and Griff, Griff and her, being apart, simply because they had been so long together.

In fact, for over half her life. Dianne was now forty-two. She had met Griff aged eighteen at a student party; they were both Film Majors, serious cinephiles, and they had chatted on till dawn. But they were good friends before they were lovers, in a group household, and maybe in some way this lay at the root of it, for there had never been the unuttered hope and blazing spark, just cohabitation with sex then thrown in. So they had never taken the thing as seriously as they might, invested what they should; always there was this idea, lurking unseen, that each was free to go their own way if and when they chose, although neither of them had, until now. And just as nothing in particular had engendered the relationship, there also seemed to be no outstanding reason or any reason at all, for Griff's departure.

He had left a note, maddeningly brief, he had ever been a man of few words, like many men, unlike herself, and actually this was a gender novelty Dianne had always found attractive, natural taciturnity, which she, probably falsely, interpreted as self-possession. Then again, it was a trait that obviously might (and did) cause problems in a relationship. On to the final problem, his absence, Griff characteristically enigmatic: 'Time to move on for me. Sorry Di. I've taken a job in Adelaide.' Adelaide? He'd never been there in his life, well far as she knew.

All her calls went to message bank, her texts, emails, all unanswered, and then she stopped. Oddly, they had never discussed marriage or children, things that might have bonded them more. Why? She never had the guts is why, suspecting, worrying, that either of these prospects would push him away. Now he was away anyway, and it was too late for her to have a family. She could probably find another partner, she was still slim and attractive, she knew, but one big possibility of life for her had inadvertently slipped by. When she dwelt on this anger boiled up, at him, but also at herself. She had spent, wasted, over half her life with a man she had maybe never really loved—she wasn't entirely sure on this point—in a manifestly unequal relationship she had nevertheless taken completely for granted. Now she had nothing.

Not even property. They had always rented, it was another unspoken feature of the 'deal', the no-real-ties, she'll-be-right, we can live in a better place, dine at smart restaurants, buy nice clothes, travel, and anyway we have one another, it's enough. Obviously not. Dianne felt totally hollowed out, angry, betrayed, all those things, but of course, she had let herself into this, gone along for the ride. She had made her bed and now had to lie in it, by herself.

And that was another weird thing: now that she could no longer have sex with Griff, she wanted it, needed it. Probably for comfort or self-esteem. She began recalling their various sexual encounters and habits down the years; idling at work or waiting at the bus-stop defunct erotic images would pop into her mind. Then she started imagining Griff having sex with other women. She couldn't see the other women, or woman, only Griff, his moves which she knew so intimately, what they had enacted together, which surely had to be more powerful and meaningful than with this other woman. Why? No reason. Nonsense. Well at least she'd shifted from herself to someone else, a progression of sorts. Or was it? Most likely he was with no-one. It was all crazy.

In the streets she caught herself looking at couples. They seemed to be everywhere. Where had they all come from? Better to stay home. But as she shuffled around the empty house, doing this, doing that, dishes, washing, dusting, she'd forget Griff wasn't there, set two plates, make space in the wardrobe, avoid playing music he didn't like. Then she'd catch herself and would have to sit down and claw back. He was present, he was absent. Like a phantom limb; part of her had been lopped off but her brain hadn't fully processed this and was still registering response. Or she was an actor that had not learnt her updated role and had been caught 'going through the motions', that shop-worn phrase, how apt it was.

One positive, sort of: he had walked out leaving pretty much all their possessions, taken his clothes and that was it. He'd organized his move the weekend she was in Launceston for her mother's birthday, planned it all in advance, well he had to if he was going to skedaddle without so much as a word, and a job and all. The books, CDs, DVDs, the lounge suite, the bloody bed, presumably it was now all hers. But of course it all reminded her of him. He'd got rid of her but she couldn't get rid of him.

'He left you his stuff as well?'

This was Marianne, her oldest friend, going back to Kinder, who Dianne had always suspected of having a thing for Griff, and was no doubt enjoying some schadenfreude amongst her genuine sympathy. She was fine, rock-solid husband, good earner, bit dull, played golf every Saturday, but still, around, mostly, plus three bonny boys, five, three, two. Who this Saturday morning (Richard on the green), were proving quite a handful in their different ways. Would she really have been up for this? But boys are always a problem. Or, the problem.

'Yeah, I mean it's all mixed up with mine. We shared everything. There's a heap of junk in the basement.'

'Basement? Can you still afford the rent here?'

'Couple of months, then I'm going to have to move.'

'Okay Di, you need to go through this stuff and work out what you want and start throwing the rest out. You need to purge.

First step in making a new start: getting your shit together. Then you move. Then you find another man.'

'I don't know if I want another man. Certainly not for a while. The other though, yes, you're right. I do need to tackle it. I'll start this weekend.'

'That's my Di.'

Yes, she definitely missed his physical presence. One big reason Dianne had hooked up with Griff originally was that he was so damn attractive. All her girlfriends had mooned after him, so that when he started paying her attention, she felt he was too good an opportunity to pass up. Then she became addicted.

She remembered how she had marvelled at his long sleek form, his beautiful hands and back and thighs that belonged just to her. After a while she felt at the mercy of his face and body. Which was the first step in engendering a sense of inequality between them, so that gradually, casually, also very naturally it seemed—although she could and did note it as it was occurring—he began to dominate her. Not sexually, but personally. Dianne felt powerless to prevent it, she was not experienced enough, or strong enough. Griff was the original adored spoilt child, charismatic and confident, always with the knack of knowing the right thing to do or say. His whole life all the people he had known—parents, teachers, friends—had deferred to him, and therefore so must she. His looks, and the rest, were an amour she could not crack.

Dianne had chafed at the unfairness, but came to see that these were the only terms on which the relationship could survive, because it was how all Griff's relationships had evolved—never had he known anything different. If she wanted him, she must accept them. So it went on. In everything his beauty and self-possession gave him the advantage. Her present jealous fantasies were probably founded on the truth that Griff would have no problem whatever picking up a much younger partner and having the family he was not going to have with her.

'What you need is three piles: things you want, things you don't, and undecided.'

Why was she listening to this?

'Tell me Marianne, do you think there might have been another woman?

'Nothing I ever heard of, he was a dish, still is, I guess. You know, honestly, I don't think he was the type.'

As soon as she heard her friend say this, Dianne knew it was right. The women were no doubt there, as opportunity presented, but infidelity would have been too complicated, too fraught for Griff, too much effort all round for the reward. He liked a simple life, no pressures, no worries. If he wanted sex he could always screw her, not that, generally speaking, he was particularly motivated. A 'once-a-week' man at most. More often than not Dianne had to initiate proceedings. But still, there must have been something she wasn't seeing.

Two coffees, boys' noise, and Marianne's chatter were doing her in. She needed to disengage. She pleaded a headache and took off on a long looping walk through Wentworth Park, which Marianne's faux-mansion fronted. Good earner hubbie.

Dianne had not been in this park since she couldn't remember. Wild fires were presently burning beyond Mount Wellington down in the Huon valley—there had been weeks of hot dry days—and the air was infused with smoke. The summer light caught all the particles, making it like an unnaturally bright dusk when it was midday. The surface of the river was a sun-illumined turquoise backed by a scree of smoke. Everything was unreal. Everywhere was a strange vacancy. Life had lost a tension. She felt insubstantial. She was responsible only for herself. There were no demands. She could do anything, it didn't matter, nothing seemed to matter. Griff's going had left this great slack gap. Did she need to fill it? She didn't feel the need.

The basement, Saturday night. She'd bought takeaway, butter chicken, gobbled it down, all that salt and grease, and was sitting alone in silence in the empty living-room enjoying one of Griff's fine cold Rieslings. This had come from the basement. Of course she would keep all the wine, although it would take her a lifetime to get through it. Boxes of wine, boxes of God-knows-what. How had they accumulated all that stuff? Dianne felt exhausted just thinking about it but, yes, she would make a start tomorrow. What else was she going to do?

Alone in the silence and the space she sipped her wine.

Truth was, right now she wasn't feeling that bad. Solitude rather than loneliness. In the madly interconnected world everyone lived these days, solitude had been given short shrift. If you weren't constantly occupied you were missing out, a loser. This was horseshit. Solitude used to be prized. You would need to cultivate it a bit, but still, even at this early stage Dianne could see how it might become deeply satisfying. And silence, she listened to it, the silence of the large empty room. It was a natural companion to solitude.

It was a pity to have to ditch the house. Dianne had a good job—Film Conservator at the State Library—a job she loved and which would probably see her out, but she couldn't afford this, a stately sandstone Georgian in South Hobart, run down, mates rates, the owner an uncle of Griff's. But she could enjoy it for a while, the elegant high ceilings, regal proportions, they knew how to make 'em back then. On the other hand, it did represent the 'old' life. If she stayed here, the ghost of Griff, of their shared time, would no doubt haunt and oppress her. And it was too big for one, even leaving aside the cost, really too big for two; she needed something that would fit her better, fit her new life, whatever that would be. She would see out the lease, then go.

So, here she was, forty-two. She'd lived half her life, and half of that she was at present not so proud of. It was not the life she could and should have lived. Certain things, important things, had been foregone. But still, there was plenty of time ahead.

No partner, no kids, but even in the short term this opened out other prospects. She could binge on all those quality Netflix and Amazon series she'd never got around to, the whole television-as-the-new-cinematic-art-form thing. And as for film, there was vintage this, classic that, even old T.V. series, everything. Catch up on what had passed her by over the years, or re-watch what she loved. Go down the alphabet listings section by section: drama, comedy, adventure, thriller, foreign, horror, get totally film literate as she'd always wanted.

Or if she ever tired of film, which she couldn't imagine, she could read, say, Gibbon or Proust. She had always wanted to read Proust. Learn Beethoven's late quartets. Or learn an instrument herself. What about the cello. She loved the cello. If that proved too difficult she could sing. Join a choir. She had to work, but other than that she could do anything she liked. Which after years of Griff was a strange thought (although she could have done any of these while still with Griff). Or, of course, as Marianne said, because Marianne could imagine nothing else, she might meet another man. Or alternatively, she might do nothing at all. Sit in solitude, like the ancients.

But first she had to clean out the basement.

The basement was actually a cellar. The house, convict built, dating back to the 1820s, a heritage listed money pit (not that the uncle was splashing out), was originally owned by a wine and rum merchant, one of the early mountebanks of the Colony. She and Griff had lived here for well over a decade and the cellar inevitably had become a junk dump. What did they call it? De-cluttering. There was a whole industry, how-to books and everything. A right and wrong approach/method. Throwing out junk as a science.

Dianne had considered hiring a skip but there was simply too much for her to do it in one fell swoop. Little by little would be best. Chip away. It was Sunday morning; she was fresh, primed for action. As she grasped the iron knob handle on the solid slanting door to the stairs, she had a strange feeling of presentiment. Her skin prickled; someone stepping on her grave as her Gran used to say. Nerves on edge while descending the unsafe wooden slats into the low room, poorly illumined by a single bulb. Why? No reason. Cobwebs in her brain as well as the room. Work would soon dispel all that.

The wine boxes were clearly labelled and grouped together, so that was easy. They could be left for the while. But there were myriad other boxes and suitcases of all shapes and sizes scattered around in the gloom. She had a clutch of bin bags, yellow for keeps, black for not. Aside from the clothes, she needed to choose those things that were her, not Griff, which could tell her who she was without him. Re-define herself through what was previously shared.

Where to start? The suitcases would probably contain clothes which would be easiest to sort and carry. She took a deep musty breath and set to it with a vengeance, summoning up the manic energy with which she'd attacked the house the day after he'd left. Four hours later she was clogging the living room with her two piles, by far the larger that for St. Vinnies. She knew she also couldn't keep most of the clothes in the yellow bags. Maybe she could give them to relatives or friends or sell them at a market somewhere.

Dianne finished the suitcases, hauled them up too, and paused for a proper break, a sandwich and a cuppa. While she recouped, sanity struck. She didn't want to spend her entire Sunday doing this, there was no need. Another hour on the boxes and she would leave it till next weekend. More than enough up here already to further sort, and somehow disperse.

She plunged back in. Books, CDs, videos, photo albums, old crockery; this was all more labour intensive. She was nearing the end of her energies when she came across an odd wooden box with a lid, that seemed to have nothing in it but screwed-up tissue paper; but nestled deep within the paper was a solid oblong object the size of a forearm, that when unwrapped revealed itself as a stone carving. Dianne held it up in the murky light. It was a figure of a man, legs and torso foreshortened, with a long fierce scowling face. The weight of it seemed unnatural, as though it were denser than the stone from which it was carved.

She recognized it. From where? She looked and looked and slowly realization dawned. It seemed incredible, but the more she looked, the more certain she became.

Dianne had last seen this figure as part of a travelling exhibition, from the New York Metropolitan Museum no less, of pre-Colombian indigenous art. She remembered joking to Griff that this little man's face in some indefinable way resembled his own. When the exhibition had moved on from Hobart the item was missing. Although naturally the collection was insured, this incident was a major embarrassment at the time for her workplace, the State Library, which had hosted the collection en-route to Melbourne, and security was considerably upgraded as a result. This was what, six, seven years ago. And here it was, in her basement, in her hand, the missing artefact.

Griff had nicked it. Incredible! How? Why? She sat on her haunches for a while, dumbfounded, then carried the carving up into the clear light of the house. It looked undamaged, actually it looked in excellent condition for something so old, the features sharp and expressive. Dianne brought it into her study and placed it next to the computer. Ten minutes later she knew what it was: a funerary jade figurine from the Mezcala Culture in south-western

Mexico, circa 300-100 B.C.   And more incredibly, what it was worth: three-hundred-thousand American dollars on the open market. She stared at the figure in amazement and saw a distorted avatar of Griff staring cold-eyed back at her.   In mockery? Amusement? Wordless as ever.

'You're looking great. Taken off weight.'

'Actually, I think I've put on a couple of kilos.'

'Put on. Right. Anyway you're obviously thriving without him.   Tell you the honest truth, never wanted you to know, obviously, but I didn't really like Griff much, too up himself and all that.'

This was codswallop. Marianne had been totally charmed like everyone.

'Marianne, there's something I wanted to sound you out on.'

'What are friends for.'

'When I was going through the stuff in the basement, I found something that I'm pretty sure Griff stole.'

'Stole? Are you sure? What is it?'

'I can't tell you, it's nothing really important. But I'm not too sure what to do about it.'

'Well, I guess you should return it.'

'I can't.'

'Why?'

'Because it's stolen.'

'I would have thought that would be the reason to return it.'

'I'm worried if I return it, Griff might be charged. Or if he denies any knowledge, I might be. And if that happens I might lose my job. And there's something else bothering me.'

'Yes?'

Marianne was clearly captivated here.

'Why didn't Griff take it with him? What it is, he could hardly have forgotten it.'

'Maybe he felt embarrassed, guilty at what he had done, and couldn't handle keeping it.'

'If that was the case he could have thrown it away or left it anonymously somewhere. No, I think he wanted me to find it.'

'Are you sure?'

'There's no other logical explanation.'

'But why? What is it?'

It had been a mistake to bring this up with Marianne, but Dianne had been bursting to discuss the business with someone, even in these ridiculously abstract terms.

'All I can say is, I really don't know what's been going on in his head. But if that was his plan, I guess in due course I'll find out.'

'Well Di, you know I'm always here to talk these things over.'

Dianne had been keeping the idol locked in a drawer, but after a while she considered this unnecessary. No-one knew she had the thing, save Griff. No-one visited her these days. Why not bring it out and enjoy it, give the little man some air after having been cooped up for so long.

She was well into the habit of the evening silences, just sitting alone after dinner in front of the fireplace doing absolutely nothing. It was March and the air was turning crisp. She began lighting the fire. She and Griff had always ignored it and used the heat-pump—organizing wood and cleaning the grate seemed too much effort—now Dianne seemed to have time in abundance, and the soft crackle of the flames was a fine accompaniment to the silence. She could sit there contentedly for hours.

It was dusk, the dishes were stacked, and she set the idol beside her on the coffee table next to her comfy fire-chair. The flames had settled down, just one large log burning sombrely. There was no internal light save from this, and as the external light gradually waned, as the shadows in the room around her shifted and deepened, the idol began to softly glow of its own accord. No doubt a feature of the jade. Finally, when it was completely dark outside, inside, the log and the idol held luminous conference.

Dianne held herself still, scarcely breathing. What did the idol represent? What properties had been invested in it by those ancient peoples? She fancied she could sense its totemic power. As the night-hours drifted on, she further fancied that she herself was drawing some kind of power from it. Just her, the log and the idol, and the spell of deep silence.

Each morning when she woke, she felt, knew, she had been dreaming about the idol, but she could never recall her dreams. Each night, night after night, she sat before the fire, autumn deepening to winter, all day-work forgotten, her and the fire and the idol, trying to think it through. Why had Griff wanted her to know about this? Why now, after all this time? What was he expecting from her? Was it some kind of test? Yes, surely, Griff had revealed this secret and shameful act of his—by this object that spoke of it, which also physically recalled him—and was giving her time, all the time she needed, all these long winter nights, to come to some kind of decision, concerning him, or concerning him and her.

Griff leaving the idol for her to discover was an act, but a passive act, that gave her a certain power over him, of possible betrayal. And if betrayal was not followed through then the business became a bond, like a sort of bond of thievery. The stolen idol bound them together, particularly since it was so valuable, and with the ongoing leverage of her knowledge of his original theft—a more serious crime than her complicity—yes, gave her a power she had never had in their relationship.

The stone glowed.

She remembered once coming across him staring at himself, half-dressed, in their full-length wardrobe mirror. He was absorbed and did not notice her. One odd thing: despite his beauty, and his casual use of it, Griff was not vain, not one of those men always trying to catch sight of themselves reflected elsewhere. This moment he looked at himself almost querulously, head tilted, as though he did not quite understand what he saw, dissatisfied too, she fancied. Maybe, Narcissus like, he had wished to disappear into his image, if not for Narcissus's reasons, but knew he could not. While she was with him, because of that image, Dianne had not been able to see this.

She regarded the idol, with its perverted Griff face. The idol spoke of another Griff; that's why he had taken it. He also could not work against his charisma, just like all the others, and he saw it was eventually going to wreck his life. He needed a strategy to counteract it. And maybe this other Griff could somehow provide this for him.

She rose from her chair, took the stone up in both her hands, and stared into its depths.

The idol was a statement of his love, and a test of hers. It could enable their relationship to change, and so endure. This was the source of its power, now flowing from it to her. At some point

Griff had grasped, as she now was doing, the agency of this strange talisman.

So finally, when through successive nightly deliberations Dianne had arrived at this poised, but equivocal point, one late-winter Saturday morning, after she had just lit the fire, there was a familiar knock on the front door. Heart in mouth, she raced over, hardly believing, but sure enough, there on the porch before her, a little thinner and worn, stood Griff.

There was something new in his handsome face, a subtlety, maybe a depth, that either had not been there before or, more likely, she had never noticed. Then a sudden rage possessed Dianne and with her clenched fist she struck him full in the mouth, a thing she had never done in her life. He took no evasive action, just stood there. She saw that she had pushed in one of his front teeth. He carefully positioned it back in place as the blood welled past his lips, and staunched the flow with the sleeve of his shirt. Dianne saw he had no luggage, not even a backpack. She looked down at her hand which was sore and skinned, throbbing. Griff also looked at it, then took it gently and wordlessly led her back into the house almost as though he'd never left.

She trailed wonderingly. Griff led Dianne directly to the idol beside her fire-chair. He picked it up and, still with her in hand, carried it back down to the basement. He carefully repacked the idol, now also smeared with blood, in its wrappings and its box, straightened, and took her hand once more. He led her back up to the fireplace, placed a chair next to hers, and sat there with her, her bloodied hand in his, dabbing his mouth from time to time and staring into the growing flames.

30 Domboshawa Road
Ant Dry

These days, 30 Domboshawa Road in Harare is a bird park, and a popular attraction for visitors, both local and foreign. You can google it if you like, it's called "Birds at Thirty."

It boasts a collection of hundreds of exotic birds, and visitors are free to wander around the various cages and marvel at the residents, who squawk and preen for the benefit of their guests.

There is a tearoom, and offices, and plenty of staff to cater to the needs of both residents and visitors.

Decades ago, 30 Domboshawa Road was my home. No bird park then, it was a sprawling home on eight acres with a tennis court, a pool, a jacuzzi, an outside bar in a thatched gazebo, and stabling for five horses who spent their days wandering freely in the paddocks.

We purchased the place for ten thousand pounds, sixty thousand US Dollars in cash wrapped up in a brown paper packet, and a few suitcases full of worthless Zimbabwe Dollars. The previous owner was desperate to leave, running from an accusation of money laundering, gun running, and being a supporter of the opposition party. He could not believe his luck that he would be able to secure some foreign currency on the sale. We both thought we had secured the deal of the century. We were both right.

We lived there for six years only, but it became one of the defining periods of our collective lives.

Friday nights at number 30 were especially good. They were tennis nights. They started off small but grew and eventually we would regularly have up to thirty people "playing" tennis. The "playing" is in inverted commas because only eight or so people actually played the game. The rest were there to escape reality for a while.

Preparations for the evening would start in the early afternoon when our gardener would collect wood and load it into a wheelbarrow ready for the barbeque (we called it a braai, back then). In the early evening he would lay the fire and light it so that by the time it came to cook, the coals would be perfect.

Our cook would prepare a range of salads, mostly home grown, as fresh vegetables were a luxury, seldom found in the shops.

The grooms would secure the horses in the stable block.

My wife would make sure the bar was stocked properly. She knew what everyone drank, and she made sure there was sufficient for everyone. There was never a shortage of alcohol in the shops. Some things are simply too important.

The guests would begin to trickle in at about five in the evening. They would arrive with plates of food and drinks. Some were dressed to play tennis, but most didn't bother. We would already be in the gazebo, and when they joined us the drinking would start.

In those days drink driving was not a crime; it was more of a national pastime. The police were too involved in intimidating and harassing members of the opposition party to be concerned about such trivial matters as the rules of the road. Consequently, no thought would be given to allocating a designated driver, or even to thinking about how anyone was going to make it home. We were there to drink, enjoy ourselves and dull the memories of the week, that was all there was to it.

The gazebo had a built-in stereo, and we had a large collection of music from the 70s and 80s, and it would be playing all evening. As the evening wore on, so the dancing would start, becoming wilder and more erratic as time moved on.

Our servants moved silently in and around us, collecting dirty glasses and plates and replenishing supplies.

The kids entertained themselves. They would fill up the jacuzzi, sometimes with bubble bath so dense that it was impossible to see anyone under the bubbles. Thank God no one drowned in all those years. They would move from the hot jacuzzi to the swimming pool and back, shrieking with delight. The girls would visit the horses and the boys would chase the girls.

We would turn off the power at the mains and run the property on generator power for the evening. The power supply was too erratic and weak, and we did not want to blow the tennis court lights by turning them on and off too often. Quite often there would be a general power cut while we were playing, but we would only notice when we could no longer see either our neighbour's houses or the streetlights. I did wonder at these times why we, as the only lighted place in the neighbourhood, were not invaded by the neighbours and passers-by, but guessed that the six-foot wall, the electric gate, the alarm beams, the razor wire, and the pack of dogs was probably sufficient to do the job.

More often than not my tennis partner for the evening would be Theresa, a friend of my wife's. She was blind in one eye, and very unfit, and her response to any ball that came within striking distance of her was to yell "yours" in my direction and wait for me to retrieve it. I got a lot of exercise playing with Theresa. We also had lots of fun.

The dogs thought that their job was to act as ball boys. They were wrong. Retrieving the ball from the dog meant that that ball's trajectory was temporarily impaired. A wet ball comes off the racket differently and sprays the receiver with spittle. Consequently, the dogs were chased by us, just as much as they chased the ball.

Jonathan and his family were regular attendees. He was a quiet, shy man, and a doctor. He would arrive exhausted and when asked, would grumble how most of the ailments of his patients were due to stress. By the end of the evening's drinking and frivolity, he had de-stressed sufficiently to tell some excellent jokes.

Lorraine and JJ were frequent visitors too. They had been tobacco farmers, whose farm had been invaded by war veterans. JJ had been sitting fixing his tractor when there came a tap on his shoulder. On looking up he saw the barrel of an AK47 an inch from his eyeball, while at the other end of the rifle stood a grinning man with a bandana around his head. He had been told he had 48 hours to leave the farm. He had protested, but had agreed quickly once the grinning man stated that he knew where JJ's daughters were. JJ was lucky. His neighbour, John Stevens, had been taken to the police station and shot dead in front of the indifferent police. Lorraine and JJ had moved into town, leaving their farm that they had nurtured from virgin bush to a prosperous workplace employing 200 staff. Curiously, on these evenings of tennis, they never spoke publicly of their ordeal, and could not be drawn out on it, but often Lorraine and my wife would disappear for a while and would re-join us, both red-eyed, but somehow more cheerful than they had been.

Theresa's husband Tim worked in Mozambique and flew back home every Friday. He was a lawyer, but couldn't practice in Zimbabwe, as he found it too difficult in a place where the law courts paid such little attention to the law, preferring to follow the rules laid down by whatever bullying official held the most sway at the time. Tim had found a job in Mozambique after a friend of his, defending a member of the opposition party from some trumped up charge, had been found dead in a car crash, coincidentally with a bullet hole through the middle of his forehead. Occasionally, after a few drinks Tim would speak of this incident, but his mumbling would become incoherent until eventually Theresa, weaving, would collect him and drive him home.

Friends of the kids would drift in and out, often aiming to collect people to take them to parties, and mostly staying with us instead. They would disappear inside, and play music, play computer games, and hold their own party. Sometimes they would spend the night, not wanting to go home to their parents, and we would find them in the morning, sprawled on the floor cuddling up to the dogs.

Our younger son Michael, eight years old when he started, would make chocolate brownies for everyone. These brownies became legend, and remain so to this day, so much so that when we reminisce with our friends and acquaintances about those tennis nights, they all without exception, firstly talk of the brownies with affection and awe, before mentioning anything else.

I sometimes wonder if those brownies were truly as good as everyone claims, or if the taste was imbued with the sense of freedom, relief, relaxation and love that number 30 exuded.

Living & Loving
Kathleen Bentley

We met in the autumn of our lives.
We were perfect for each other
Our cultures entwined
As did our minds.

Being old was just part of life,
Part of us and all that meant.
We lived, we loved, we shared
Our lives, our hearts, our souls.

We brought each other such joy,
An incredible ending to our days.
Love is the same, no matter what
Young people think – Love belongs to everyone.

We are approaching the end of life's journey –
We are older, weaker, frailer
But our love is just as passionate
Even if mostly in our heads!

We can still share the quiet moments –
Sitting reading together in the garden.
Our spirits soar when we are together
Walking our pathways through Life.

Thank you for the joys you have given me,
For accepting me without reservations,
For being quick to forgive and to forget
For being – well, just who you are.

Know that we shall see each again,
Not in this Life but the next.
Oh, what joy that will bring
   When I hold you and tell you how much you mean to me.

The Hunter of the Forest
Brenda Slavoff

We met in the forest
Where day kisses night
Joy and sorrow meet
Time light-footed as a deer ......

I was the deer
Swift dweller of the forest
Timid of heart
Nervously shy
I heard your steps
I felt your shadow
I saw your face
I touched your heart;

Carefully you wooed me
With soft gentle words
Warm loving words –
Oh why, kind stranger?
Caught by kindness
I would eat from your hand,
Entranced by love
I gazed into your eyes,
I trusted your voice
I worshipped your power
And above all others
I ran to you.....

Long hours we spent
Together in the forest
Earth and sky blessings
Peace and love shelter
You brought me bright presents
I taught you rich joy
You remembered your childhood
I forgot to be afraid;

Then sudden as a storm
Loud thunder awoke
And the hunter awakened
And took up the arrow,
You forgot who I was –
You forgot what had been –
And you brought me down
Transfixed to the ground
Pierced through the body
To the depth of my heart –

You have brought me down
Down at your feet
Pierced to the heart
With the hunter's arrow!
Oh why, kind stranger?
Oh why? Oh why?
I was true, I was loving,
I was strong, I was yours

Now by my side
Come stroke my head
While one last time
I gaze into your eyes
– Your trembling hand
Your frightened eyes –
My last faint cry
Oh why, why, why?

Sudden Illumination
Jake O'Mara

Electricity was a mystery to most older people in the 1960s, especially so where I grew up. Our rural district was "off the grid" meaning that, as with alcohol during prohibition, you either went without electricity or made your own. Making your own electricity required an engine, a generator and a sizeable bank of batteries.

Here's where we meet Ted, a local farmer not known for sharp intellect or finesse with things even slightly technical, but Ted does own a lighting plant. He lives a couple of miles from the shop-cum-garage and often finds reason to call in, but now the more observant souls note that Ted has not been seen for over a week. When he does show up, he parks his battered truck and makes a bee line for the garage. The garage adjoins the drive-through storage area for the shop and is run by Laurie. Laurie works alone, his budget doesn't run to paying wages.

Now Laurie is a mechanical prodigy, able to fix anything mechanical, electrical, or both, but the wowsers think his language is like his workshop, where everything, including the floor, is coated with a thick layer of dirt and sump-oil. Some – who "wouldn't say shit for a shilling" my dad reckoned – fear contamination with his filth, either literal or linguistic. But Laurie is a great raconteur and there are plenty of willing listeners, including me.

Laurie hears someone call his name and pokes his grease-smeared face out from under the bonnet of Bert Schinkel's old International truck. The caller is only a silhouette in the bright square of light from the garage door, like a saint in a stained-glass church window. But Laurie, who avoids all churches like the plague, recognises a familiar voice and calls out,

"Giday Ted! Haven't seen you for a while, wouldn't Maisie let you off the chain?" Only when the visitor is fully inside the building does Laurie realise that Ted has been in the wars. He has a black and partly closed eye, severe bruising on his neck, plus various partly healed cuts and burns on his arms and hands. And that is only the bits that Laurie can see.

"Holy smoke Ted, you look terrible!" Then, witty as ever, he adds, "…What's the other bloke look like?" But Ted never had much of a sense of humour, especially now. He looks at the floor and replies,

"Um, …I've been in 'ospital."

"Hospital! Did yer have a flamin' heart attack or somethin'?"

"Er …no, Maisie threw me a fiftieth birthday party."

"So there was a fight then?"

"No, it was all good, but people stayed late an' the lights were fadin' fast."

"Don't tell me Ted. You'd had a few drinks, decided to fix the hay baler from the inside 'an it started up." If Laurie expects a laugh at this, it doesn't come. Ted looks glum.

"No, I just went to bed, but first thing in th' mornin' I went out to the generator shed ter start the engine."

By now, Laurie's attention is fully focussed on Ted's story, and he is wondering what the hell could've caused all that damage. He begins to feel more kindly, almost fatherly, toward Ted than he ever expected to.

"Well, what happened?"

"I started the gen-set and went to do the milkin'." Laurie waits while Ted is lost in thought, reliving the mystery of it all.

"…When I came back from the factory I checked to see if the batteries were chargin' properly. I took the caps off, but it was too dark in me little shed to see if they was bubblin' like they're s'posed ta."

"So what did you do?" Laurie asks, suddenly afraid of what might be coming.

"I struck a match for light, an' that's all I remember."

"BLOODY HELL TED, THOSE BUBBLES ARE HYDROGEN, IT'LL EXPLODE!!"

"Well um, …Maisie heard a loud bang and came out to the shed. She says half the batteries were in pieces and I was on the floor."

Ted pauses, looks intently and seriously at the mechanic and says,

"Tell me Laurie, will batteries always do that?"

More Fallen than Standing
Susan Austin

Hot blood storms my torso,
bypassing hands
on this steep hike.
The long, grey, wet road stretches and veers.
Yellow lines scream at me
to stay the course.
Snow smirks from the verge –
you think you belong here!
There are more trees fallen than standing
and cloud shrouds us all.
Why did I think this was a good idea?
I try not to think of the beds that need stripping,
the shrubs that need clipping or
the groceries calling from the shelves.
I direct my focus to the sparse landscape,
the ghostly serenity,
the sensation of moving my body forwards,
step by crisp-snappy step
but the forest seems to abandon me
the more I walk towards it.
My calves aren't the only parts aching.

Confined (hind) Quarters
Pete Stratford

Adapted from an article, all efforts to identify the original author having been in vain.

Excited by the invitation to attend a wedding, where many of the respected gentry would also gather to celebrate the event, my dear wife insisted that she would require a new outfit for that occasion. So a few days later she returned from a well patronised store, aptly named Ladies of Style, laden with packages. Trying on her tailored shell-pink linen dress, with matching jacket and similarly colour matched accessories, she became aware that it was just a tad close fitting. However, with a month before the event she was determined to shed "a couple of pounds" and then it would be a perfect fit.

When the time came for us to travel to the town where the event was to be held, she discovered that she had in fact gained that couple of pounds. Never mind, a new girdle would rectify that little problem, so we duly called back to the Ladies of Style, en route to our destination. Knowing that a new, elastic sided girdle, size L, would be just what was required, and having insufficient time for a fitting, she emerged from the store clutching her $49.95 purchase nicely boxed and wrapped. Having stayed over-night at a motel near the old stone Catholic Church, we awoke to one of those days already uncomfortably warm, even before the sun was above the horizon. So, of course the process of getting ourselves all dressed up was delayed until there was only just sufficient time to do so.

Upon opening the box it was quickly discovered that while the container was marked "size L" the girdle was in fact labelled "S"! Too late for any exchanges, she puffed, squirmed, and contorted in her efforts to get into that garment, finally calling upon my assistance. With me, laughing uncontrollably while heaving either side of it, coupled with her own desperate efforts to redistribute parts of her anatomy, we eventually got her installed. Picture if you will, trying to shake 20lbs of potatoes into a 5lb sack. Then, snug within her girdle, the new outfit fitted rather well, although by then she felt that the pink didn't really go so well with her purple face, but we were ready to go.

Along the way to the church I became concerned at how she was looking and frequently asked if she was ok, because she was becoming rather watery eyed at that stage. She gasped that she was fine, adding that we men didn't understand or appreciate what women do to look good. Struggling not to laugh again, I dutifully drove on until we found a park in the church yard. Although I assisted her walking into the church, I was getting worried at the funny way she was breathing by then. Assuring me she was fine, and that I not make a fuss, because she knew wedding ceremonies at our own church take about thirty minutes, and we'd be outside again soon. Unfortunately this particular mass lasted for one hour, twenty three minutes and eight and a half seconds, as the priest blessed everything except that new girdle. Over on the other side of the church the brides' mother was in tears, as was my wife on our side, which caused a little old lady nearby to nudge her companion saying, "Oh look, she's so touched."

They were right about that, she'd never been touched so tightly in her life! She was whispering to me that her ankles were swelling, her knees had gone blue, and she'd lost all feeling from her hips. Meanwhile I had begun fanning her with one of her pink accessories, as sweat was beading on her face, at the same time still trying to comfort her, without drawing undue attention our way.

As soon as the priest pronounced the couple married and the wedding party began their way back up the aisle, she hobbled as quickly as she was able, supporting herself on my arm, as she squeezed into position behind the wedding group, like a "fifth bridesmaid," while I was still whispering if she would be alright, could she breathe, can I help, etc? Her gasped, "just get me out of here" added urgency to my quest to do just that. Eventually having hop-danced her all the way to our car, she promptly opened the front and rear passenger doors to almost touch the next car and thus partially screened from the eyes of both God and the crowd, squeezed her bruised and battered body out from that elastic torture chamber once and for all. Perhaps much like a butterfly emerging from its chrysalis, but nowhere near as graceful, as attempting one final little kick to free her foot from the offending garment, it catapulted directly beneath the car beside us. That was just too much for me, and doubled over with laughter I was quite unable to retrieve it from there. So we just got into our vehicle and drove away.

Over the years we have both speculated on the reactions of those devout parishioners as they arrived to attend morning mass next day and then finding that $49.95, bright pink, very badly stretched, small sized, elastic panelled girdle, on display in all its glory in the middle of their church parking area.

The Siren Song of Little Country Creeks
Jennie Herrera

She always said: Put on your boots.
Not—take care, don't forget the time,
Don't go too far—
Just boots. She knew—the compulsion.
When it rains, to follow, to pursue, unheeding,
The beginnings of gullies, long dry, years-long,
Becoming trickles, now streams, now rushing …

The way they turn a jumbled stone into waterfalls,
An incline to a gorge, then race away bending
Dry white grass so it seems to float on the rising tide,
Seed heads, streaming; swirling, making ripples …
The way banks cave and fall where cows have
Walked Indian file. Small tributaries joining in,
Clods melting away, great black cracks across the paddocks
Expanding, filling, a secret underworld glued over and gone.

The landscape changed within an hour of that first roll of thunder;
A landscape we thought we knew; and now we must re-acquaint—
These whirlpools, those wild daisies uprooted and forming dams
To hold water beetles and softened twigs; and with the first shaft
Of sun again there are dragonflies. Branches collect along
The fence lines, catch in barbed-wire, gather in nameless clots.

And the sound of boots sucking, squelching, sighing, drowning,
And squeals: Did you see that! Hey! Look at this! Wow, see
The way it bubbles in the bends! And old ironbark roots
Are left bare by the water's swirl. Little creeks, child-size creeks.
Places where the magic lingers; the metamorphosis of world
Into world … and back again. A few pools lingering in gullies.
Worth another traipse or not? … Put on your boots.

AUTHOR BIOGRAPHIES

MARILYN ARNOLD

Marilyn Arnold is a published Tasmanian writer and poet. She has been writing for over 30 years; inaugural president of the Tasmanian Branch of the Society of Women Writers, and has long been associated with FAW Tasmania. She also runs the well-known 'open mic' poetry readings in Launceston, "Poetry Pedlars."

Marilyn participates regularly in poetry readings, and has been a guest reader at three Tasmanian Poetry Festivals. In 2014 she won the annual Launceston Poetry Cup. Currently she is on the committee of the Tasmanian Poetry Festival, runs a fortnightly poetry workshop in Launceston, and has taught life-writing classes, and writing as therapy.

She has recently published two books of poetry: *Capture* with Carol Easton, and *Lies, Lovers and Other Constructions,* which has eighty of her poems; about the everyday, childhood, relationships, motherhood, siblings, lovers (and their many lies), family, travel, dementia, the spiritual journey, place, conversations stolen from others … "Semi-autobiographical, but like any life under construction, there are always lies."

SUSAN AUSTIN

Susan Austin is a poet, eco-socialist activist and occupational therapist. She facilitates group programs, including a creative writing program, in a mental health clinic in Hobart. Her first poetry collection, *Undertow*, was published by Walleah Press, after being First Commended in the Best First Book category of the IP Picks 2011 competition. She was awarded an Australia Council for the Arts grant to work with Dr Gina Mercer on her verse novel, *Dancing With Empty Prams*, published by Walleah Press this year. Susan won the Fellowship of Australian Writers Tasmania Poetry Prize 2021 and has been a guest performer at several writers' festivals. She has been widely published in newspapers and journals including this year's Australian Poetry Anthology.

KATHLEEN BENTLEY

I retired to Ulverstone from Kalgoorlie with my husband Max in 2012 and became involved with the artist community – my speciality became pastel painting of Indigenous animals plus land and sea scapes of Tasmania. I was successful in selling my art to tourists from all over the world, but then came the Coronavirus and the whole world seemingly went into lockdown. That meant I couldn't exhibit my artworks so I turned to writing.

One story had crystallised during a cruise around South East Asia then, when COVID struck, I wrote a trilogy within 18 months of the enforced lockdown. I had not written anything before but the characters seemed to speak to me so I had no trouble writing. Of course there was research to be completed, which I enjoyed. My first book *The Divided Heart*, has recently been published with the second book *Divided No More* due to be published by the end of July and the third book *Eternally Yours* is expected to be published prior to Christmas 2023. I have had several short stories published and now I am happy to contribute several of these and some poems to this Anthology. I hope you find these interesting.

ANGELA BISCHOF-JOSEPH

Angela is a retired Nurse and Midwife of forty-four years. She has worked in Singapore, England, Saudi Arabia and Australia. Widely travelled, Angela settled in Tasmania with her Swiss-born Australian husband from New South Wales. They run a hobby cattle farm of sixty acres in the hills of Natone.

Her first book, a biography, was published in April 2023. Besides writing, Angela is an enthusiastic cook and loves travel, the theatre, walking and sewing. She coordinates a Burnie Social Club for older adults. She has qualified in Public Speaking with Toastmasters International.

ANNE COLLINS

Anne Collins writes poetry and creative non-fiction. Her sixth book is a collection of poetry and prose with Spanish themes titled *Listening to the Deep Song* and was published in November 2022 by Bright South press.

Her previous poetry books are *How to Belong* (2019); *The Language of Water* (2014), *Seasoned with Honey* a 4-poet anthology (2008) and *The Season of Chance* (2005). Another collection of poetry and prose is titled *My Friends, This Landscape* (2011).

Anne co-curates the successful quarterly poetry event Seasonal Poets in Hobart.

Further information about Anne and her work can be found on her website at www.annecollins.com.au

ANT DRY

ANT DRY moved from Zimbabwe to Tasmania in 2007. He has lived in the Burnie area since then with his wife, Yvonne. Their four children live on the mainland. He sees himself as the most contented person on the planet; after all, who could ask for more from life than living in Tasmania and having the world's most wonderful family?

LAURENCE HARROULD

In 2016 my wife, Danita, and I moved to Tasmania from Sydney, in search of sanity and a healthier lifestyle. It has proven to be the best decision of our lives.

For decades I have been thinking about writing a book called *How to Love Your Pain: Why Bad Things Happen to Good People.* Since retiring from the IT industry and having some time on my hands, I decided I finally needed to front up and get it done. It's now with a group of reviewers and I'm excited that it's actually happening.

Before moving to Tasmania, Danita and I were house-sitters in Sydney for five years. During that time, I wrote a weekly blog called *Adventures of an Urban Nomad.* You can read it at: https://aviel.com.au/adventures-urban My next project is to turn it into a set of books

I owe a debt of gratitude to the members of the Fellowship of Australian Writers (North West) for their encouragement and support.

JENNIE HERRERA

Jennie Herrera was born in Toowoomba but has lived in Hobart for 36 years. She is President of FAW TAS and some of her novels, short stories, and poems can be read at https://jlherrera.com Her work has also appeared in a number of anthologies.

She works on issues such as West Papua and the Sue Neill-Fraser case and loves reading.

GRAEME HETHERINGTON

In my first 13 years, I went to Rosebery, Renison Bell, and Zeehan state schools before going to boarding school in Launceston. I was a lecturer in the Classics Department of UTas for over 25 years. Given the nature of the subject matter I taught, life in Europe was more appropriate and congenial for upwards of thirty years of my adult life. I returned to Tasmania in 2013, finally settling in St Helens.

Poetry has been my mainstay since about 1970 when I had the good fortune to be incidentally mentored by sympathetic friends James McAuley and Gwen Harwood to whom I owe much.

I am the author of *'Remote Corners'*, *'In The Shadow of Van Diemen's Land'*, *'Life Given'*, *'A Tasmanian Paradise Lost'*, *'A Post-Colonial Boy'*, *'An Inherited Epic of Gilgamesh'*, *'At Large'*, *'Another Love, Another Life'*, *'The Divided Self: A Tasmanian Odyssey'*, and with Ralph Spaulding, I co-edited *'Upper Heights and Lower Depths'* a Tasmanian anthology of poetry. An epic poem takes me up in my old age. My tenth collection, *'The Persistence of History'*, essentially a response to paintings by David Keeling, is due out towards the end of 2023.

ALLAN JAMIESON

Allan Jamieson retired in 1999 after a long working life as a chemical engineer in the pulp and paper industry, living on four continents and visiting 21 countries for business purposes – averaging one plane flight every four days through 35 years. He has resided in Burnie since 1981.

He began writing books in the early 2000's. So far, he has published six non-fiction books, one novel, one novella and one compendium of short stories.

Currently Allan is President and Secretary of FAWNW.

For more information, see
<https://fawtasnorthwest.blogspot.com/>
For copies of Allan's books, email Allan at jamtin79@gmail.com

DONNA & HANK KOOPMAN

Spending all their adult life entertaining and touring Australia and several overseas destinations with their songs and humour, this duo was "never famous, but very successful" as Donna explains.

Hank and Donna-Marie have witnessed a kaleidoscope of people during their travels, interacting and listening to them, finding inspiration for stories and songs over many years.

In their mid-seventies, they have retired from performing and decided to impart some of those interesting and sometimes comical stories to others. Hank has self-published three autobiographical books relating to their personal experiences. Donna has self-published her first book of poetry and prose called *Reverie*.

By joining the Fellowship of Australian Writers North West, they hope to gain further experiences from other members in the group as to processes involved in writing and distributing their many and varied stories.

ANNE LAYTON-BENNETT

Anne is a published writer both in Australia and overseas in both print and online publications. For several years she juggled writing commitments with a part-time job in a school library, and running a commercial flower growing business with her partner. She now writes regularly for specialist magazine *The Veterinarian*, and occasionally writes features for www.tasmaniantimes.com, an online journal.

Anne co-edited: *An Inspired Pursuit*: 40 years of writing by women in northern Tasmania, (Karuda Press) 2002, and has essays included in *An Inspired Pursuit*: Volume 2, (Tatlers) 2012; *Breaking the boundaries*: Australian activists tell their stories (Wakefield Press) 2016, and *The Fabric of Launceston* (Launceston Historical Society) 2016.

Challenged several years ago to try her hand at writing poetry, Anne also has a growing portfolio of poems – some of which have been published. She still writes letters.

MEG McLAREN

Meg was born on the island of Trinidad, in the West Indies. She had a happy and colourful childhood and her writing is influenced by these experiences. Over the years she has travelled extensively and has come into contact with many different lifestyles. She is now retired and lives in Tasmania where she is able to pursue her love of writing.

ANDREA McMAHON

Andrea McMahon writes short stories for adults and children. Her short stories have appeared in literary journals and anthologies, including *Island* and *Forty South magazine*. In 2020 Andrea's story, *Damselfly*, won the Forty South Tasmanian Writers' Prize. In 2008 her short story collection, *Skin Hunger*, was published by Ginninderra Press with the assistance of a grant from Arts Tasmania. Andrea lives in Hobart/Nipaluna and more of her writing can be found at andreaswriting.wordpress.com

DAWN MEREDITH

Dawn has authored 14 fiction and non-fiction books for children and young adults and contributed pieces for curriculum based publishers such as Cambridge University Press and Rigby Heineman. Her most successful book to date is *12 Annoying Monsters – Self Talk for Kids with Anxiety* (2013), reaching children all over the world. Dawn has produced a wide variety of work, including the five year project with WWII veteran Jim Haynes to produce his memoir *The Boy Who Went to War* (2016).

In 2016 Dawn won the SCBWI Andrea Davis Pinkney Writer Award for her then incomplete manuscript *Letters From the Dead,* which was published in 2017 as an adult novel. More recently she has focussed on Young Adult fiction, producing fantasy *Rebel* (2017), urban sci-fi *Elkwood* (2021) and urban fantasy *The Whispering Stone* (2023). Currently she is writing *Runaway,* the sequel to *Rebel* and finishing a non-fiction book for children, *10 Ridiculous Robots – Socialising Skills for Quirky Kids.* Her middle grade urban fantasy story, *Secrets of the Water Meadow,* set in 1970s Norway, is due for release in 2024.

www.dawnmeredithauthor.blogspot.com

IAN NETTLETON

From school days Ian discovered that he could string a sentence together. This was put to some use in uni. assignments and, later in life, writing eulogies for family members, Christmas newsletters, grant applications for the local Men's Shed, and a periodic newsletter including biographies of Men's Shedders.

As the family historian and genealogist he joined the Fellowship of Australian Writers, NW Tasmania chapter, to gain advice, expertise and motivation to write a family story that has been incubating for years. He is enjoying the company, wisdom and shared experience of a group of like-minded folk at the monthly meetings, and the stimulating exchange of emails between times.

JAKE O'MARA

Jake grew up on a farm in regional South Australia. He tried several occupations in widely separated parts of Australia before graduating as a registered nurse in 1987. He later completed a Graduate Diploma in Tropical Medicine at James Cook University, Townsville and worked in Indigenous communities in many remote areas. These included the Torres Straits and Cape York, the Gibson Desert, the Kimberley and Arctic Canada. Since then he has worked in both inpatient and community mental health in Queensland and Tasmania.

TATIANA PETROVSKY

Tatiana Petrovsky is a published poet and writer; a passionate supporter of health, education and the environment – a protector and enhancer of wetlands of national significance.

Tatiana has won the Nairda Lyne Award three times.

BRENDA SLAVOFF

Brenda has written poetry, plays, short stories and novels. Many of them were based on the author's vivid dreams. One of her novels has been read in serial form on radio, two of her plays have been performed and she has published many short stories and poems – and all this between gardening, theatre, composing music, playing the harp and dancing the tango.

EDITH SPEERS

Edith Speers was born in Canada, migrated to Australia after university, and for many years has lived in the far south of Tasmania. Her poetry has been published in most of the Australian journals and many anthologies of the past forty years. Several overseas literary magazines have also published her poems and she has won many awards for her poetry and short stories. Three books of her verse have been published and, as the proprietor of Esperance Press, she has published the work of many other Tasmanian writers.

ADAM STOKELL

Adam Stokell's poems have appeared in numerous journals, including *The Honest Ulsterman*, *Porridge*, *Cordite* and *Meniscus*. He lives on the outskirts of nipaluna/Hobart.

PETE STRATFORD

Born in New Zealand, I lived there until well into adulthood, and being in a rural community, farming life has had a significant influence on what I write. Later in life, came a change to working for over a decade as night care worker and counsellor at a shelter for homeless people. Coupled with an interest in observing people in general, this has provided me with a rich source of material to draw from.

Mentally composing poems while working at repetitive activities, such as shearing sheep or fruit picking, kept my brain cells active, but was rarely recorded. However while on "grey nomad" trips around Australia, brief notes were made for me as we drove along so that I could expand on the ideas of an evening. Thus was the gestation of my first book of verses. Having now self-published a third book of poems, I continue writing for the pleasure of it.

LEIGH SWINBOURNE

Leigh has written for the theatre as well as fiction and non-fiction work. Resident in nipaluna/Hobart, he has had plays produced and/or read by Old Nick, Hobart Repertory, The Australian Script Centre, The Tasmanian Theatre Company, Mudlark and Blue Cow. His play *The Mark of Cain* was shortlisted for the 2005 Patrick White Playwrights' Award. Six scripts are currently listed (digitally published) with *Australian Plays Transform*.

Leigh has had short stories and articles published in journals and anthologies. He is the recipient of writing grants and residencies from Arts Tasmania and Varuna. He has published two short story collections, *The Shark* (2011), and *Away* (2014), through Ginninderra Press, both selected for 'Pick of the Week' in *The Age* and *The Sydney Morning Herald*. In 2013 he was shortlisted for the University of Tasmania Prize for an unpublished manuscript, subsequently published as the novel *Shadow in the Forest* by Ginninderra Press in 2019. A second novel MS has been awarded an A.S.A. Mentorship for 2023. More about Leigh's writing can be found at www.leighswinbourne.com.au

www.ingramcontent.com/pod-product-compliance
Lightning Source LLC
Chambersburg PA
CBHW071920130726
47909CB00014B/2119